CAUGHT ON TAPE . . .

The murderer looked exactly like me.

His hair was darker than mine and slightly longer than I wore it. But everything else about him was identical.

"You! You killed her!" Neil backpedaled, raising up his hands in case I was going to grab him and twist his head off.

"I didn't kill her, Neil." I was shocked, but kept my voice even. "That's just someone who looks like me. A disguise. Or someone with facial reconstruction. Might even be a clone."

Neil's voice was shaky. "He's your age. He would have had to have been cloned at the same time as your birth."

"Look, I'll prove it isn't me."

I zoomed out and switched the resolution from the visible spectrum to a preprogrammed wavelength and frequency, bringing up an electromagnetic radiation resolution. The effect was similar to old-fashioned X-rays. The killer and Aunt Zelda became phosphorescent skeletons. I used the joystick to focus in on the man's wrist, then zoomed in.

His chip filled the screen. A twenty-digit ID number, followed by the birth name.

I paused it, and then got an even bigger shock.

The ID number and the name were mine.

"You killed her," Neil whispered . . .

TIMECASTER

JOE KIMBALL

ACE BOOKS, NEW YORK

THE BERKLEY PUBLISHING GROUP
Published by the Penguin Group
Penguin Group (USA) Inc.
375 Hudson Street, New York, New York 10014, USA

Penguin Group (Canada), 90 Eglinton Avenue East, Suite 700, Toronto, Ontario M4P 2Y3, Canada
(a division of Pearson Penguin Canada Inc.)
Penguin Books Ltd., 80 Strand, London WC2R 0RL, England
Penguin Group Ireland, 25 St. Stephen's Green, Dublin 2, Ireland (a division of Penguin Books Ltd.)
Penguin Group (Australia), 250 Camberwell Road, Camberwell, Victoria 3124, Australia
(a division of Pearson Australia Group Pty. Ltd.)
Penguin Books India Pvt. Ltd., 11 Community Centre, Panchsheel Park, New Delhi—110 017, India
Penguin Group (NZ), 67 Apollo Drive, Rosedale, Auckland 0632, New Zealand
(a division of Pearson New Zealand Ltd.)
Penguin Books (South Africa) (Pty.) Ltd., 24 Sturdee Avenue, Rosebank, Johannesburg 2196,
South Africa

Penguin Books Ltd., Registered Offices: 80 Strand, London WC2R 0RL, England

This is a work of fiction. Names, characters, places, and incidents either are the product of the author's
imagination or are used fictitiously, and any resemblance to actual persons, living or dead, business
establishments, events, or locales is entirely coincidental. The publisher does not have any control
over and does not assume any responsibility for author or third-party websites or their content.

TIMECASTER

An Ace Book / published by arrangement with the author

PRINTING HISTORY
Ace mass-market edition / June 2011

ISBN: 978-0-441-01918-2

ACE
Ace Books are published by The Berkley Publishing Group,
a division of Penguin Group (USA) Inc.,
375 Hudson Street, New York, New York 10014.
ACE and the "A" design are trademarks of Penguin Group (USA) Inc.

PRINTED IN THE UNITED STATES OF AMERICA

10 9 8 7 6 5 4 3 2 1

For Talon Ace Konrath

Ecopunk—(ē-kō-puhngk)

1. A subgenre of science fiction set in a green, utopian future, with a libertarian government. The opposite of nihilistic, authoritarian sci-fi, where no one smiles because everyone is so fucking oppressed.

2. A narrative typified by high-tech gadgetry, over-the-top action, copious amounts of sex, gratuitous and often rude humor, and theoretical physics, taking place in a society that emphasizes personal freedom and respect for the environment.

3. A Joe Kimball story where people get kicked in the groin a lot.

Nothing is improbable until it moves into the past tense.
—GEORGE ADE

I wasted time, and now doth time waste me.
—WILLIAM SHAKESPEARE

Time is on my side, yes it is.
—MICK JAGGER

ONE

Chicago 2064

Exactly nine hours and eleven minutes before I was charged with the complete destruction of Boise, Idaho, and the murders of the four hundred sixty-two thousand and nine people living there, I was mowing my roof and collecting the clippings like a good little taxpayer when I noticed a raccoon hiding in one of my hemp plants.

Raccoons were on the endangered list. That meant if one took up residence on my city-mandated green roof, I wasn't allowed to disturb its habitat. No mowing. No trimming. No planting. No gardening at all. Which meant instead of paying my weekly biodiesel tax in foliage, I'd have to pay in credits.

I had no desire to part with my hard-earned credits. Or my wife's hard-earned credits. That was why I cut off the lawn mower and pulled my regulation Glock 1MV Taser from my side holster and aimed it right between the animal's adorable masked eyes.

I'm not a monster, even though the world news would make me out to be one later that day. The Taser was meant for human-sized opponents, but I didn't think it would kill the little guy. It would just stun him long enough for me to toss him on my neighbor Chomsky's roof only six feet over. Worst that would happen was a little singed fur. Probably.

The raccoon stared back at me without fear, like he knew he was protected by the government. The fine for harming an endangered species was considerably more money than the biofuel tax. But even if the creature didn't survive, I could still throw it on Chomsky's property. Then I could arrest Chomsky for its murder. Chomsky was a dick.

Still, I hesitated. The raccoon grew bored with our staring contest, turning his attention back to the hemp bush. He began to snack on a large bud. I holstered the Taser. Maybe if I left him alone, he'd OD.

"Sergeant Avalon?"

I turned. Neil Winston was standing on my roof, between a large hydrangea and some bamboo stalks. He was wearing a bathrobe and slippers. Though it was a cool sixty-five degrees, he had sweat on his forehead, and I resented what that implied.

"What do you want, Neil?" My voice was hard, clipped, pure cop. He took a step back, but didn't leave.

"Victoria, uh, she said you might be able to help me."

I didn't like what my wife did for a living, and didn't like her clients. Neil was a skinny man with a big Adam's apple, a few years older than me, a banker or an accountant or something uptight like that. Victoria respected me enough to not talk about her work, but I did routine background checks on everyone she associated with. Call me Mr. Concerned Husband.

"Help you with what, Neil?" I could feel my shoulder muscles bunch up.

"You sound, um, a little angry. Victoria said you weren't

a jealous man, that I could come to you without any fear whatsoever. I have to be honest. I'm feeling a little bit of fear."

I thought about the Taser, and allowed myself a small grin imagining what he'd look like flopping around on the ground, doing the million-volt boogie. He'd look pretty damn good, I decided.

"That, uh, scowl makes you seem even scarier." Neil took another step backward. "Sergeant Avalon, there's no competition here. I'm a thin, homely, lonely little guy who has to pay a social worker for sex."

I hated the term *social worker*. It sounded like Victoria was helping poor people with their family problems instead of being a state-licensed prostitute. A state-licensed prostitute who made more than double my peace officer's salary.

"But you," Neil blabbered on, "you're a hero, you're handsome, with large, intimidating muscles, you own a beautiful home, and you married a goddess. There's no need to be jealous of me, Sergeant Avalon."

My wife bought the home with her savings, but the rest of what he said was close enough to true. It looked like Neil's knees were knocking together beneath his robe, so I eased off the throttle a bit.

"What is it you want, Neil?"

"You're a timecaster, right? I mean, well, of course you are. But do you still do it? Use the machine?"

"Yeah," I said. "All the time."

I hadn't turned on the TEV in about eight months. No need to, with crime practically nonexistent these days. All I used it for was show-and-tell at grammar schools.

"Well, I, uh, wondered if you couldn't maybe help me with something."

I let my frown deepen. What errand did Victoria expect me to run for this poor shlub? Find his missing kitty? Discover who was peeing on his doorstep?

"Help you with what, Neil?"

"It's my aunt, Zelda Peterson." Neil's voice got lower. "I think someone murdered her."

I sighed. Besides being thin, homely, and lonely enough to pay for sex, Neil was obviously fuct in the head. There hadn't been a murder in the taxpaying sections of Illinois for more than seven years. There hadn't been a violent crime in more than five. The closest thing to a crime spree these days was a parking ticket followed by pinching an apple from a street vendor.

But since this was one of my wife's clients, I responded with restraint.

"You're fuct in the head," I told him.

Believe me. That was restraint.

"Look, Sergeant Avalon, I know it sounds crazy. I know nobody gets murdered anymore. Heck, there hasn't even been a fatal car accident in as long as I can remember. That's because of peace officers like you. Because of time-casters. Since everyone knows there are no more secrets, everyone is more careful. I was serious when I said you're a hero, Sergeant Avalon."

If he laid it on any thicker, I could insulate my house with it. And, truth told, he appeared pretty shaken up. Normally, anyone who spent time with Victoria had a happy, satisfied look. A look I normally wore, except on the days she worked.

"Why do you think she was murdered, Neil?"

His eyes got glassy. "Aunt Zelda is the kindest person on the planet. Everyone loves her. I visit her once a day. We have coffee after work. Yesterday, I went to her apartment, and she wasn't there. I let myself in and waited around for her to come home. She didn't."

"Did you call her headphone?"

"Aunt Zelda never got the implant. But she has a regular cell. I called it, and it was in her purse, in the bedroom."

"How old is your aunt, Neil?"

"She's in her seventies. But her mind is perfect, Sergeant

Avalon. She wouldn't go anywhere without telling me. She calls me when she goes to the corner download kiosk to buy a magazine, and that's just a block away. Plus there was blood."

"Blood?" I was becoming curious, a hazard of my profession. I kept it from showing.

"A few drops. On the sink."

"Any pets? Cat? Dog?"

"No pets."

"You're sure it was blood?"

He began to shift his weight from one leg to the other. "It was definitely blood."

"If you're so concerned, why not go to the Peace Department?"

"I did. I spoke to another sergeant there, a man named Teague. He laughed me out of his office."

No surprise. Teague was a dick.

"Was your aunt chipped?"

"Of course. But she's not showing up on GPS. Teague said maybe the chip shorted out. But they're bioregulated, aren't they? They run organically. They don't short out. They just cease some of their functions when the host dies."

I thought about it. Having a chipped person not show up on GPS made this whole thing even more intriguing. A few years ago, a tanker sank, and they were able to find the bodies under four hundred feet of water. Chips eliminated the need for paper money, identification, and keys. Each one was unique to a person's DNA, and operated as credit and keys only while the owner was alive. After death, they could no longer open doors or buy things. But GPS still worked.

The only way to short out a chip was to destroy it on purpose, like the dissys do.

"Please, Sergeant. I'm willing to pay for your time. Name a price, I'll pay it. Any price. Ever since yesterday, I've been worried sick. I can't think about anything else."

Worried sick, but he still managed to enjoy an afternoon

with my wife. I glanced back at the raccoon still happily nibbling away. That was a vicious circle going on there. Eat marijuana, get the munchies, so you eat more marijuana. Maybe I'd be lucky and he'd pop.

"Two months' worth of foliage for my property size," I said. "That's my price."

He frowned. "I live in a condo, Sergeant Avalon. I don't have a roof, just a little garden on my porch, and some kudzu in the bathroom. I could pay you the equivalent amount in credits."

"No deal. If you can't get the foliage, you can come up here once a week and work my roof."

A fair compromise. He came here to get a little trim. Why not give a little trim back?

"Done. When can we do this?"

"Now is good."

"Now. Excellent. I'll go get dressed." He turned to leave, then turned right back around. "Thank you, Sergeant."

I shrugged. "Meet you out in front in ten."

Neil disappeared. I gave my little pot thief one more glance. "If you feel like dropping dead, please go next door to Chomsky's roof."

The raccoon's mouth was full, his cheeks puffed out with weed, but he probably wouldn't have replied anyway.

TWO

Victoria was in a red silk kimono one shade lighter than her hair, and even though we'd been married for three years and had known each other for five, the sight of her still took my breath away. She was beautiful, sure. And it was natural beauty, not surgically enhanced. But the thing that drew me and countless others to her was how she radiated life. Vicki had something beneath her superficial looks, something she exuded that made you want to be near her. Charisma times ten. And it had nothing to do with her being one of the last real redheads in the country.

I walked to her in the kitchen, where she was at the sink, peeling the potatoes I'd dug up earlier, setting the skins aside. I came up from behind and wrapped my arms around her.

"You're going to help him?" she asked, dropping the spud and squeezing my forearms.

"Yeah. He agreed to do our foliage for two months."

"You're the last of the nice guys, Talon."

I considered nuzzling her neck, but figured it had been

nuzzled only a few minutes prior. The thought made my arms tense up.

"I didn't mean to bring him over while you were home." Victoria must have sensed my mood swing. She was good at reading people. "But the reason he wanted to see me is because he wanted to see you. He tried your office first. You weren't there, so he made an appointment."

"So you guys didn't . . ."

"Of course we did. He's a regular client, obviously very upset. I did my best to relax him."

I kept the jealousy down. I had no right to judge her. Victoria kept her relationship with her clients business-like and professional. No kissing. Always protection. And since she married me, she drastically reduced her schedule. Women of her attributes could have been making four times the amount she did, but she worked only two days a week, and picked days when I was at work so I wouldn't have to see or hear anything that might make me go on a Tasing expedition.

Besides, the only reason I knew Victoria in the first place was because I was a former client.

"Kiss me," I said.

She turned, my arms still around her. Her green eyes were wide, her pupils huge.

"Sometimes I think that's the only reason you married me, Talon. Because you knew how much I wanted to kiss you."

"That, and it was cheaper to marry you than keep hiring you."

We kissed, and it tasted just as fresh and new as it did that very first time, at our wedding ceremony. Victoria had been extremely rigid on that no-kissing policy.

I nibbled her lower lip, dropping my mouth to her neck, and she leaned slightly back.

"I've got another client coming in twenty minutes. I doubled up today so I could have tomorrow off. I got us space elevator tickets. How does a day in low-earth orbit sound?"

Unfortunately, my alpha-male mind didn't zero in on the extra day I'd have her to myself.

"Who's the client?"

"Barney. The dentist."

"I hate that guy."

"He's a harmless old man."

I knew I shouldn't go there, but there I went. "Quit," I told her.

She pushed me away. "Don't start. We have bills, Talon."

"We can move someplace cheaper."

"I like Chicago. I like our big house."

"You're not the one who does the gardening for a property this big."

"I thought Neil was doing it."

"For two months. Then it's back to me."

Her eyes flashed challenge. "If you hate it so much, we can hire someone. I'll take on an extra client to pay for it."

"Boise, Idaho, is nice," I managed to say through clenched teeth. "Let's move to Boise. We could each get normal jobs. Maybe we could farm. There's still affordable land out there. Buy four acres and raise blue-green algae. There's a new strain that's almost sixty-five percent lipid."

"You hate gardening. You think you'd like farming?"

"I would if it meant having you to myself."

She rolled her eyes. "If I thought you were serious, I'd do it, Talon. But I know you. I know you're a city guy. If you moved out to the country, you'd go crazy within two weeks."

She was right, but I wasn't going to back down.

"If you loved me, you'd quit."

Vicki folded her arms. Just like she was able to project warmth, she was now projecting anger.

"I shouldn't have brought anyone here while you were home."

"You could have gone to his place."

"You don't let me go to my clients' homes. You don't trust any of them."

"And why would that be? Maybe because they're nailing my wife?"

If freeze-vision were possible, Vicki would have turned me into an iceberg right there.

"It's my job, Talon. Nothing more. I can't believe we're having this conversation. You promised you'd stop doing this."

The hurt in her face made me want to take her in my arms again, but I was on a roll.

"How would you like it if I slept around?"

Her temperature dropped even further. "I'm not sleeping around. I'm earning a living. A very good living that lets us have a big house in a nice city. Sex is a natural, wholesome, biological need, and you know the only person I make it personal with is you."

Now I folded my arms, too. "But what if I did? What if I slept with someone else?"

Victoria's green eyes narrowed to slits. "Our prenup doesn't have a monogamy clause. You go right ahead. Just make sure the next time you're in my bed you have a full medical exam in your hand, and you sure as hell better not kiss her."

She stormed past me. I shook my head. SLPs. Sex with strangers was okay, but I'd better not kiss anyone else.

Unfortunately, I didn't want to kiss, or have sex with, anyone but her.

"Sergeant?"

Neil again, standing in the kitchen doorway. He was wearing a rumpled suit that made him look even thinner and wimpier. I might have even felt sorry for him, but he got laid today, and I hadn't.

"Let's go," I told him.

We walked through my admittedly large and beautiful

house, each step representing several square feet of very expensive real estate. My background check on Neil showed he didn't own a vehicle, so I lead him to the garage. Like everyone else who sees my ride, his eyes bugged out when I turned on the overhead lights.

"You have a . . . *car*?"

"A 2024 Corvette Stingray, retrofitted for biofuel."

"It must have cost a fortune," Neil said.

"A gift from my wife." I stared at him pointedly, letting him know his visits helped pay for this baby. But he apparently didn't need a reminder.

"With biofuel prices these days, it must cost a fortune to run. How many clients does Victoria have?"

I shot him with my eyes, and he cowed. He was right, though. Funny how history repeats itself. During the energy crisis of the early-twenty-first century, desert sheiks artificially inflated the price of oil. Western countries decided they'd had enough, and half the world switched to a renewable energy source. Biofuels, made from cheap and plentiful vegetation. Extract the oil, then compost the rest for methane. But the population kept growing, and soon the foliage grown specifically for biofuel began to compete for space with the foliage grown for human and livestock consumption. That jacked up the prices of both fuel and food, and now everyone in the civilized world used every square inch of land they could spare to grow plants to make more fuel.

I've seen pictures, movies on the intranet. Chicago, and the world, once looked industrial. Now every apartment had a garden, every roof a farm, every building covered top to bottom in vines. The urban jungle was, truly, a jungle.

I hit the security button on my keys—this thing was so classic it still used keys—and we climbed into the front seat. The garage door, however, was chip operated. I waved my wrist over the remote box on the dashboard, and the door automatically levered open.

I started the engine, listening to it purr and enjoying the look of wonder on Neil's face. Chances were high he'd never been in a car before. I hadn't, until Vicki bought me one.

"Address?" I asked.

"Thirteen twenty-two Wacker."

I squeezed my earlobe, turning on my headphone implant. The familiar dial tone came on in my head.

"Car nav," I said. "Thirteen twenty-two Wacker."

The message was sent to my car's navigation system, and the semitransparent map flickered and then superimposed over my windshield. Another addition that wasn't available back in 2024.

The garage let out into the alley. I tapped the accelerator, eased out of the garage, and fishtailed. The greentop road was spongy, and needed to be harvested and replanted. Normally I did that myself, but this week Neil would get to enjoy that particular task.

The alley let out onto the main street, Troy, and the city kept the greentop well maintained with regular uprooting and reseeding. If I'd been able to really floor it, my tires would have had no problem sticking to the road.

Of course, with four million biofuel bikes on the street, I'd be lucky to hit thirty miles an hour anywhere within the city limits. It was like driving through a gaggle of geese. Fast geese, who enjoyed cutting you off. Even more annoying were the kermits, who were so green they rejected even biodiesel. They powerbocked; bipedding around on frog legs, which were flexible leg extensions that added thirty inches to their height. You could run forty miles an hour in a pair, perform a fifteen-foot vertical jump, and still manage to look like an idiot with that awkward, hopping gait.

We weaved our way through the green skyscrapers, avoided injuring any utopeons, and even managed to cut off a few city buses, their roofs sprouting flowers arranged in a Cubs logo, to celebrate their eighth consecutive World Series win.

"So why do you think someone murdered your aunt, Neil? Does she have enemies?"

"Not that I know of. But she does have credits. Quite a bit. Came into it late in life. She's a tech-head."

"You can't murder someone for their credits. Credits don't exist IRL. To make a transfer, both people would need their biochips. There would be a record of the transaction."

Neil lowered his voice. "Some people don't use credits."

"Who? The dissys? Did your aunt associate with any dissys?"

"One of her nephews is a dissy. And he's a bit . . . *unstable.*"

I filed that away.

It took ten minutes to drive the twenty-four blocks. Parking in Chicago was even more competitive than driving, and the car didn't fit into the pay carousels. But being a cop had its privileges. I parked up on the clover-covered sidewalk, flipped down my sun visor with my badge number on it, and climbed out of the Vette.

Aunt Zelda's apartment building, predictably, was green. But the wall ivy had tiny red flowers on it, making the building appear orangish. I popped the trunk and grabbed my utility belt and holster, mostly out of habit. I didn't expect any trouble, but it never hurts to be prepared. After cinching on the buckle and adjusting my holster, I reached for the TEV, winding the carry strap over my shoulder. Next to it was my digital tablet, and when the sun hit the solar panels it powered up, beginning a slide show of crudely drawn stick-figure pictures. Neil was nearby, so I quickly pocketed it before he noticed.

"Were those pictures of you?"

Apparently he'd noticed.

"Mrs. Simpson's third grade class. I, uh, do a lot of school demonstrations. Community relations stuff. I tell kids to stay out of trouble, only take recreational drugs in moderation, that kind of thing."

"Sounds important," Neil said.

But I knew he was thinking the same thing I was: it wasn't nearly as important as working Homicide. I'd become a cop to save lives, to make a difference, and now I was basically just a walking public service announcement. Not that I longed for violent crime to come back. That would be monstrous.

And yet, there was a spring in my step as we walked to the apartment door.

The lobby had UV grow lights in the ceiling, artificial sun for the bamboo lining the walls. As expected, the elevator also sported UV, the railing lined with hemp seedlings. Along with the vine kudzu, hemp and bamboo were among the fastest-growing plants, but most people favored hemp. If Chicago caught fire, everyone within three hundred miles would be stoned for a week.

Aunt Zelda lived on the thirty-second floor. Whether it was habit or nervous tension, Neil picked and pruned the tiny plants as we took the ride up. Like a good little citizen he palmed the tiny bits he'd pinched off, then dropped them in a biorecycle container when we reached our floor.

We walked past more plant life, found the correct door.

"I'm programmed with her key code," Neil said. "I check up on her a lot."

He waved his wrist chip in front of the doorknob, and it opened automatically.

When I walked into the apartment I whistled in awe.

Aunt Zelda's home was completely packed with contraband.

THREE

"Oh, I . . . uh . . . I forgot about those," Neil said.

I folded my arms across my chest. "Just the biorecycle price alone would be worth a bunch of credits. But on the black market, we're talking some major duckets."

Neil shrugged. "My aunt, she's from an older generation. She grew up with paper. I told her to give these up, but she can't."

There was a fortune around us. A fortune in books. Thousands of books. All of them illegal.

Not that their content was illegal. Their content was public domain. It was the paper that was illegal.

Sometime back around when I was born, thirty years ago, the biofuel shortage began, quickly followed by the food shortage. To stem off the inevitable, plants were no longer used to make anything but fuel or food. So natural cloth, wood furniture, and paper, among many other plant-derived products, were banned. Those that already existed were gathered up and recycled for fuel.

Not that anything was actually lost. Even back then synthetics could imitate, or improve upon, most natural products. And digital memory had become so cheap and plentiful, every word ever written had been digitized and could be stored on something called a hard drive, which was about the size of many of these smaller books.

Those were dark ages, compared to today. Now you could fit 300 petabytes on a memory card the size of my fingernail. Enough to store every piece of media ever created by human beings. This base of information was given away freely when you bought a digital tablet. It also came with an intranet operating system, so you could access and search the vast volumes of knowledge and entertainment, accurately updated IRT by a team of experts and technicians. If you wanted a recent bit of media, like a new book or movie or magazine, you could download it at a news kiosk for credits with a flash of your wrist, and it would transfer directly to your digital tablet.

Years ago, when DTs needed separate monitors and processors and were called *computers*, people used the Internet to communicate and exchange information with other people. These days, the Internet was an underground thing for bored hobbyists and fanboyz, saturated with untruths Wikied by the uninformed, conspiracy flakes, and pr0n. Basically just a big mess of nut jobs jerking off and shouting lies at one another. And don't even get me started on the malware.

That was why, when Web 4.0 became a wasteland, the tech geniuses took everything off the Internet that was worthwhile—basically every bit of knowledge, media, and art in human history—and created the intranet. Now everyone owned everything, and no one missed the flame wars and inaccurate half-truths of the Internet. It was much easier to communicate using headphone implants and digital tablets. And why waste time looking for unverified information when you could spend fifteen lifetimes sorting through the accurate information on your personal intranet and not even come close to viewing it all?

Since these books were old, I could guarantee Aunt

Zelda, and everyone else on the planet, already had copies of them on their intranet cards, so there was no real reason for her to keep them, other than sentiment. Especially since digital books were interactive and versatile and just plain better. I pulled a volume off the shelf, and peered at a random page. It was medieval. You couldn't adjust the font size, couldn't change the contrast, and it didn't even have a button that made it read to you.

Still, if Zelda had met with foul play, here was a monetary motive.

"She, um, gave up everything else," Neil continued. "Cotton clothing. A real particleboard desk. Some cherrywood frames. But she couldn't part with her books."

"How about these bookcases?" I asked, pointing to the wood grain on them as I replaced the book. Truth was, I didn't care at all about an old lady's book collection. But I did enjoy freaking Neil out.

"Synthetic," he quickly said. "All fake."

I frowned, pretending to think things over. "Is there any other contraband I need to be aware of?"

Neil got even paler. "She, uh, also has a still."

I raised an eyebrow. As the twenty-first century marched onward, liquor also joined the ranks of illegal products. Again, not for its effects—the Libertarian Act of 2028 made all recreational substances legal. But alcohol was made from plants, and plants could be used only for food and fuel. While the synthetic forms of drugs were cheap, plentiful, and popular, synthetic alcohol supposedly didn't taste right. It was eventually made into pills like all other drugs, and I sometimes liked to kick back with a few whiskey tablets when I was off duty. I'd never tasted the real thing, and I was curious.

"You'll show that to me later," I told him, my voice stern. "But first, show me the blood you found."

Neil nodded quickly, then led me into the kitchen. I lugged the TEV after him, setting it down next to the sink.

"There," Neil said, pointing.

I squinted at some brown splotches on the stainless steel. It was blood. If I went back to my car for my crime-scene kit, I could have analyzed the sample on the spot, compared it to a hair sample from Aunt Zelda's brush, and instantly matched the DNA, proving this blood was hers.

But why bother with that when I could actually see what happened here instead?

I took the tachyon emission visualizer off my shoulder and set it on the floor. The TEV sort of looked like an antique film projector. It was box-shaped, with a lens on the front, and two large spinning disks on the side. The top contained the control panel, recording software, and input pad. On the other side were the contrast dials. It had a handle on top, and a shoulder strap.

"Do you know your aunt's Tesla ID number?" I asked. I could have used my own, but preferred to save the credits when I could.

"I have it written down. Hold on." He dug a digital tablet out of his pocket and powered it on. "B-D-R-five-two-nine."

I punched the code onto the keypad, and the TEV accessed the airborne electricity and powered on. Just ten years ago, electronic devices still needed to be plugged into wall outlets, fed by generators that used enormous power lines.

Now Tesla generators threw electrons into the atmosphere, which were zone-coded so customers paid for only what they used in their prezoned area, using specific serial ID numbers. It got rid of all the wires, making room for more plants. But the generators ran on biofuel, so I wondered exactly what we gained in the transition.

The TEV hummed. I picked it up by the handle and moved it onto the kitchen table, using the monitor to aim the lens at a wide-angle view of the sink. That was the rudimentary part. The next part was all finesse.

From what I understood, out of everyone who took TEV

training, only .001 percent became a timecaster. It wasn't that the controls were difficult to use. But the average person couldn't use them well enough. My instructor likened it to playing a musical instrument. A lot of people could play the notes, but only a few could make those notes really come alive.

Tuning a TEV required a fair bit of skill, but a lot of intuition. The basic premise was kid stuff, taught in first grade science tablet texts. Until their actual discovery, tachyons were only theoretical particles. Their claim to fame was they moved faster than light. According to classic Einsteinian physics, anything that moved faster than light could go back in time. Einstein was proven correct, but time machines never materialized. Apparently it's possible to send particles back in time, but not anything larger.

Some scientists warned against tachyon experiments, saying that they could rip holes in spacetime and create miniature black holes and wormholes. Others insisted that tachyons, if applied at a proper frequency, could travel back through spacetime and record it. The mathematicians still couldn't figure out how it actually worked, but knew it had to do with the eighth imploded dimension.

The TEV, used properly, allowed a timecaster to set up in a certain vantage point, and then record everything that happened from that vantage point up to two weeks prior.

In layman's terms, mankind now had a rewind button.

It altered how people behaved, and ultimately changed the world. Pretty much all crime could now be solved. The TEV could record the crime in progress. Even if the perpetrator cut out his chip, it was simply a question of following him backward in time, usually right to his house.

Within two years the jails—previously empty from back when all the drug-related offenders went free—were once again filled.

With the violent element removed, the USA became a much nicer place to live. Especially since the rest of society wised up. If, at any given moment, you knew your actions could be recorded, you tended to not break any laws. And legal drugs meant even crimes of passion were kept to a minimum.

Eighteen years ago, when I became a peace officer, there had been more than thirty timecasters in Chicago. We were now down to two on the payroll.

Virulence wasn't good for diseases. A highly contagious, highly lethal virus was so efficient that it would rip through a population, killing all the hosts, and then dying itself. The same thing with timecasters. We were so effective, we put ourselves out of business.

"Can I watch?" Neil asked, peering over my shoulder.

"Only if you stay quiet."

I pressed the emitter start switch, and the generator reels began to turn. As they gathered tachyons, they did a disconcerting thing. For brief flashes, lasting a few microseconds, the rotating wheels would disappear. This made them flicker, like jump cuts in an old movie.

"Whoa," Neil said.

"Shh."

I closed my eyes, listening to the room, to the hum of the TEV, and to spacetime itself.

That's an embarrassing thing to admit—believing I could feel spacetime—and certainly not something I was taught by Michio Sata, my timecasting instructor. But I'd done a lot of research on the intranet to try to figure it out, and I thought I had a possible solution.

Years back, supernatural phenomena were proven to be bunk by science. Ghosts, ESP, monsters, God, magic, religion, and all of that other mumbo jumbo was abandoned by the majority of society. But a small fringe group hypothesized that belief in the supernatural was genetic. In certain situations, people were able to sense and sometimes control aspects of the eleven dimensions. Little things, like knowing the phone was going to ring two seconds before it did, and bigger things, like Indian swamis who could stop their heartbeats and balance on two fingers, were all related to the interaction among dimensions.

Certain people were more sensitive to this interaction than others. Throughout recorded history, these people were attributed with divine or supernatural powers. Magicians, prophets, mystics, miracle workers, clairvoyants, soothsayers; these folks could tune in and channel other dimensions. Some were treated like gods for having this ability. Others were burned at the stake.

This hypothesis never graduated to a theory, because only a few of the imploded dimensions could be proven mathematically, and the only one that could be seen was the eighth dimension, through tachyon emission visualization, and we weren't even completely sure how it worked.

But, strange as it sounded, I believed when I was tuning the TEV into spacetime, I could sense if I was hitting the fabric or not, then adjust accordingly.

Nothing supernatural about it. Just a genetic ability, like being good at basketball, or having 20/20 eyesight. Still, I didn't talk about it much, for fear of being laughed out of the Peace Department.

So I took a deep breath, let it out slow, then reached for the dial to see where this blood came from.

FOUR

When I'm tuning in to the spacetime fabric, my brain sort of splits in half. Not literally, or even figuratively. But I don't really know how else to describe it. One part of my mind is intensely focused. The other part just spaces out, like I'm daydreaming.

Each click of the focus dial is one-hundredth of a millimeter, and most people can't distinguish the movement. But to me, each click feels like a huge chasm that I'm traversing in slow motion. People watching me have commented that my fingers aren't moving at all. But they are, on a very sensitive, very minuscule level.

First I needed to locate the eighth membrane. According to Michio Sata, the world's first timecaster and the genius who helped invent the technology, there was no way to actually locate its physical presence. Either you could sense it, or you couldn't. I could, and when I tuned in to the 8M I sensed that it looked and felt like a furry, bloated, red raisin. But the descriptors *looked* and *felt* aren't appropriate, because I really couldn't see or feel anything. It was all happening in my head.

Even though I hadn't done a visualization in a long
time, I focused in on the 8M pretty quickly. But it seemed
strange. A little too small. A little too orange. I chalked
that up to being out of practice, and then switched from the
focus dial to the fine-tuning dial.

If one out of a thousand could locate the membrane, only
a fraction of them could fine-tune. Unlike the raisin sensation, fine-tuning appeared in my imagination like a long,
winding road. I had to follow its twists and turns, using the
dial, maneuvering this way and that way until I reached the
pinpoint of light at the very end. But it wasn't actually light.
It was more like a single point that pulled light in.

The point itself was weird as hell, and supposedly different for everyone who found it. But if you could sense the
point, getting to it wasn't any more difficult than driving a
vehicle.

"Oh, my . . ."

I opened my eyes and looked at Neil, who appeared to
be disappearing and reappearing, switching on and off like
a flickering monitor. Actually, it was me and the TEV who
were disappearing. Though I didn't understand the science
or the math, I was getting close to the octeract point; the
center of the spacetime eighth-dimensional hypercube.
While I didn't understand what any of that meant, I knew
what it felt like when I got there.

Strangely, it felt like petting a bunny between the ears.

As I got closer, the octeract point unfolded, and I sensed
my mind being stretched, like it was made of chewing gum
and someone was tugging on either end. One more deli-
cate twist of the fine-tuning dial and the light enveloped
everything, providing me with the very real but decidedly
unmacho bunny sensation.

I locked the dials. The flickering had stopped. The world
was tangible and real again. Neil's jaw was hanging open.

"Close your mouth, Neil, or you'll accidentally swallow
the eighth dimension and your head will explode."

His jaw clicked shut at my lie. Newbies were so much fun to mess with.

I directed my attention to the TEV monitor. It looked like a live video. The lens was pointed at the sink, and the monitor showed the sink. But when I waved my hand in front of the lens, it didn't appear on the monitor.

That was because we weren't looking at the sink in present time. We were looking at the sink from seventy-two hours ago. The liquid display was round and full-color, highly realistic, on par with the best real-definition displays. It had filters to compensate for the way light reflected off objects. Unfiltered, the center image was tinted blue, and around the edges was a deep red—blueshift and redshift due to the Doppler effect.

I checked the filters and tweaked them, because the current image was a bit too orange. Unable to lock it in, I played with the hue, trying to match the colors in the room. Eventually I got it looking pretty close.

"Incredible," Neil said.

"Shh. Mouth closed."

He obeyed, pursing his lips. I hit the fast-forward button, resuming play again when I saw a woman go to this sink. She was older, gray hair, comfortable shoes, wearing a combination of purple and green that only the elderly could get away with. I watched her place an empty plate in the sink, then drain the last drops of what looked like liquor from a rocks glass. Enjoying her alcohol still, apparently.

I looked away from the monitor, into the sink. The plate and glass were still there.

"Oh . . ."

At Neil's gasp I glanced back at the monitor.

It was ugly.

A man in a black jumpsuit and gloves had come up behind Aunt Zelda and was ramming her face into the sink. After the third crack, he placed his hands on her ears and with one violent turn—

—he twisted her head 180 degrees, so it was facing the opposite way.

Neil made a gagging sound. I hit the pause button. From this angle, all I could see was the back of the man's head. He had dark hair, a muscular build, and his jumpsuit looked like a uniform of some sort. I picked up the TEV by the handle, and walked it to the other side of the sink. While the action on the monitor remained paused, the angle changed as the lens moved, allowing me to view the scene from a different perspective. I set down the TEV and zoomed in, getting a close-up of the bastard's face.

"Totally fuct!" Neil uttered.

Totally fuct was right.

The murderer looked exactly like me.

His hair was darker than mine and slightly longer than I wore it. But everything else about him was identical.

"You! You killed her!" Neil backpedaled, raising up his hands in case I was going to grab him and twist his head off.

"I didn't kill her, Neil." I was shocked, but kept my voice even. "That's just someone who looks like me. A disguise. Or someone with facial reconstruction. Might even be a clone."

Neil's voice was shaky. "He's your age. He would have had to have been cloned at the same time as your birth."

"Look, I'll prove it isn't me."

I zoomed out and switched the resolution from the visible spectrum to a preprogrammed wavelength and frequency, bringing up an electromagnetic radiation resolution. The effect was similar to old-fashioned X-rays. The killer and Aunt Zelda became phosphorescent skeletons. I used the joystick to focus in on the man's wrist, then zoomed in.

His chip filled the screen. A twenty-digit ID number, followed by the birth name.

I paused it, and then got an even bigger shock.

The ID number and the name were mine.

"You killed her," Neil whispered.

"The . . . uh . . . chip has to be a counterfeit."

"It's impossible to counterfeit chips. They're specific to individual DNA."

I zoomed in even more, to a microscopic level, seeing the nanocircuits trading electrical impulses with nerve endings. The chip had indeed fused with this guy's biological system. It was real.

That was all the confirmation Neil needed, because he turned tail and ran for the door, yelling, "Fuct! Fuct, fuct!" and waving his hands in the air.

So I did the only thing I could do.

I drew my Glock and shot him in the back.

FIVE

My Glock 1MV fired wax bullets, each housing a barbed needle attached to a microprocessor that was directly linked to my account. The slug hit Neil between the shoulder blades and the wax broke away, leaving the needle embedded fifteen millimeters into his shirt and skin. At the speed of light, the processor accessed my Tesla billing ID number, and a tiny lightning bolt shot out from the ceiling and gave Neil a taste of one million volts. The same wireless electricity system that powered the city also powered my bullets.

For a nonlethal weapon, the Glock Taser was still pretty nasty, and I knew from experience it hurt like hell. Neil plopped onto his face, unable to break his fall with his hands because his entire skeletomuscular system locked up. He flopped around on the floor for a bit, and I hit the remote control on my utility belt, shutting off the juice. Then I removed a supplication collar from its case and locked the thin strip of anodized plastic around his neck.

"Fuct . . ." Neil moaned into the carpeting.

I holstered my roscoe and took the EPF activator—a

silver sphere no bigger than a hypergolf ball—and placed it next to the front door, setting the distance at two meters.

With Neil taken care of, I went back to the kitchen and stared at the TEV monitor, my face staring back at me. Tachyon emission visualization technology was foolproof. It couldn't be compromised. It couldn't be faked. The TEV was better than any eyewitness, because it showed the truth without perception or bias getting in the way.

But this wasn't the truth. At the time of the murder, I was home with Vicki. I had an alibi.

Of course, the famous court case of the State of Illinois v. Joseph Andrew Konrath showed that alibis meant nothing against TEV evidence.

I picked up the unit and hit rewind, keeping the lens on the killer. I watched the murder in reverse, and then saw him sneak away from Aunt Zelda, walking backward. I followed him, through the hallway, to the apartment door.

Outside the door, I watched him use a smart magnet on the lock. Smart magnets were used by locksmiths, when electronic entry failed due to mechanical error. Prior to the invention of timecasting technology, burglars used them to gain entrance to homes. But B and E was a thing of the past, because all a timecaster had to do was follow the thief all the way home, either forward or in reverse. Which was what I planned on doing with my double.

He led me to the elevator. But right before he stepped out, the monitor flickered.

And he disappeared.

I pressed fast-forward and watched it again.

One millisecond he was there. The next he wasn't.

I tuned in to the exact frame of his vanishing act, trying to spot where Alter-Talon went.

Alter-Talon didn't go anywhere. He completely dematerialized. Which was, of course, impossible.

The only difference between the before and after frames was the hallway lighting. Before he disappeared, it was slightly bluer. When he appeared, the light became a bit oranger.

"Fuct!" Neil screamed, high-pitched and decidedly un-macho.

I glanced over at Aunt Zelda's open door, then walked back inside her apartment.

Neil was on his ass, eyes bugging out, both hands gripping the supplication collar. His whole body shook. I grabbed his shirt and dragged him away from the door, back into the hallway.

"I put an electronic perimeter fence by the door. If you get within two meters, it shocks you. But you apparently figured that out."

Neil was gasping like he'd been underwater. "You . . . killed her."

"I didn't kill her."

His eyes welled up. "Please let me go."

"Sorry. I can't do that just yet. If you go running to the Peace Department, they'll put me away before I have a chance to figure out what's going on. So you'll have to stay put for a while."

Neil pouted, and a trembling hand reached up for his earlobe.

"It also jams your headphone. And if you try to cut it off, it explodes, blowing a hole in your neck."

The last part was a lie, but I wasn't too concerned with Neil getting the collar off. It was reinforced with carbon nanotube fibers. They were the strongest things on the planet, and were used to tether space elevators to earth. Unless Aunt Zelda had a diamond bit drill, the supplication collar would stay on until I took it off.

Then I went back to the TEV. Instead of reverse, I let the past move forward. The murder was just as horrible the second time. Even more so, because I zoomed in on the killer's face as he snapped her neck, and the SMF was smiling.

It got worse. After her death, the alter-me pulled something out of a sheath on his belt. From my viewing angle, it appeared to be nothing more than an empty handle. But I knew what it was.

A Nife.

The Nife, or nanoknife, was yet another miracle courtesy of carbon nanotubes. It had a tensile strength sixty times greater than diamonds. From the side, it looked like a military KA-BAR knife. But the Nife was invisible while looking at it edge-on because it was incredibly thin—1/10,000th the width of a human hair. This also made it incredibly sharp, and equally dangerous. Only the mentally compromised carried Nifes. It was too easy to cut off your own leg sheathing it, and you wouldn't even know until you tried to take a step and your leg stayed behind.

The killer used his Nife to fillet the skin away from the vic's arm, layer by layer, down to her chip. Then, with an expert flick, he dug the chip out and walked off.

Neil made a gagging sound.

I kept the lens on the killer, watched him approach the microwave. He set the timer on twenty minutes.

I paused the TEV and went to the microwave, wincing at the smell when I opened the door. All that was left of the chip was black ash. Hence Neil's inability to locate his aunt using GPS. I went back to the visualization, letting it play out.

After the cut and bake, he focused on the refrigerator, unloading all of the food and placing it in the biorecycle chute. Then he removed the shelves and stacked them in the cabinet under the sink. It didn't take a timecaster to see what was going to happen next. I paused the transmission and stared at the fridge for a few seconds, my stomach becoming unhappy. Then I tugged open the door.

Aunt Zelda's frozen, lifeless eyes stared back at me. Her jaw was stretched open, impossibly wide, in a horrifying silent scream.

"You put her in the icebox?" Neil blubbered. "You're inhuman."

I ignored him, following protocol and checking for a pulse that I knew wasn't there. Her skin was cold to the touch. I patted her down, checking her pockets, and came up empty. Then I let the TEV play out the rest of the crime. After stuffing the vic into the chill chest, Alter-Talon walked out the front door. I followed him into the hallway, over to the elevator—

—where he disappeared into thin air right before he climbed on.

SIX

The Mastermind checks the time. He wonders how long this is going to take. Wonders if it will play out according to plan.

The tension is delicious.

It all began as an experiment. One he wasn't even sure he'd go through with. But it fed on itself. Got bigger. More seductive.

Planning and scheming had to become action. Knowledge is for using, not hoarding.

The testing period had been heady. Exhilarating. But the true potential of what he'd accomplished hadn't been realized until now.

What started as a solo was quickly becoming an ensemble piece.

So many layers. So many variables.

Such fun.

He waits, forcing patience, while he really wants to run around and cheer. Shout. Scream.

There's much left to do. But too many variables.

So he listens. And he waits.

The mouse has found the cheese.

Soon the trap will spring.

SEVEN

WTF?

I played the rewind/pause/fast-forward game again, but the results were the same as before. One moment Alter-Talon existed. The next moment he didn't. If I wasn't 100 percent positive I was watching an actual past event, I'd think someone somehow tampered with the transmission.

But TEV was tamperproof. The past was the past, and couldn't be changed or faked. The only reason I didn't think I killed Aunt Zelda was because I didn't kill Aunt Zelda. Even though every bit of evidence pointed to the contrary.

I turned to Neil, who was sitting at the breakfast bar on a stool, one eye on me and the other on the EPF at the front door.

"Neil, did your aunt have any enemies?"

His nose was running, and he sniffled. "Are you going to kill me?"

I sighed. "I'm a peace officer, Neil. I don't kill people."

"I'm sure that's a huge reassurance to the dead woman in the refrigerator."

"Enemies, Neil. Did she have any?"

"You mean besides you?"

I thought about hitting a button on the remote control and activating either the Taser needle or the supplication collar. Or both. But as a representative of the law, I was limited in the use of force when questioning subjects. In fact, I wasn't legally allowed to ask Neil anything without counsel present on both sides. But then, I wasn't placing Neil under arrest. The only one who could be brought up on charges in this room was me.

"Your aunt has a lot of nice things," I said, noticing a painting on the wall. It was real art, not a monitor. Old paintings, and the organic canvases they were painted on, were spared from the Great Recycling Effort with a grandfather clause. You didn't see too many of them outside of museums. "Was she employed?"

"Retired."

"From what?"

He sniffled again, a big one that sucked in a long line of snot that had been hanging down his chin. "Are you going to kill me?"

He looked like a whipped dog, and if he had a tail, it would surely be between his legs. But when I stared at him, I couldn't help but see him on top of my wife, grunting away. That didn't leave me much left in the sympathy department.

"Honestly, Neil, I'm starting to consider it. Can you tell me anything at all relevant to what might be happening here?"

His shoulders shook. "I shouldn't have gone to you. This was a huge mistake. Are you going to put me in the icebox?"

Neil started to cry. I rubbed my jaw and decided to take a closer look around. Aunt Zelda had books and a painting, both indicators of wealth. I wondered what else she had around the old homestead.

I began in the bedroom. There were more books, and the pillows and comforter were stuffed with real feathers. Two other paintings, both real, and taking up valuable wall space that could have been used for growing ivy or hemp. Her clothes closet was filled with synthetics, save for one spectacular piece: a raccoon fur coat. I thought of my four-legged friend on my green roof. Maybe if I put this on, I could make him think a giant had moved in and scare him away.

I checked all the drawers, but didn't find her DT. Aside from accessing the personal data on a chip implant, a person's digital tablet usually revealed the most about them.

I tried the living room next, and uncovered more contraband. A collection of antique tech magazines. There were paper issues of *Wired*, *PCWorld*, *Science Digest*, and a number of others. Some of them were almost as old as she was, which meant she must have bought them off the black market, or new when they came out. But why? The content of these magazines was available on the intranet on every DT. Why spend what had to be a small fortune for paper copies?

In the bathroom, I discovered cotton towels and a silk kimono. She also had one of those new ComfortMax toilets—the kind with a seat warmer, heated bidet, music player, scent control, and an autoflush so powerful it could suck down a boot without getting clogged. This went way beyond rich. Aunt Zelda was easily the wealthiest person I'd ever encountered during my years on the peace force.

Who was this woman?

I went into the kitchen. Neil had abandoned the breakfast bar and opened a utensil drawer. He had a pair of scissors against his neck and was getting ready to cut the supplication collar.

"Neil, that won't work. And if you try it—"

He squeezed the scissors. They didn't cut through the nanotubes. But they did activate the tamper sensors, sucking electricity from the Tesla field and giving him a harsh jolt.

"—you'll get shocked again."

Neil dropped onto his butt. The jolt continued.

"Neil, you need to let go of the scissors for it to stop."

He probably heard me. But the muscles in his hand remained locked on the blades, and the collar kept shocking him in self-defense. I saw a small cloud rise up and hover above his head. It wasn't smoke. It was the tears on his face turning into steam.

I gave his hand a kick—away from his neck so he didn't stab himself—and broke the connection.

"I want to go home," Neil cried.

"I know, buddy. Tell me how your aunt got so rich."

He touched his face, then his forehead. "Do I still have eyebrows?"

"Most of them."

I lost Neil to another sobbing binge, and took the opportunity to search through the kitchen. Still no DT. But I did find a can of blackstrap molasses that was worth more credits than I earned in a month. I'd never tasted the real thing before, and was tempted to try it.

Government subsidies, and competition with biofuel companies, caused food farmers to sow what could be grown and harvested the quickest. Things that took longer to grow were proportionally more expensive. The universal availability of synthetic food drove the price up even higher.

Indulgent as the molasses was, it was downright decadent when I figured out what she was doing with it. In one of the cabinets, Aunt Zelda had a Mr. Distiller.

Alcohol was never actually outlawed. In fact, the biggest manufacturer of alcohol in the world was the US government, which sold it as fuel. But it became illegal to drink it. Stupid, too. Alcohol pills were safer, and cheaper, than the real thing. And from what I understood, the pills didn't damage your liver, or give you bad breath and hangovers.

I stared at the antique silver device, retrofitted to function off of the Tesla grid, and noticed behind it on the shelf were several full bottles with *Rum* written on the sides.

Next I searched the bathroom to see what sorts of pills she took. I found the standards. Morphine. LSD. Ibuprofen. Penicillin. Antacids. Methamphetamine. Antihistamine. Pretty much the same contents as every other person's medicine cabinet, mine included. Except for two exceptions. Antiandrogen and Estrolux. Both in high doses.

Time to power up the intranet and see what I could see.

I took out my DT and accessed uffsee. While having every bit of human knowledge accessible on a digital tablet was an overwhelming experience—so overwhelming that many folks had to go into therapy because of their DT addiction—information was essentially useless unless you were able to find it. When I was a child, pre-intranet, the Internet was the place to go to learn things. But search engines were limited back then, and you spent most of your time trying to sort out the good information from the ads, inaccuracies, and plain old bullshit.

Then a man named Franklin Debont created UFSE. An acronym of Use the Fucking Search Engine, the uffsee search algorithm was intuitive and user-specific. In layman's terms, it learned what the user was seeking, and pinpointed data to match individual search requests.

No more wasted hours searching. WYSIWYW technology had made the overwhelming wealth of accumulated human knowledge as easy to navigate as a walk around the block.

I hit the voice button on my touch screen and told uffsee, "Detailed biography of Zelda Peterson, thirteen twenty-two Wacker Drive, Chicago, Illinois."

Three-thousandths of a second later the screen filled with data.

Or perhaps *filled* was too optimistic a word.

It listed all the standard stats. Height, weight, age, eye

color, chip number, previous addresses, and assorted public information like the charities she supported, moped license, estimated biofuel consumption, etcetera. No criminal record. And strangely, no mention of education or work history.

"Peace officer eyes only," I told my DT.

That brought up the private info. No known associates. The excessive amount she paid in taxes, which was more than Vicki made in a year. Credit history. But it came up blank in regard to family, college, and previous employment. No mention of how she got so rich, or how she managed to avoid penalties for the contraband she made no effort to conceal. It also didn't list her medical history, or the obvious reason she took Antiandrogen and Estrolux.

The average ten-year-old kid had more information available about them than Aunt Zelda did. Which meant it was time to have another chat with Neil. I set the voice-stress analyzer on my DT to record a neutral baseline.

"Oh, no." Neil's eyes were as wide as dinner plates when I walked up to him. "You're going to kill me now."

"Soon, Neil. But first I have some questions. Your aunt Zelda was a billionaire. I'm assuming you knew that and just neglected to mention it."

"I . . . uh . . . didn't know that."

My DT said it was the truth.

"Did you know Aunt Zelda was once Uncle Zelda?"

"Excuse me?"

"She was TG, Neil. Transgender. She took hormones because she used to be a man. Did you know that?"

"Uh . . . no."

I checked the touch screen. *Truth.*

"You apparently weren't very close. Did you know the intranet didn't actually mention you as a next of kin?" I moved closer to him, making him cringe. "Are you really her nephew, Neil?"

"Yes."

Inconclusive.

"Say it. Say she was your aunt."

"She was my aunt."

Inconclusive.

"Do you know how she got so rich?"

"No."

Truth.

"Do you know who murdered her?"

"Yes."

Truth.

"Who murdered her, Neil?"

"You did."

Truth.

Shit. Neil wasn't helping the investigation much. I decided to take it in another, unprofessional direction.

"Okay, Neil. One last question. Are you ready?"

He gave me a small, frightened nod.

"Do you love my wife, Neil?"

Neil swallowed, his Adam's apple bobbling. "Uh . . . no."

Untruth.

I made a fist, and he cowered away, covering his face. While hitting him would have felt pretty good, it wouldn't have accomplished anything. Of course he loved Vicki. All men who met Vicki fell in love with her. Guys like Neil were the reason I drove a Corvette.

Guys like Neil were also the reason my wife had a dozen more orgasms a week than I did.

My shoulder muscles bunched and I threw the punch, feeling the solid connection when my fist hit its target.

Neil screamed and scurried away. I stared at the hole I made in the plasterboard wall, and glanced at my knuckles, already beginning to swell.

Nice one, Talon. Hitting walls was about as mature as jealousy. Pretty lame coming from a man who helped rid Chicago of crime.

I glanced at the refrigerator. Apparently I hadn't done a good enough job in the crime department.

A feeling somewhere between panic and despair began to take root in my head. I seriously considered grabbing a bottle of rum, and some of Aunt Zelda's LSD, and zoning out for the rest of the day.

Instead I pressed my earlobe to activate my headphone. I wanted to call Vicki. Wanted to apologize for being a dick.

"Service not available."

Shit. Neil's collar must have been jamming my phone as well.

The rum and hallucinogens called, but I decided to man up and do my damn job. I couldn't hide the evidence of this murder forever. And once the news broke, I'd be arrested and convicted within an hour. With so few criminals these days, trials were often faster than the time it took to get dressed for them.

I still had no idea how the TEV showed me committing the murder.

But I did know someone who might be able to figure it out.

"Neil, there's some food in the cabinets when you get hungry," I said, heading for the front door. "Remember to stay out of the refrigerator. I'll BRB."

Then I left the apartment and went to see Michio Sata.

EIGHT

Outside the building, I called Vicki from my headphone as I walked to my car. She didn't pick up. Probably blocking my calls because I had acted like a cretin. I left her a message.

"Look, babe, I'm sorry I was an asshat. It's just that I love you so much, I can't stand thinking about you with other guys. Call me old-fashioned, but the only man you should be with is me. When I picture some tool like Neil . . ."

No. That wasn't an apology. That was continuing the fight.

"Erase. Restart. Vicki? I'm sorry. I knew when I married an SLP that you would spread your legs for other men . . ."

That didn't sound good either.

"Erase. Restart. Vicki, I'm sorry, but how can I help feeling jealous knowing you're sucking some other guy's . . . Shit. Erase. Restart."

"This isn't working, Talon."

Uh-oh.

"Vicki? Were you listening to that?"

"If you're not mature enough to accept what I do for a living, maybe we shouldn't be together."

I felt my heart stop. "Vicki . . . I'm sorry . . ."

"I've been discussing this with my therapist. She doesn't feel like this marriage is healthy for either of us."

I leaned against the hood of my Corvette. My Corvette, paid for because she boffed other men. "You discuss this with your therapist?"

"Don't you discuss it with your therapist?"

Both of our jobs required us to see therapists once a week, Vicki to retain her SLP license, me to remain a peace officer.

"No. We don't discuss anything. We spend the session watching hyperbaseball."

"My therapist thinks it's unhealthy for me to feel guilty about my profession because you're too insecure—"

"Insecure? I'm always one hundred percent sure of myself! Aren't I?"

"—too insecure to realize sex is simply a biological need that is completely wholesome and natural and impersonal. It's no more intimate than a massage."

"Then why can't you become a masseuse?"

"Dammit, Talon, you're acting so twentieth century. Other animals don't get jealous. This is your hang-up, and it's ruining our marriage."

I didn't like where this conversation was heading.

"Ruining? I thought our marriage was solid. We rarely ever fight about this."

"You mention it at least once a week."

"That's not a lot. Is it? Do you really think I'm insecure?"

"Maybe we need to take a break from each other for a while."

I thought about Aunt Zelda, and the speedy conviction that awaited me. "Maybe we'll get a break, whether we want one or not."

"So you agree with me?"

"What? No. I don't agree at all. But something came up at work that may—"

"Is it Neil? Did you help him? Is he okay?"

"You sound awfully concerned about Neil, babe."

"There you go again. He's just a sad, lonely little man."

A sad, lonely little man who nailed my wife today, while I was mowing our lawn.

"He's in love with you," I said.

"He's just got a crush. That's all."

"No. It's love. I asked him."

"You had no right to do that!"

"You say sex is harmless, but this tool would jump off a building for you. Is that harmless?"

"Where is Neil? You didn't do anything stupid, did you?"

"Can you give me a little credit, maybe?"

"I'm calling him."

"Vicki . . ."

She hung up.

"That went well," I said to my car. I stared out into the urban jungle, green buildings scraping the sky, thousands of anonymous biofuel scooters flooding the roads. My city. Vibrant, alive, and beautiful in its way.

The thought of living here without Vicki was unbearable.

The thought of living anywhere without Vicki was unbearable.

I climbed in the Vette and plotted a route to Sata's house. One crisis at a time.

Michio Sata lived in the northwest suburbs, in the city of Schaumburg. The twelve-lane highway was predictably stop-and-go, bikes clogging everything. Even the frog-leg lane was full, the kermits going slightly slower than the rest of traffic, probably because they enjoyed stopping every so often and bouncing around like idiots.

I glanced longingly at the cargo train alongside the road—used to move goods since trucks were outlawed—and not for the first time wished I was a bag of grain, which undoubtedly traveled faster than I did. Or maybe a hobo. Dangerous business, hopping onto trains, but at least those who survived reached their destinations on time.

To kill some time I linked my DT to the car stereo and listened to some blues, but every damn song seemed to be about cheating women and jealous men. So I asked it to filter the content for infidelity, and listened to eight straight songs about drinking, which made me want to turn around and grab that rum from Aunt Zelda's cabinet. After that I switched to laser radio and drummed my steering wheel to mc chris, Ice Cube, and Pink, but I tired of oldies pretty quick and went back to blues.

I managed to make it to Sata's neighborhood within an hour. Unlike Chicago, where ivy-draped buildings dominated the scenery, Schaumburg's architecture was placed far enough apart to turn it into a giant bamboo maze. Six-foot stalks sprouted from every bit of free land space, making it look like many of the shops and houses were sinking in a swamp, only their roofs visible from the street.

My GPS led me to Sata's driveway, a green clover road being squeezed on either side by overgrown hemp. The size of his lawn was commensurate with his wealth. Sata's patent rights in timecasting tech had made him a rich man. I parked next to a fountain—two concrete mermaids spitting water on each other—then grabbed my TEV and rang his videobell.

Sata's face appeared on the monitor. His long gray hair was plastered to his forehead with sweat, and I saw he was wearing a *keikogi*. He nodded when he saw me.

"Talon. I was hoping you'd come by. Enter."

At his voice command, the door unlocked. I walked into his home and slipped off my shoes, setting them in a cubbyhole of the *getabako* he kept in the foyer. Then I made my way to the gym.

Unlike Aunt Zelda, whose small apartment was light on greenery and heavy on contraband, Sata's wealth was

apparent only by the size of his home and land. Every wall
had ivy growing on it, and the tile floors were bracketed by
dirt patches growing sunflowers. The high ceilings were
inlaid with magnifying windows and solar lights, so no
matter the time of day his home was always bright. Every
few meters was a Doric pedestal supporting a bonsai tree.
According to Sata, some of them were more than a hundred years old.

The house smelled of plant life, of greenery and humid
oxygen and lavender that grew from hanging pots. The odor
changed when I opened the doors to the training room. The
gym smelled like sweat and determination.

Sata was barefoot in the center of the faux-wooden
floor, wearing a blue *keikogi*—the traditional long-sleeved
shirt—and black *hakama*—the baggy black pants that
looked like a skirt. In his hands was a bamboo sword,
a *shinai*. He was beating the absolute shit out of a faux-
wooden training dummy, his strikes as loud as thunder, but
coming in such rapid succession that they sounded more
like a group of people wildly applauding.

When he noticed my entrance he yelled out a terrifying
cry of, "*Ki-ai!*" and ran straight at me, his sword raised.

NINE

He swung the sword down, and just as I lifted up my forearm to block he switched from an attack to a hug.

"Great to see you, Talon-kun!"

I hugged him back. Then he held me at arm's length, his eyes twinkling as he looked me over. I felt a surge of affection, and a pang of guilt because I hadn't visited him in so long.

"Great to see you as well, Sata-san."

His *keikogi* wasn't tied, and it revealed a sweaty, bare chest cut with muscles. At sixty-four years old, Sata was built like a bodybuilder. He'd gotten even bigger since the last time I'd seen him, two years ago. While some of his appearance was the result of training, I knew Sata took various roids and hormones to stay so big. It looked like he'd been upping his dosage lately.

"There are clothes and *bōgu* in the closet there." He pointed over my shoulder. "Get dressed and we'll train."

"I would love to, sensei. But I'm really pressed for time, and I need your help."

"And I need yours as well, old friend. Ralph there is a

terrible training partner." He pointed to the wooden dummy. "His *kakari-geiko* is woefully predictable, and his blocking is lackluster at best. Suit up. After a quick match, I'll be at your disposal."

I couldn't say no to Sata. "You're going to beat me."

"Of course I'm going to beat you. You seem distracted, and you're thinner than I remember."

"I'm the same I've always been. A hundred and ninety pounds soaking wet. You've just gotten huge. What are you, two hundred thirty?"

"Two fifty. The wonders of modern chemistry. I'm thinking of gaining another twenty pounds, competing as a hyperheavyweight in the next nationals. Now, suit up. Let's see if you can last longer than eight seconds this time."

I pursed my lips. The only reason he'd beaten me that quickly was because I'd tied my *hakama* too loosely and had tripped over the cuffs. Sata knew this, but it tickled him to bring it up every time he saw me.

I dropped the TEV and stripped down to my boxer briefs, dressing quickly. Sata helped me put on the *bōgu*. Kendo armor consisted of a padded chest plate, called a *dô*, padded gloves that covered the forearms, called *kote*, a padded belt with five hanging panels called a *tare*, and the instantly recognizable helmet with the metal grill faceplate, known as the *men*.

When fully suited up, you felt kind of invincible. Like a medieval Japanese robot. If given the choice of combat wearing *bōgu* or hyperfootball gear, I'd pick the kendo armor every time.

But there was a reason the armor was so protective. The kendo sword—the *shinai*—was more than a meter long, made of four slats of bamboo lashed together. A ninth-*dan kendoka*, like Sata, could kill someone with one thrust of his bamboo sword.

This was not a sport for wimps.

I quit practicing kendo on a regular basis seven years

ago, when Sata retired from the peace force. At the time, I
was a capable *sho-dan*—eight *dan*s below Sata. But what
I lacked in experience I made up for in speed. All of his
chiding aside, I knew Sata respected my skills.

"Where is your armor, sensei?" I asked.

"It isn't worth the time it will take me to put it on to go
against you, Eight Seconds."

Cocky bastard.

I grabbed a sword and we walked to the middle of the
training room. The floor was cool under my bare feet, and
already my hands had begun to sweat inside my gloves.

On first glance, kendo rules were simple. The first person
to land two strikes wins. The only strikes that counted were
to the head, sides, and wrists.

But scoring was complicated by something called *ki-ken-tai-itchi*. It translated roughly as *spirit*. Simply tapping
your opponent's target zones wasn't enough to score. You
had to hit them hard, and your leading foot had to slap the
floor the same moment contact was made. You also had to
scream out, "*Ki-ai!*" with feeling.

The first time you did it, it felt silly. But in the heat of a
match, swords swinging with full force, each man trying to
cream the other, the *ki-ai*s came naturally.

Sata faced me on the floor and bowed. I bowed back.
Then we raised our *shinai*, and the whoop-ass began.

For the first match, I lasted longer than eight seconds,
but not by much. After circling each other, I managed to
block twice before Sata slapped me upside the head, rocking me backward. To show it wasn't a fluke, he won his second point by hitting me in the exact same spot. The armor
protected me from most of the pain, but it still felt like my
head was inside a large bell, being rung.

Second match, Sata focused on my sides. I saw this was
his intent, and focused my parries at waist level, trying to
keep him from scoring. Since I left my head unguarded,

I was able to hold him off for longer, and it took him about two minutes to win.

For our third match, Sata went after my *kote*. The intensity really kicked up. He was swinging at my wrists, and I was doing my damnedest to block his strikes and protect my wrists. After clashing swords sixty or seventy times in rapid succession, my arms felt like they'd turned into lead, and the lactic acid buildup in my muscles made them ache. Each time I struck his *shinai* with mine, it was like smacking a brick wall with a hyperbaseball bat. But I kept him at bay, kept him from scoring.

"Better," Sata said, pausing his barrage. "You still have the speed."

"You've gotten faster. And stronger."

"I've also managed to keep my boyish good looks."

Sata advanced again, creaming me on the side of my head.

Apparently he'd judged me good enough to no longer focus on specific targets. I took a bit of pride in that. But what I really wanted to do was score a point. I wasn't big into competitive sports. I preferred competing against myself. Beating my last marathon time. Increasing my bench press by five pounds. But when I did face an opponent, I didn't like to lose.

I was going to lose against Sata, no question about it. But I wasn't going to make it easy for him.

Sata advanced again. I had a headache, and my arms hurt, but I'd become used to moving in the bulky armor. I'd also been reacquainting myself with Sata's technique. He was strong, and fast, but his attacks followed patterns. Perhaps he was so used to drilling on a training dummy that he'd forgotten what it was like when someone hit back.

I aimed to show him.

It was unlikely Sata would let me get to his head or throat. Not that I wanted to go there anyway; without his armor, I could seriously injure him if I landed a lucky blow.

So I focused on his sides and wrists. He was so used to my defense that if I attacked, I might be able to land a strike by surprise.

Sata went for my *kote* again, and our bamboo swords clacked and bent as we traded blows. But I didn't back away this time. I blocked his shots, saw him go in for a thrust, and spun away, bringing my *shinai* around toward his ribs.

He blocked it, but barely. The attempt apparently delighted him.

"Excellent, Talon-kun!"

He launched into another attack. But either his speed wasn't as great, or I was anticipating his strikes, because I was able to parry him with much less effort. I could guess the look on my face matched his grim countenance—eyebrows furrowed, lips drawn down in a scowl, veins popping out in the forehead. I continued to block his swings, and then saw the surprise in his eyes when I advanced, making him step backward, and finally catching him off guard and slapping him across the forearm with my *shinai*, yelling, "*Ki-ai!*" as I did.

Sata's eyes went wide in surprise. He looked at his arm. The welt had already begun to raise, his pores leaking tiny droplets of blood.

TEN

It must have hurt like a bitch. Sata's reaction was not what mine would have been.

He let out a belly laugh.

"Terrific! You've saved face, and made me pay for my arrogance, Talon. I was wrong to taunt you by not wearing *bōgu*. Please forgive an old fool."

He bowed. I bowed back.

"So you want to put on the armor for the last point?" I asked.

Sata shook his head. "No. You won't land another strike."

Like hell I wouldn't.

I rushed at Sata and began a steady, deliberate offense. I knew it wouldn't lead to a point, but maybe I could trick him into making a mistake.

My offense lasted all of five blocked strikes, and then I was on the defense again, my hands a blur as I kept him at bay. Once again, Sata's strength and skill forced me back, my parries so violent I had to fight to keep my balance. Then, incredibly, he went even faster, his *shinai* twirling

like a heliplane propeller, me practically jogging backward
to stay out of harm's way.

My back hit the wall, surprising me, and Sata thrust at
my throat. I jerked to the left, and the tip of his *shinai* hit
me in my unpadded chest. I'd never been attacked with a
sledgehammer, but I could guess this was what it felt like.
As I dropped to my knees I managed to lash out one-handed
and catch Sata on his left side, under his raised arms.

Point. Win.

Sata fell onto his knees next to me, wincing as he held his
kidney. He'd hit me harder, but I'd had my ribs to protect me.

We stayed there for a moment, breathing heavy, clutching our respective injuries, and then Sata began to laugh.
"Excellent match. Go again?"

"Your pride can't handle losing, old friend?"

"I may not be able to sleep tonight, I'm so distraught
over it."

"I'll take a rain check. I really need you to help with
something."

"Of course." Sata stood and offered his hand to help me
up. I took it. My right arm was going a little numb, and I
wasn't as steady on my feet as I would have preferred.

"Are you all right? Ribs cracked?"

I lifted off my helmet, then worked off the gloves. "I
think they're okay. But you may have pinched a nerve."

"Should we go to the hospital?"

I couldn't tell if Sata was being sincere, or busting my
balls. His twinkling eyes betrayed nothing.

"I'll be fine. Is there someplace we can talk?"

"The study. I'll meet you there after I've changed.
Would you like a morphine pill?"

I took a deep breath, wincing at the pain. Morphine
sounded pretty good. But I needed a clear head.

"Aspirin would be better."

He nodded, then walked off. I managed to extricate
myself from the remainder of my uniform and get dressed.

The buttons on my shirt were nearly impossible. My fingers had that pins-and-needles sensation, like I'd lost circulation to my arm. He'd gotten me good. I may have won the match, but if it had been a real fight, Sata would be bashing my head open right now.

I hoped I was in that good a shape when I was his age. Maybe there was something to roids after all. While I had no aversion to better living through chemistry, I pursued my health goals the natural way, with regular exercise. The fact that roids were known to harm the libido also gave me pause, and excessive use led to a condition called roid rage, where basic mental faculties collapsed. Neither would endear me to Vicki, so I avoided the stuff.

I left my last few buttons undone and made my way to the study. His sofa, chairs, and wall screen seemed overrun with wild vines. But a closer look saw the vines were carefully pruned to avoid interfering with the walkway, furniture, and electronics. Sata was already on the sofa, a green drink in his hand. On the table in front of him was another full glass, and a bottle of aspirin. I thanked him and swallowed two pills with the liquid, which had a wheatgrass base that tasted like a freshly mown lawn. Knowing Sata, the drink probably had a wealth of micronutrients in it. But that didn't make it any easier to stomach.

"Thanks. Can I use your projector?"

"By all means."

I synced up the TEV to his screen. "I have to warn you. The man in the transmission looks like me. He even has a chip that says it's me. But he's someone else. I was with my wife when this took place."

I let the scene from Aunt Zelda's play, beginning where Alter-Talon materialized out of the elevator.

Sata watched without a sound. The expression on his face was somewhere between confusion and repulsion. I let it play until the killer disappeared again in the hallway. Then I paused the image, waiting for his response.

"It's been a very long time since I've seen a murder," Sata said. "And I've never seen a friend committing one."

"That wasn't me, Michio. The hair is different. And did you notice that the man in the transmission is left-handed?"

"Yes. He also has a mole on his cheek. You don't have a mole. But all of that could be easily explained. And it's inconsequential compared to seeing you break that poor woman's neck."

"If I wanted to hide it being me, I wouldn't have changed my hair and pretended to be lefty. I would have worn a mask or veil. This guy didn't care that his face was seen. Because it isn't his face. It's my face."

"And you got this on-site?"

"Only two hours ago."

Sata stood up, rubbing his jaw. "It's impossible. TEV can't be faked."

"Something's going on. You saw how he appeared and disappeared near the elevator. Wouldn't that be enough to cast reasonable doubt?"

"No. Remember the State of Illinois v. Jack Kilborn?"

I nodded. Rape, but it had happened in a high-rise building that burned down. So it was impossible to get the TEV in the exact location of the event. Timecasting worked only when you occupied the same physical space where past events occurred. I was dangled from a crane for ten hours, trying to get a good image of the guy's face. I wound up getting one, but it lasted only for a few rough frames. The judge allowed it. So there was a precedent for dodgy TEV footage.

"Sensei, if I can't get a close friend to believe me, how will I get a jury to?"

Sata appraised me. His face was kind.

"Do you have any enemies, Talon?"

"Of course. I helped put away over a thousand guys."

"We'll need to see if any of them have been released. Or have escaped. You might also want to put together a list of anyone currently on the street who'd like to frame you."

"So you'll help me?"

"I should say no. The transmission is pretty cut-and-dried that you're the killer, and if I assist you, I'm an accessory after the fact. But something about the recording bothers me."

"The disappearing and reappearing?"

"That. And the color. Did it look orange to you?"

"It was orange. I had to adjust the hue to get it to appear normal."

"There's something definitely strange here. This is the original, unaltered recording?"

"You can check the time stamp."

"Getting someone to look like you would be difficult. Getting them to have a duplicate ID chip would be impossible. But there's no way they could alter a timecast."

"Some sort of digital image?"

"Was the dead woman a digital image?"

I shook my head. "She was real."

"I've seen enough of these to know that killer was real as well. You know digital imagining. The movies spend hundreds of millions of credits on special effects, and you can still tell it's fake. That wasn't fake. Can you play it again?"

"I have a lead to follow up on. I'll transfer a copy to you now." I pressed a button and saved the transmission to Sata's projector. "You wouldn't happen to have an Internet connection, would you?"

"Why on earth would I? Do I look like a whack job?"

No matter. They had one at the office.

"Thanks for helping me on this, Sata. And for trusting me."

"You were one of my best students, Talon. I'll do what I can."

He offered his hand. I shook it, but the feeling still hadn't returned to my fingers. If anything, the numbness had gotten more severe.

I probably should have gone to the hospital. Instead I went to work.

ELEVEN

Area 4 Peace Headquarters was located in the Loop, on Wabash. Ever since the El train was updated to carry three times as many passengers back in the fifties, Wabash had been off-limits to civilian traffic. But city officials and peace officers were exempt from the ban.

Though I had to steer around the massive support pylons for the El, Wabash was still my favorite street to drive on. No glut of biofuel bikes. No traffic signals. If pedestrian traffic was light, I could even get the Vette up to fifty mph.

But today the ride to the office was perfunctory. I had a lot on my mind, and my arm was giving me some serious trouble. Adding to my woes was the fact that Vicki refused to answer her headphone. I wondered if she had blocked me. I wondered if I could blame her if she had. So I let my DT compile a list of potential enemies, and cruised at a comfortable thirty-five until I reached A4.

I parked in the underground garage, in a reserved spot next to Teague's vintage Porsche 911. Ours were the only two cars in a lot crammed with bikes, and his was worth more than mine. Back when we were rookies, we spent a lot of our spare time hanging out in P&P bars, getting wasted, discussing what kind of cars we'd buy if we could ever afford them. The Porsche was his way of thumbing his nose at my Vette, and our prior friendship. To pay for it, he lived in a shithole apartment the size of my right shoe.

I took the elevator to the forty-ninth floor. A4 was the largest area in Chicago, so it had the largest main building, home base to more than twelve thousand cops. The majority of them worked Traffic and Pedestrian Control, and the rest were vice regulators, making sure everyone played nice. No more Homicide Division. No more Violent Crimes. Fewer than a thousand cops still wore sidearm Tasers.

On one hand, living in a green utopia had a lot of perks. With the serial violent offenders all locked up, and average citizens obeying the major laws, the city was safer than it had ever been.

On the other hand, it was pretty boring. Which was why, for the first time in years, I came to work energized. I actually had a case. An important case. And even though it was my neck on the line, it was almost worth it just to feel useful again.

Even that asshole Teague couldn't ruin my buzz.

Since the Timecaster Division was down to just two people, we shared an office. It was a big office, but we still managed to get in each other's way. I'd rather do demos at a dozen third-grade classrooms than have to talk to Teague for more than five minutes.

He had his feet up on his desk and was watching a projection of CNP—Cable Network Pr0n. He muted the action—which from my limited observation seemed to involve bondage, midgets, and a very fat goat—when I came in.

"Well, if it ain't the second-best Van Damme in the state."

There were only two full-time timecasters still in Illinois, me and him, and he'd graduated Sata's class two points ahead of me. Van Damme was a slang term, going way back to a classic 2D movie called *Timecop*.

I ignored him, heading to my desk. I had a terminal link there, which would allow me hook into the Internet.

"Well, don't we look determined today?" Teague swiveled his chair in my direction. "What's on your mind, bro? Marital problems?"

I shouldn't have let him bait me, but I still said, "You wish."

"How is your dee-liscious whore of a wife? She miss me? Or does she have more than enough cock to satisfy her?"

"She sends her love."

"And she charges out the ass for it. Maybe I'll stop by, give her a tap for old times' sake."

"That won't work. She's got a new policy. No clients with a penis under three inches." I stared at him, hard. "But I heard your mother doesn't have standards. Maybe you should give her a call."

His eyebrows creased in anger, and I wondered if he was actually going to get up and make a try for me. Teague was taller, but we weighed about the same. The one time we did scuffle, years ago, it had been a draw.

But the moment passed, and he snorted and flashed his teeth. "FU, Talon. FU and your whore."

He popped a nicotine pill, and went back to his pr0n. I checked the program compiling my enemies list—82.656 percent complete and already up over two thousand names. Then I punched in some passwords and wirelessly connected my DT to the Internet.

I hadn't been online in a while, and in my absence the World Wide Web had gotten worse. Even though the CPD had the latest blockers and antimalware programs, I was immediately assaulted with pop-ups. For shits and grins, I kept a window open of the programs and sites my blocker assassinated while I surfed. In the eighteen seconds it took for me to get to WikiWorld, I'd been attacked three hundred and seventeen times. That didn't include the forty-two hijack attempts and eight attempted trojan-bot hacks.

The Internet sucked.

WikiWorld, which had a decent reputation back when I was a kid, was now a cesspool of unsupported and imaginary garbage that any n00b and b00b could edit at will. Most of the time it was useless. But there was a chance Aunt Zelda could be in there somewhere.

I projected a keyboard onto my desktop, preferring typing to voice commands Teague could hear, and punched in Zelda's name. WikiWorld gave me a hit and a brief definition, but some prankster had replaced every noun in the entry with "hairy weasel dick," making it pretty much unreadable. I tried to access the edit history, but his hack had encompassed that as well.

I heard bleating, and looked around. Teague had turned up the volume on his pr0n, just to annoy me.

"Check out that flexibility, bro. Vicki ever get freaky with dumb animals? Other than you?"

I pressed the remote on my belt, switching the projector to the Homeschooling Network and putting a jam on the button. Now no matter what Teague tried to watch, it would be stuck on six-year-olds perfecting their recyclable macaroni art.

"WTF?"

As he tried in vain to change the channel, I went from WikiWorld to an old search engine I used to use. All it came up with were ads, pr0n, and ads for pr0n. I tried a pirated version of uffsee, but UFSE didn't work well on the Internet, and it crashed before the Boolean results could be compiled.

Then my browser did get hijacked, by a 3D ad program that flashed some very fake holographic breasts in my face. I had to kill my connection and start over.

This time, I injected my search parameters into a CPD metaspider and crawled WikiWorld, trying to find an un-

tampered entry in the script. The spider got caught in an
adware loop, pop-ups coming faster than my antivirus program could kill them.

I disconnected again, and used a brunt force attack with
a hundred metaspiders.

"The projector is fuct. Did you do something to it,
ass-munch?"

The pop-ups came again, and I set my DT to open each
one in its own browser, trying to slow them down.

Incredibly, it worked, and I got the unaltered Zelda
page. I captured the screen before some malware could eat
it up, and went from elation to confusion to outright shock
when I learned who Aunt Zelda used to be before her gender transformation.

Zelda Peterson was born Franklin Debont, the multi-
billionaire who invented UFSE.

"Live! Murder in Chicago!"

I looked up at the projector. The macaroni art had been
replaced with an emergency news bulletin. Some serious-
looking anchor said, *"We interrupt your regularly scheduled program for this late-breaking report. Warning. What
you are about to see is shocking."*

It shocked me more than anyone. There, on Teague's
projector screen, was Zelda Peterson in her kitchen, next to
the sink, as a man snuck up behind her.

TWELVE

I knew what happened next and fumbled for the remote, changing the channel.

It didn't matter. Each channel I flipped to was showing the same thing. Poor Aunt Zelda getting her head bashed in, and her neck broken. The image was circular, with telltale red edges. A TEV transmission.

Sata? Had he gone to the authorities?

No. This wasn't the transmission I'd recorded. This one had a different perspective, different angles, and a tighter zoom. Zelda was dead, and it still hadn't shown the killer's face.

But if this wasn't my recording, whose recording was it?

I stared at Teague. The only other timecaster in Chicago.

Then my DT beeped. It had finished compiling my list of 3,342 known enemies. And the name at the very top was Joshua Teague VanCamp.

"Talon? Shit!"

I looked up. Alter-Talon was on the projector screen, carving up Aunt Zelda's arm.

Teague stood up and spun around, reaching for his Taser holster.

"Hold it!" I yelled. My hand hovered over my holster as well. But I still had limited sensation in my right hand. I doubted I'd be able to draw, let alone fire.

Teague stared at me, hard. Hate smoldered in his eyes.

"You fucking psycho. You really popped a gasket, didn't you, bro?"

"Put your hands behind your head, Teague." I kept my voice steady, hoping it didn't betray my fear. My heart was beating so fast I could hear it. "You know I can outdraw you."

"The victim is still as yet unidentified," the projector droned on, *"but the murderer has been positively IDed as Talon Ace Avalon."*

"I knew you were unstable, Talon. But an old bitch? Aren't you getting enough at home?"

"Hands behind your head!" I yelled.

Time seemed to stand still. If Teague drew, he'd Tase me first. Then it would be a speedy trial and a conviction by dinnertime. I'd spend the rest of my life in a maximum-security prison with three thousand guys I helped put there.

Teague seemed to read my mind. "You won't last ten minutes in jail, Talon. They'll eat you alive. But don't worry . . . I'll comfort Vicki for you while you're gone."

"Why the games, Teague? Why didn't you arrest me when I walked in?"

"You know me, bro. I love games."

His hand moved an inch closer to the butt of his Taser.

"Don't," I warned. "We've gone shooting together. I'll put a Taser needle right up your nose."

"And then what? Snap my neck? What the hell happened to you?"

"Hands behind your fucking head."

For a bad moment I thought he was going to make a try for his weapon. I could see in his eyes he was considering it. But it passed, and he complied, lacing his fingers behind his neck.

"Doesn't matter." He shrugged. "You're in A4 headquarters, for fuck's sake. How far you think you're gonna get?"

I used my left hand to shove my DT into my pocket, staring hard at my former friend. He must have been the one to give the footage to the news. But could he have actually set this whole thing up? Framed me somehow?

He had the opportunity. He also had the motive. But did he have the smarts to pull it off?

This wasn't the time or place for an interrogation. Hundreds of cops, in this very building, had to have seen the broadcast. Because I was a peace officer, required to be located if needed, my chip ID was fully trackable by GPS. They were probably on their way up right now.

"Your hand is shaking, Talon. I bet you're too scared to draw."

"Don't try me."

Teague made his move, his hand coming down off his neck, reaching for his weapon. I reached across my body, left-handed, and dug out my piece, pulling it from the holster and aiming it upside down, my pinkie finding the trigger, squeezing off a shot just as Teague cleared faux leather.

Not my fastest draw, and my aim was way off, but unfortunately for Teague the bullet still hit him. In the groin.

A Tesla bolt of lightning materialized and zapped him right in the junk. He dropped, shrieking, and I ran past, out of the office and into the hallway.

"There he is!"

Twenty cops in the hall raised their weapons.

I darted left, keeping low as wax bullets pummeled the walls on either side of me, exploding in jagged bolts of electricity. I managed to get to the stairwell without getting hit, and took the stairs three at a time. When I reached the fiftieth floor I paused, listening.

A person was running up the stairs, toward me.

Make that *a lot of people* were running up the stairs. I exited the stairwell, running like crazy, realizing it was futile, that I'd never make it out of this building.

I ducked into an office, ignoring the worker bees, wondering where I could go. Hiding wouldn't work; they'd track my chip. The windows on this floor wouldn't open, and they were undoubtedly safety glass. Desperation even made me briefly consider attempting a hostage situation. But I didn't have a lethal weapon, or adequate protection from their Tasers.

Maybe I should just play it cool. Try to hide my face and walk calmly out of there.

"It's him!"

So much for that.

The cop who spotted me was young, eager, pointing his finger when he should have been pointing his weapon. I was on him in three steps, snapping my hips around, kissing his cheek with a spin-kick. Another cop, a woman, had her Taser already out. I ducked under her first shot, diving at the floor and rolling, coming up next to the biorecycle chute.

It had a push door, no wider than twenty inches. I stuck my hand inside and gave it a swift yank. The aluminum cover popped off, revealing a wide metal duct. But wide enough for me to fit inside? And did I really want to go in there? The smell was rank; rotten food and decay. I had no idea where it ended. Might be a six-hundred-foot drop into a mulcher.

The air around me exploded in electricity, the sharp scent of ozone overtaking the garbage stench. Without thinking it through I shoved my legs into the chute just as a Taser bullet drilled me in the breastbone.

Though it reeked of cliché, the pain was indeed electrifying. At the area of impact, it felt like someone pressing a hot coal against my chest. The million volts locked my muscles rigid, my jaw slamming shut, my arms and legs stiffening like iron bars. I heard crackling and sizzling, my eyes open and paralyzed as the Tesla energy struck the needle in my chest like a lightning rod.

Then gravity took over and I fell down the chute.

THIRTEEN

The drop was vertical, the metal duct wide enough so my shoulders barely grazed the sides as I picked up speed. Held rigid by the Taser and wracked with pain, I did a quick calculation in my brain.

Vicki conned me into going skydiving once. Not too many things scare me, but I'm not a huge fan of heights, and the control freak in me dislikes heliplane rides because I'm not the one driving. Jumping out of a heliplane seemed like a really bad idea, but being a big macho peace officer and a new groom who wanted to impress his bride, I did it. Vicki jumped first, which was perfect, because she didn't see any of the three times I vomited.

Prior to jumping, I did a fair amount of research on skydiving and the speed human beings fall. In open air, terminal velocity—when the force of gravity on a person is equal to wind resistance—takes about fifteen seconds to top out, at around 125 mph.

There was no air resistance in the chute. And the vertical position I was in meant I'd be accelerating faster, and hit a higher speed.

On the fiftieth floor, roughly six hundred and twenty-five feet high, I'd probably have a terminal velocity of thirty feet per second.

Which meant I had twenty seconds, maybe less, before hitting ground zero. And even if I fell onto a stack of air mattresses, at my speed it would be the same as hitting concrete.

The chute was dark, except for the zigzag of light that continued to drill into my chest as I plummeted. Just as I wondered what the transmission range of Taser bullets was, the electricity shut off, plunging me into complete darkness but allowing my muscles to move again.

My arms and legs felt heavy—the jolt had filled my bloodstream with lactic acid. I spread out my feet, trying to get a grip on the sides of the chute. No good. The metal had been treated with polymer-slick, so recyclables wouldn't stick. Polymer-slick was a carbon-based surfacer made with buckyballs. I might as well be trying to grip crude oil.

With ten seconds wasted and ten left to live, I slapped at my utility belt, seeking my nanotube reel—

Nine seconds . . .

My right hand fumbled for my gun, so I had to release the reel catch with my left—

Eight seconds . . .

I hit the catch and pulled the blank, my plummeting body brushing against the side of the chute, burning all the skin off my knuckles—

Seven seconds . . .

The pain in my hand brought instant tears, but I managed to hold on to the blank, while I willed my right hand to somehow pull the Glock from my holster—

Six seconds . . .

I brought the Glock around, manually inserting the blank into the chamber backward, through the barrel—

Five seconds . . .

I fired at waist level, straight into the side of the chute, the blank embedding itself in the metal and forming a molecular bond—

Four seconds . . .

The nanotube line whirred out of the reel, only a few millimeters thick but stronger than steel, and I kept my hands away so it didn't slice them off—

Three seconds . . .

The autosensor in the reel adjusted tension, my belt digging into my gut like I'd been hit by a bus, slowing me down, but not fast enough—

Two seconds . . .

The chute ended, and I fell into open air, the line on my belt tugging me so I went from vertical to horizontal—

One second . . .

Light blurred by, and I gasped and choked on the strong reek of rotting garbage just as my back slapped into the ground with a wet *splat.*

Was the splatting sound my skin splitting open and spraying out blood? Was it my head exploding like a pumpkin?

I stared up at the chute, twenty feet above my head, and watched an orange peel flutter out and hit me in the chest while I waited for pain and death to overtake me.

But neither did.

I did a body inventory. Left leg worked. Right leg worked. Left arm worked, but hurt. Ditto the right arm. Head and neck okay. Shoulders and back seemed fine.

I snorted, amazed I had not only survived, but did so intact.

So what made that splatting . . . ?

Then the ground seemed to melt beneath me, and I realized I wasn't on the ground at all. I was on a huge vat of decaying plant matter. The putrescent sludge swallowed me up like a flesh-eating blob, and I took one more gulp of air before sinking into the muck.

FOURTEEN

The Mastermind muses on the absoluteness of uncertainty.

He wishes he knew more about what was happening. But his reach is limited. His ears are silent. His eyes restricted to newscasts.

What's going on? Where is the mouse?

Better not to know, he muses. The mouse is both on course and off course. Dead and alive. The Copenhagen interpretation of quantum mechanics. Once you measure it, wavefunction collapses.

Perhaps instead of referring to Talon as a mouse, he should think of him as Schrödinger's cat. For the Mastermind, Talon is everything and nothing at the same time. Best of all, the math backed it up.

There's much left to do. Calls. Travel. Meetings.

The search has run its course, but there are other searches to perform.

He reaches up, feels his own heart. It pounds with excitement, and some trepidation.

Killing the woman was necessary. The cheese to lure the mouse.

But it was more than that. She gave him a precious and unique gift. Her life, for his amusement. He respected her for that. Even honored her.

However, she was only a footnote in the eventual history of his endeavors. An insignificant warm-up act for the magnificence to come.

It isn't like comparing walking to crawling.

It's more like comparing walking to breaking the light-speed barrier.

There will be more deaths.

Many more deaths.

His heart beats faster at the thought, and he smiles.

FIFTEEN

The effect was like quicksand. The viscous pool was somewhere between a liquid and a solid. Buoyancy wasn't working, and every tiny struggle created a minivacuum that
sucked me down farther. While I was grateful I couldn't
smell anything while holding my breath, I knew I'd have
to breathe eventually, and the idea of taking this crap into
my mouth, my lungs, was almost worse than the thought
of dying. To make things even more disgusting, the goop
was warm—probably due to bacteria activity, which generated heat.

Garbage was gross. Warm garbage was unbearable.

I dared not open my eyes, concerned what diseases
would permanently blind me. But after more than a minute
without air, blindness became the least of my concerns.
When I kept absolutely still, I sank. When I moved, I sank
even faster. There was no way to get on top of the stuff, to
pull myself—

The nanotube line.

I moved my left hand toward the reel. Even using all of
my strength, it was like pushing through mud, and I could

manage only an inch or so a second. The energy expended
by my effort depleted the remaining oxygen in my blood,
and my head began to spin. Even through closed eyelids, I
saw flashes of red and yellow.

I wondered if my body would ever be discovered. Or
if I'd be recycled just like all of this biomass, eventually
winding up in someone's scooter tank.

My brain began to fool itself. It told me it was okay to
breathe this shit. In fact, this shit had a high oxygen content
in it. All I needed to do was take a big gulp and I'd be fine.

My hand touched something. A dial. Something familiar about it. Something important.

My utility belt reel.

I turned it counterclockwise and felt a tug on my belt.
My sinking had stopped. But had it reversed? The sludge
was too thick, too warm, for me to tell if I was moving
through it.

I had no idea how much time had passed, but my will-
power was gone. Betrayed by my body, I could no longer
keep holding my breath. My immediate future would be
choking, gagging, and dying, accompanied by a horrible
taste.

My mouth opened with a will of its own, my diaphragm
spasmed, and I gasped for air I knew I wouldn't get.

I was right. The taste was terrible. Like taking a bite out
of a rotten egg coated with sour milk and dog feces.

But I was also wrong. Because it was, indeed, air.

I opened my eyes, squinting against the sting, and
saw the nanotube reel had brought me to the surface of
the muck and was slowly winching me out of the vat. My
peace officer training had apparently paid off, because
one of the things drilled into our heads was to never let
go of our weapons. I was pleasantly surprised to see I still
clenched my Taser. I shoved it into my holster, then shifted
my weight so I rose vertically.

Thirty seconds later I was hanging in midair, above the

biomuck. I hit the reel, pausing the ascent, and then moved my arms and legs to swing. Slowly at first, then picking up speed as momentum kicked in. Timing it right, I pressed the release on the reel just as I cleared the edge of the vat.

The fall could have been fatal—a fifteen-foot drop onto grass. But I twisted my body around as I fell and managed to catch the lip of the vat, my body slamming alongside it. I released my grip and hit the ground hard, flexing my knees to absorb the landing, then slamming onto my side and slapping the ground with my open palms, like a judo fall.

I lay there for a moment. Then I laughed. A wet, garbled laugh that ended in me turning over and throwing up on the floor, the fear and the stench too much for my stomach.

I wiped my good hand across my face, trying to squeegee away the goo from my eyes, nose, and mouth. Then I got on all fours, and eventually my feet, and tried to figure out where I was in the building.

The smell was supernatural. Besides the biomass vat I'd crawled out of, there were six others of equal size, plus two toilet vats. Like plant and animal matter, human waste was also compostable and recyclable. I'd never given much thought to what happened after I flushed, but it apparently ended up in a holding facility like this one. The pools were even larger than the biomass vats, making me glad I chose the right chute to drop down.

Keeping my nostrils pinched together, I staggered past the vats to the near wall, which I followed until I found a door. I didn't encounter anyone, but that didn't surprise me. This wasn't a part of the building where you'd hang out for fun.

The door led to a hallway. I tugged out my DT, wiped off the screen, and brought up a schematic for this building. One room over was the furnace, and then beyond that the stairwell to the parking garage.

Every step felt slow and ponderous, like I was still in the muck. As anxious as I was to get out of there, I also had an irrational desire to curl up in a corner and get some sleep. Two near-death experiences within four minutes really took a toll on the body.

I managed to find the garage, and incredibly it was empty. It took me a moment to get my bearings, and then I half ran, half stumbled to my Corvette. It was hardly anonymous, but they could already track me with my chip, and I chose horsepower over a less auspicious ride. I fished my keys out of my pocket and hit the security button.

Then the garage filled with cops.

They came streaming in from all directions. I pulled out my Taser and shot twice, each shot hitting a peace officer.

But there was no bolt of Tesla lightning. No falling over in spasms. They kept coming at me, pulling out and aiming their own weapons.

They'd suspended my electricity account.

I managed to get behind my car door as the firing began, the blue storm starting off with just a few bolts and then gathering speed and strength until the wax bullets hitting my car sounded like hurricane hail. I jammed my key into the ignition—grateful it was a real key because if they'd killed my electric account, they'd probably disabled all other chip functions—and then gunned the engine and slammed the Vette into gear.

It was like driving into a supernova, too bright for me to be able to steer, so much light it hurt like someone was poking my corneas with splinters. I turned sharply, plowing through parked biofuel bikes, getting ahead of the barrage just enough to be able to see again. I gunned the engine, drowning out the electric bullet maelstrom, and then was whiplashed into my seat by a rear impact.

I squinted into my rearview mirror.

Teague. In his Porsche 911. As I watched, he rammed me again, jerking my head backward.

"You want to play, old buddy? Let's play."

I pinned the accelerator, throwing dirt and clover onto

his windshield as my fat rear tires dug two trenches in the greentop.

I squeezed my earlobe, activating my headphone. No dial tone. Disabled. So I flipped on the dashboard microphone.

"Sirens," I told the car.

The police lights came on, embedded in my front and rear fenders, strobing red and blue and accompanied by the piercing wail of the emergency horn, belting out the familiar *weeeeeeeeee-oooooooooooooo-weeeeeeeeeee-oooooooooooo*.

When was the last time I'd hit my siren? Months? Years?

Hectic as the situation was, I managed a tight smile. Being a cop felt pretty good.

I shot out of the garage, my chassis taking to the air, and burst out onto Wabash, the El train racing by overhead. I jerked the wheel, fishtailed, and floored it, chasing the El, weaving through the metal beams that supported it. The siren would automatically change all the signal lights to green, giving me the right of way.

In six seconds I was doing eighty miles an hour, my tires losing traction on the greentop. I turned the wheel slightly. The car didn't respond, beginning to skid.

"Ice treads!" I hollered.

Metal spikes poked out of the rubber in my tires, finding traction on the bioroad, digging into the greens and dirt. The traction returned, and I finessed the car past a support pylon, clipping off my driver's side mirror as I scraped by.

"GPS. Route to home."

The video superimposed over the windshield, plotting a map through the streets to my house. But it wanted me to get off of Wabash. Since Wabash was the only road without traffic, it was best I stayed on it as long as possible.

"Reroute. Wabash primary."

The display changed, keeping me on this street for the next two miles.

"Rearview. Bottom left."

My rearview mirror switched to the lower left-hand side of my windshield, which was easier for me to see. Teague was still behind me, a pinpoint blur in the distance.

I had to get home, had to talk to Vicki before I went underground. Chances were high that every peace officer in Chicago was plotting my course and knew my destination. But the only one I really feared was Teague. He knew me. He had a TEV. He'd be able to find me no matter how far underground I went.

That meant I had to stop him, and stop him now.

I cut around a pylon and stomped on the brakes, doing a one-eighty, three-sixty, and finally a five-forty, facing south on Wabash. I could make out the flash of Teague's police lights in the distance.

"You want me? Come get some."

I mashed down the gas pedal and headed right at him.

SIXTEEN

Teague and I were childhood buds. Grew up in the same neighborhood. Went to the same schools. Both majored in peace studies and law enforcement down in Carbondale. We applied for the CPD on the same day, and both joined the Timecaster Division on the same day. I loved him like a brother, and would have died for him, knowing he felt the exact same way about me.

Then Vicki came along.

Teague was the one who found her.

"She's the most incredible woman I've ever met, Talon. She makes other women seem like they're from a different species. You have to book her months in advance, but you really need to try her out. Trust me, man."

I trusted him. And I booked the time, expecting the most incredible sexual experience of my life.

I didn't expect to fall in love.

I really didn't expect her to return that feeling.

And it completely blindsided me when Teague showed me the engagement ring he'd bought for her, because he was in love with her as well.

I was no idiot. I wouldn't trade a woman for a brother. Not even the greatest woman in the world.

I kept my mouth shut. Teague proposed, and was politely turned down. I swore I'd stop seeing her, out of respect for our friendship.

But I didn't. I kept seeing her. And I bought an engagement ring of my own, one that Vicki accepted.

Teague went ballistic. Our fight was so brutal that if we both weren't peace officers, we would have spent at least a decade each in jail. My left arm, right knee, and six ribs all have carbon nanotube weaves thanks to Teague, and his jaw, right arm, and skull suffered similar damage.

When I healed, I married Vicki, and lost my best friend.

I knew he hated me. But I didn't think the hate ran so deep in him he'd frame me for murder. Or that it ran so deep in me that I'd be clenching the steering wheel and barreling at him at sixty miles per hour.

Since he was matching or surpassing my speed, there was no time for second thoughts. No time for dwelling on actions or consequences or repercussions. I was going to run the fucker off the road or die trying.

I expected no less from him, which was why it really threw me when he hit the brakes.

In the millisecond before impact I swerved, my tail end clipping his front bumper, enough energy, speed, and momentum to send both of our cars rolling end over end like dice.

The airfoam package Vicki insisted I install—because it was far superior to air bags—deployed as advertised, filling the interior of the Vette with a protein foam matrix as I flipped, turned, and eventually came to a stop on my hood.

The foam was clear, permeable enough to breathe in, but strong enough to keep me pinned in my seat without a bit of damage. I was dizzy, but unharmed.

"Solvent," I said.

The solvent sprayed out of the dashboard jets, instantly

dissolving the foam. Gravity kicked in, and I felt the weight of my body as I hung upside down from my seat belt.

"Seat belt."

It released me, dropping me onto my shoulder.

"Door."

The twisted door blew off, the recessed explosives ejecting it into the street. I crawled out of the tight opening, kissing the greentop.

I may have been fine, but my car . . .

Oh, shit. My beautiful car.

It looked like an angry god had crushed it in his fist. I shook away the motes floating around in my vision and locked onto Teague's Porsche. The same god had smote him as well. But Teague hadn't opted for the expensive airfoam package, and an old-fashioned air bag pressed him into his seat. I hobbled over, knowing I needed to get out of there, but not willing to leave my former friend if he needed help. An odd feeling, since moments before I'd been ready to kill him.

I unclipped my folding knife from my utility belt and jabbed the air bag, pulling it away from him. His nose looked like a mashed tomato, and his arm hung at a funny angle. I felt for a pulse in his neck.

Strong. For some reason I was relieved by this.

Then his hand shot up, pointing his Taser at me.

I ducked the shot and sprinted away, toward the intersection, blending from near-deserted Wabash onto megabusy Monroe. The people were packed so densely it was tough to walk through them. I managed to push into the street, and then stepped in front of a kindly looking old man on a biofuel scooter.

"Sorry," I said, plucking him off.

He stared at me, angry and confused.

"Are you fuct? I'll just call a timecaster."

"Don't bother," I said, taking his helmet. "I already know I did it."

I twisted the gas handle and melded into traffic. While I knew I was being tracked, I wouldn't be easy to spot in a stream of several million bikes. I kept executing quick turns, changing directions, backtracking, making it hard for the peace officer bikes—if they knew who to look for—to catch me.

When I finally buzzed past the front of my house I wasn't surprised to see twenty cops standing guard around the property.

It wasn't good for my health to try to talk to Vicki right now. But it might be the only way to save my marriage.

I kept my head down, whipping around the corner and ditching the biofuel bike in front of my neighbor's house. I hung the helmet on the handlebars, the engine still on. Then I swallowed my pride and rang his videobell.

Chomsky's face appeared on the monitor. He was bald with a big nose and looked pissed, but that was his perpetual look. We'd been neighbors for more than ten years, and friendly for the first few, until his vines grew across to my rooftop and I harvested them for biofuel tax, figuring they were on my property. He took offense and raised a big stink with the local alderman, resulting in a big fine for me.

Chomsky was a dick. But he was also my only shot at seeing Vicki.

"What the hell do you want, Talon?"

Good. Apparently he hadn't seen the news yet.

"I had an accident and can't get in my house. I need to get on your roof to jump over."

"You look like shit."

The remnants of the airfoam had become a slimy mucus, which gave my coat of stinky biomass garbage a glossy sheen.

"Please, Chomsky. I know we don't get along. But this is an emergency."

"A month of foliage."

"Excuse me?"

"I'll let you on my roof, but you'll owe me a month of foliage for biofuel tax."

I glanced at the corner. Two peace officers were coming my way.

"Sure, Chomsky. A month."

"Really? You sure agreed to that quickly. Let's make it two months."

"Two months? You're such a dick."

"That's the offer. Take it or leave it."

The cop duo had picked up their pace. One was holding his earlobe.

"Deal," I said.

"And apologize for calling me a dick."

I ground my molars. "I'm sorry, Chomsky. You aren't a dick."

"That's right. Who's the dick?"

The cops were almost on me.

"I am, Chomsky. I'm the dick. Now, please open the door."

"Wipe your feet before you come up."

He buzzed me in. I didn't bother wiping my feet. I pushed past him in the hallway, running up his stairs as fast as I could, bursting out onto his green roof. I hurried to the edge and looked down.

Cops were everywhere, many of them focused on their DTs, tracking my chip.

"Talon, you ass-master! You trailed shit all through my house! And it stinks!"

I judged the gap between my roof and his. It was only six feet, but the height made it seem a lot farther away. Did I have the strength to make the leap? I was exhausted, beaten up, covered with twenty pounds of gunk.

"The stink is making me puke! You owe me a carpet cleaning as well, mister!"

"Shut up, Chomsky! You're such a dick!"

"I'm calling the alderman!"

Dick.

Chomsky stomped off. I looked at the gap again, sure I wouldn't be able to make it across. I wondered if my dick neighbor had a pair of frog legs. A kermit could make the jump, easy.

"Talon?"

I glanced over at my roof. Vicki was there. Vicki, the love of my life. My wife. My everything. And suddenly I had the strength of ten men. I took five running steps, then launched myself into the air, sailing toward her, soaring like a bird on the wings of love.

Halfway there I knew I'd be about a foot short.

SEVENTEEN

The wings of love fuct me, and I slammed into the side of my house, frantically trying to get a handhold even as I felt one or two ribs snap. Vicki raced to me, pulling my shirt just as the bullets started to fly. I hooked an ankle up on the ledge and hefted myself over, lying on my back and panting like an asthmatic at a hayseed festival.

"Talon . . ."

My wife knelt next to me. She had tears in her eyes, her face a sad snapshot of concern.

"In order of importance," I heaved, "I love you, I'm sorry, and I didn't do it."

"I know, I know, and I know. I love you, too, baby."

She kissed me, which proved she loved me because at that moment I was the worst-smelling object on the planet.

"Cops in the house?"

She nodded. "A dozen."

"Are you in trouble?"

"No."

"They'll use you to get to me. Go to Sata. He knows what's going on."

"I tried calling you . . ."

"They cut my headphone. But I'll get in touch."

"Promise me."

"I promise. If you don't hear from me, I'll meet you at the space elevator. Tomorrow."

She nodded. I wanted to kiss her again, but she was already covered with foul-smelling gunk and I didn't want to add to it.

Vicki had no such concerns, and she leaned in to kiss me. For ten magical seconds, all was right with the world.

I heard a snoring sound, and turned left. My raccoon visitor was sleeping in the hemp bush, all four legs in the air. He had marijuana all over his whiskers, and I may have been projecting but it sure looked like he had a smile on his furry face. I pulled my knife.

Vicki's eyes got wide. "What are you doing?"

"This needs to be done. You don't want to watch."

I advanced on the animal with my blade drawn, trying to get my courage up, trying not to hesitate.

"Talon!" Vicki covered her eyes. "Oh . . . Talon . . ."

When I was finished, I tossed the raccoon onto that dick Chomsky's roof. Then I crawled to the sprinkler and turned it on, cleaning myself up as best I could and drinking at least a half gallon in a futile effort to quench my thirst.

"Talon! They're here!"

Three cops poured through my roof door, guns drawn. I struggled to my feet, got up a head of steam, and threw myself into the air again. And once again, I came up short, hanging from the edge of Chomsky's building. But my bloody hands couldn't hold on, and before I could get a leg up I lost my grip.

Luckily, Chomsky's wall was covered with thick vines— the same vines that I'd been fined for harvesting. I hooked my hands into the vines, ripping them off the wall as I fell. They lowered me gently down. By the time I reached the ground I had two hundred credits' worth of foliage in my arms. I gave them a rough yank, uprooting them. Served Chomsky right, the dick.

Cops appeared in front of me, Tasers raised. I backpedaled, squinting against the glare as the wax bullets struck my armful of vines. I dropped them and tore ass around the corner, finding my abandoned biofuel scooter, the motor still running. I put on the helmet, jumped on, and revved it, cutting into an alley, right into a swarm of two dozen peace officers.

They surrounded me, guns raised. I braced myself for the Taser attack, knowing that if more than ten of them shot me, it would likely be fatal.

But no one shot me. They all ran past, oblivious to my presence.

I turned around, confused, then saw what they were chasing.

My raccoon buddy was scurrying along the edge of Chomsky's roof. But the cops weren't looking at the animal. They were looking at their DT screens, which tracked my chip. After cutting the chip out of my wrist, I'd shoved it down the sleeping raccoon's throat. Chips ceased functioning when their biological host died, or if they were removed from the body—with the exception of GPS. That worked as long as there was some biological matter still attached. Apparently I'd removed enough tissue for it to still work for a while.

I stitched myself into westbound traffic, heading to an old friend's house.

Well, maybe *friend* was the wrong word. He was an ex–peace officer, and currently a tracer. I'd worked with him when we were both cops, and used him freelance on runaway cases after he was fired. After the Libertarian Act emancipated children, giving them the option of quitting school and living on their own if they got qualified employment, those without jobs but still yearning to be free of their parents went the dissy route. It was possible to track them by timecasting, but the process was painstaking and lengthy, especially since runaways weren't technically breaking the law.

Harry McGlade had his ear to the ground in the dissy community, and could often find people faster than a time-caster could. He also had his hand in any number of under-ground, potentially illegal activities, one of which I needed his help with.

I merged onto the expressway, heading north to Rock-ford. I hadn't seen him in a few years and hoped he still had the same address.

The three-hour ride was grueling. I was in considerable pain. My arm still wasn't fully operational from when Sata hit me. The skin left on my knuckles kept scabbing over and bleeding every time I moved my fingers. The hole in my arm where I dug out the chip had clotted, but unless I cleaned it out and took some meds I was sure to get an infection.

The worst pain of all came from my ribs. After a self-inspection I felt two that were wiggly. The stop-and-go traffic, while sitting on a biofuel bike, wasn't quite torture, but if I'd had to endure it for more than those three hours, I would have gladly confessed state secrets to make it stop.

McGlade's house was as I'd remembered it; run-down and ugly, his front yard covered with junk, half-buried by weeds. Rockford had a lower biofuel tax, and McGlade apparently paid it in credits rather than foliage, because he hadn't done any gardening here since Mary-Kate Olsen was elected president.

I parked the bike and limped to the front door, giving his videobell a ring.

His face appeared. Unshaven, sweaty, with what looked like dried egg stuck in the corner of his mouth.

"C'mon in, Talon. Been hoping you'd drop by."

The door buzzed, and opened.

Apparently, McGlade really had been hoping I'd drop by. He was standing right there when I walked inside, pointing an antique .44 Magnum between my eyes.

EIGHTEEN

"Is that a real gun?"

McGlade scratched himself in an unattractive place. He was in his midthirties, wearing a dirty undershirt and a bathrobe, both of which were too small for his pudgy body. "Fuck yeah, it's a real gun. I just saw you on the news. You know what kind of reward I'm gonna get from bringing you in?"

"There's a reward?"

"I dunno. Lemme check." McGlade pinched his earlobe. "Hello? I'm calling about the fugitive, Talon Avalon. Is there a reward for his capture?" He frowned. "Excuse me? Why not? . . . What? . . . Fuck no, I haven't seen him. Find him yourself."

He lowered the gun, scowling at me. "You're worthless," he said.

"Sorry about that." I hadn't been too worried about McGlade shooting me. At least, not with an illegal weapon. Not unless he wanted to share a prison cell with me. "Where did you get a gun? I thought they rounded them all up after CWII."

"It was my grandfather's. I ever tell you he used to be a cop? Then he went private. Just like me. They made movies about him."

"We've had this conversation, McGlade. Several times. My grandmother and your grandfather used to be partners. Remember?"

"Of course I remember. Who are you again?"

"Cute. Lemme see the gun."

He handed over the revolver, butt first. I'd never held a real gun before, and was surprised by how heavy it was.

"Don't shoot it," McGlade said. "The bullets are worth a fortune, and impossible to replace."

"If it even fires anymore. You could go to jail forever for having this."

"Fuck 'em. I'll flee to Texas."

When the US outlawed guns, Texas refused to give up its firearms and tried to secede from the nation, which lead to Civil War Two. The only person who died during the war was a Texan named Earl Stampton, who barricaded himself in a bunker with more than two hundred guns and ten thousand rounds of ammunition and then accidentally set the compound on fire while cooking some bacon. All they found of his body was a finger.

The remainder of CWII was fought with blockades and sanctions. Texas finally gave up after four years because they weren't getting the latest Hollywood movie releases.

I returned the gun to him. "I need your help, McGlade."

"I figured you did. Can you pay?"

"Eventually. I'm having a little chip problem at the moment." I held up my arm, showing him the hole.

"An IOU from a lifer ain't worth much."

"I won't be a lifer. They'll kill me in prison. I'll make sure you're a beneficiary on my insurance."

He brightened at that. "Okay. C'mon in."

The interior of his house was much like the exterior, except for fewer plants. McGlade's décor seemed to be of the *let it lie where it dropped* school of design. Dirty clothing, food wrappers, and assorted garbage competed for space amid the mismatched discount furniture. For art, McGlade plastered his walls with posters of old pinup girls. I'd asked once, and these were indeed paper. His favorite seemed to be someone named Heather Thomas, who boasted several different swimsuit poses. It was oddly quaint, because people hadn't worn swimsuits in decades.

"Have a seat in my office. I'll get some P and P."

"Nothing too heavy. I have to keep my wits."

He snorted. "What wits?"

McGlade veered off. I continued on through a hallway, and stepped in a small pile of shit.

"McGlade!" I called. "You have a pet?"

Boy, did I hope he had a pet.

"Yeah. His name is Peanuts. Don't step on him."

"I stepped on something else."

"Smells awful, doesn't it? They don't tell you that at the genipet store."

I scraped my shoe off on the carpet, figuring he'd never notice, and found Peanuts in McGlade's office, curled up on the floor. At first I couldn't tell what it was. Brown and hairy and lumpy, about the size of the raccoon I'd fed earlier. Then it looked up and me, shook its floppy ears, and gave me a deep, loud trumpet.

Peanuts was a genetically modified African elephant.

It trumpeted again, its tiny trunk sticking out like a bugle, and then padded up to me on little round feet. When he reached my leg he bumped my shin with its head. His tusks were capped with cork.

"Hello, Peanuts," I said. I crouched down—an act that brought tears to my eyes—and gave the elephant a scratch on the head.

"Not *Peanuts*," McGlade said, walking in behind me. He scooped up the elephant and held him at eye level. "*Penis.* Check out the size of his junk."

The elephant did, indeed, have impressive junk.

"It's like a second trunk," McGlade marveled. "You want to touch it?"

He shoved the elephant in my face, its lengthy dong flopping around and threatening to take out one of my eyes.

"No thanks."

"He's a bonsai elephant." McGlade set the pachyderm down. "That's as big as he gets."

"He's . . ." I searched for a word that wasn't derogatory. "Very elephantish."

"Yeah. I gotta get him a mate. Problem is, they're so freakin' expensive. I tried a few nonelephant surrogates. A cat and a poodle. He killed them both."

"His tusks?"

"Naw. Slipping them the high, hard one."

"Nice." Wasn't sure what else to say to that.

"They both sounded like they died happy. The poodle especially. Vet said it was a heart attack."

"And the cat?" I asked, wondering why I cared.

"Internal bleeding. Here, take these."

McGlade handed me six pills.

"What are they?"

"Morphine, hash, and valium."

"There's enough here to kill me, McGlade."

"The other three are speed, so you don't lapse into a coma. Take them and go shower. There's a robe hanging in the bathroom."

I noticed his apparel, which had more stains than there was space available. "Is the robe clean?"

"No. But after the pills, you won't care."

I took four of the pills, then hit the bathroom. The warm shower was both invigorating and painful, and then the drugs began to kick in and I was able to scrub my wounds with soap without crying for my mother.

I stepped out of the shower, pleasantly buzzed and feeling

no pain, then toweled off and slipped into a robe that wasn't too badly stained, though the fabric was a bit stiff in parts.

"I'm in the office!" McGlade called.

I walked to him with a spring in my step, thanks to the amphetamines. But it was a wobbly spring, thanks to the hash and valium. I'd skipped the morphine. That shit put me to sleep.

The satisfied smile on my face dropped off when I saw what McGlade had spread out on his table.

Surgical tools. A lot of them. Silver and sharp and shiny in the overhead lights.

"What's all that for, McGlade?"

"This is why you came to me, isn't it, Talon? They switched off your headphone, and you want it working again. Right?"

"Yeah." But now I wasn't so sure.

"How do you think that'll happen? Hope and a head massage?"

As I stood there the room began to wobble, so I grabbed the doorway for support. "Have you done this before?"

"Four times. Two of them successful. I'm charging you five thousand credits for this, by the way. That includes patching up your arm and hand."

"I also have some broken ribs."

"We'll call it an even fifty-five hundred. Though tipping isn't discouraged."

The doorway began to wobble as well. "I dunno about this, McGlade."

"Don't worry. Penis is here to help."

Penis was standing on the table, holding a scalpel in his trunk. I giggled, because the thought of a miniature elephant sticking a knife in my ear was pretty funny.

That alone was proof I shouldn't have been here.

"Sit before you fall over. Put your head on this semi-clean towel here."

He patted a rolled-up towel. Penis dropped the scalpel and walked up to it.

"Your pet is getting amorous with the towel."

"Just the inside. You'll have your head on the outside."

That made a warped sort of sense. I weaved over to the chair and managed to sit down without falling over. The elephant was really going at it, his tiny elephant hips a blur. After a few more thrusts he trumpeted and walked away.

"I want a new towel," I said.

"You're such a little girl." McGlade tossed the towel over his shoulder and placed a pillow on the table. "Head down, princess."

I complied, resting my ear on the towel. Just a few inches away, Penis stared at me. It was a prurient stare. His trunk extended and he sniffed my nostrils. I had a bad feeling he was judging their depth and flexibility.

"Get him off the table," I said. "I don't trust him."

"He's fine. He won't hurt you."

"He looks like he's sizing me up."

"Don't worry. He's got a long refractory period."

"Off the table, McGlade."

"Fine. Sheesh. You're some kind of animal hater, you know that, Princess Talon?"

"I want my nose to remain a virgin."

McGlade grabbed the elephant and set him on the floor. Then he picked up a bottle of iodine.

"First I'm going to sterilize the area. Then it might get a little, um, uncomfortable."

The iodine felt warm, almost soothing.

The scalpel wasn't soothing at all.

"Hold still. I don't want to rupture your eardrum."

He brought down a magnifying lens on an articulated arm, then went at it. I tried to stay still, wishing I'd taken the morphine. It felt like . . . Well, it felt like someone was jabbing a scalpel in my ear.

"All headphones have a very tiny external jack, for

updating the firmware," McGlade said. "A guy I know, he made a nanochip that can reflash the bios. It cycles WLAN channels and piggybacks on nearby users, which means free calls via Wi-Fi. Of course, it also works for people who get their headphones disconnected. Not really good with long distance, but it'll do for a hundred miles or so."

I wasn't paying attention to him, my jaw locked on the corner of the pillow in an effort not to flinch and Van Gogh myself.

"Okay, I've exposed the jack. This is the tricky part. Don't move."

He ripped open a small plastic package, taking out what looked like a dental pick.

"Chip is in the tip. I place it into the jack, and we're good to go."

"What's that slurping sound?" I said around the pillow.

"Suction hose, sucking up all the blood. Stay still."

He jammed the pick in my ear, but it was sort of anti-climactic, and I only wished for death twice instead of the five times I'd wished for it when he was using the scalpel.

"There. Now I'm going to use some living stitches. This might sting."

I'd been stung by bees before. Living stitches felt like I was having my skin pulled off with hot pliers. I may have cried a little. Or a lot.

"Okay, we're good. Let's work on that hand."

"I think I want the morphine," I said, shaking my leg. The elephant had wrapped himself around my ankle.

"Don't be a baby, Talon. Living stitches aren't that bad."

"Have you tried them?"

"Several times."

"And you didn't scream?"

"Of course not. I passed out before I could scream. Gimme your hand."

After a liberal dose of iodine, he draped some living stitches over my hand. Living stitches were a synthetic fabric seeded with genetically altered bacteria. The germs were packed with human codons, specifically the genes that repaired skin. A miracle of modern medicine. But the rapid healing involved the little buggers reopening the wound and rearranging the cells, which hurt more than the damage they were repairing.

After my third scream, Penis ran out of the room, frightened.

"You scared away my pachyderm," McGlade said.

"Aaaaaaaaaaaaaaaaaaa!" I replied.

"Now let's get started on that arm."

The arm hurt a lot worse, and apparently at some point I followed McGlade's advice and passed out.

NINETEEN

I awoke lying on the floor. Penis the bonsai African elephant was sitting on my chest, staring at me.

The first thing I did was check my nose. It seemed okay. I also smacked my lips, trying to detect any funny tastes in my mouth.

"Rise and shine, sleepyhead." McGlade was sitting at his desk. "While you were out, I injected your ribs with nanotubes. How do you feel?"

"Better," I said. My brain was still a bit foggy, and my stomach felt like I'd been on a cruise during a typhoon, but my various aches and pains had all vanished. Except for my arm, where Sata had hit me. That was still numb.

"My fingers are tingling."

"I noticed that. You've got some sort of nerve damage. That's beyond what I can do here. You need to visit an ER for that."

Penis trumpeted at me, spraying my face with elephant snot.

"Your pet sucks," I said, gently shoving him off my chest.

"Yeah. But he's really expensive."

I sat up, letting the room come into focus. The first thing I thought of was Vicki. I pressed my earlobe. No dial tone. I pressed it again.

"Try hitting yourself on the side of the head," McGlade said.

I gave myself a swift tap.

"Harder."

I reared back and really whacked myself, almost tipping over.

"Is that how this is supposed to work?" I asked, shaking away the wooziness.

"Naw. I haven't turned it on yet. I just wanted to see if you'd hit yourself."

"Asshole."

McGlade grinned, then pressed a button on a remote control he had in his hand. A dial tone came on in my head.

"Call Vicki."

The headphone connected to hers, but I got voice mail. She must have still been dealing with the cops and couldn't talk.

"Still with the SLP, huh, Talon?"

"Yeah."

"You know, she's got to be one of the last natural redheads on the planet. They're almost extinct. She is natural, right? The carpet matches the drapes?"

"She's natural." If he hadn't just saved my tail, I might have objected to where this conversation was heading.

"That's so hot. You know, maybe I could reduce my fee if she could fit me into her schedule. Is she taking new clients?"

"No."

"How about for quick sessions? I'd only need about two minutes."

"Let's stop talking about Vicki."

"What if it wasn't overtly sexual?"

"That wasn't a suggestion, McGlade."

"I like feet," he stated matter-of-factly.

I stared at him.

"Maybe she could step on me sometime," he continued.

Seeing he wasn't going to let it go, I said, "I'll check her calendar."

"Thanks, pal. I also like blow jobs."

I stood up and rubbed my neck. "How long was I out?"

"An hour. I threw your clothes in the washer/dryer. Should be done by now."

"You have a washer/dryer?"

"I get it. You said that because my clothes are always dirty. Jackass."

"Next you'll say you have a maid."

"I do have a maid. But when she comes over we spend the whole time in bed and she never has a chance to clean anything."

"Does she have cute feet?"

"No. Her toes are hairy, and they smell like cheese. But I let her step on me anyway."

I reminded myself that I'd come here willingly. "Where's my DT and belt?"

"All your shit is in the laundry room."

I walked out of the office. McGlade scooped up Penis and followed me.

"You want something to eat? I could order out. There's a place up the street that delivers. They do the best bald eagle nachos. I know most people think bald eagles are vermin, like rats. But these things melt in your mouth."

I found the laundry room. The clothes were on the drying cycle, with a few minutes left. My utility belt and gear were on top. I picked up my DT.

"Can you hack my Taser?" I asked. "Make it work again?"

"No. Wi-Fi is hackable because there are so many free hot spots. Tesla electricity is all chip-based, dependent on ID and account numbers. Unhackable."

"Can I buy one of your Tasers?"

"Mine are DNA-specific. Only I can fire them."

Just like mine and every other registered Taser out there. I couldn't even use his bullets.

"How about the Magnum?"

"Sure. Do you have half a million credits? Because that's what it's worth."

"You're supposed to be this legendary black market dealer, McGlade. Don't you have any weapons?"

"Really? Legendary?"

"Weapons, McGlade."

"No, Talon. Weapons are so 2050. I deal in books, posters, art, real denim blue jeans, that kind of shit. Didn't you hear we've given up violence as a species in favor of a green utopia?"

"I heard. But someone isn't playing by those rules."

McGlade folded his arms. "Yeah. You're that someone. I saw the transmission, you and that old ugly chick. Remind me never to play Twister with you."

"That wasn't me."

"The ID chip proved it was."

I stared at McGlade. "ID chip?"

"Yeah. The transmission zoomed in with electromagnetic radiation."

I picked up my DT and tuned in to CNN. They were playing the video of Aunt Zelda's death. But not the early one; the one I assumed Teague made. They were playing mine, which showed the close-up of Alter-Talon's ID chip.

Sata? Had he given his copy of the transmission to the police?

No. The channel cut to the wreckage of my beautiful Corvette, the newscaster saying they took my TEV out of the trunk and found the recorded footage. Teague came on next, talking to a reporter. His arm was in a sling, and he looked seriously pissed. I switched from closed captioning to sound.

"The woman is still unidentified, and I just spent the

last two fucking hours chasing a fucking raccoon. But it doesn't matter. I'm a timecaster. I'll follow him like a bloodhound until his ass is mine."

"Is that Teague?" McGlade said. "He looks seriously pissed. I thought you guys were buddies."

I switched off the sound, then accessed uffsee.

"Franklin Debont, inventor of UFSE, bio," I told the voice command.

Uffsee brought up the file on Debont. It was an extensive biography. I glossed over the early years, his fifteen search-engine patents, the global utilization of uffsee on the intranet, and got to his eventual retirement. No mention of his gender change, of becoming Aunt Zelda, or of living on Wacker Drive.

"Franklin Debont, living relatives."

It came up with one. And it wasn't Neil. It was Franklin's nephew, a man named Rocket Corbitz.

"Rocket Corbitz bio."

Rocket had a one-word intranet entry.

Disenfranchized.

"He's a dissy, huh?" McGlade asked.

I didn't answer, momentarily lost in thought. I still believed Teague had set me up, but I had no idea how. Hopefully Sata would be able to figure that out.

But why didn't the intranet have any record of Debont's sex change? Or of his nephew Neil? That was impossible.

Then again, Debont was the creator of the greatest search engine in the history of mankind. He could have easily altered the entry about himself. Maybe he was a private person, and wanted to live his new life out of the spotlight.

It still didn't make sense why Neil didn't know his aunt was really one of the richest men on the planet. And Neil had mentioned he went to Teague before coming to me. Were they in this together somehow?

I needed to talk to Teague, but I doubted I'd be able to get any quality one-on-one time with him. He was probably already tracing my steps, and as soon as he learned my whereabouts he'd call for backup. Neil might also be compromised, and Teague could very well be using him as bait.

I called Sata on my headphone, to see if he'd figured out anything about the TEV transmission. I got his voice mail.

That left only one lead to follow up on. Rocket Corbitz.

"You still have ties to the dissys?" I asked McGlade.

"You need a tracer?"

"Rocket Corbitz. He may know something."

McGlade stroked his elephant's trunk in a vaguely obscene manner. "My standard fee is a thousand credits a day, plus expenses. And if Teague is on your ass, it will lead him here, so expenses are going to include disappearing me until this shit all blows over."

"My Vette was insured. Two hundred thousand credits."

He bowed. "Harry McGlade, tracer extraordinaire, at your disposal."

McGlade smiled. Penis farted. I rubbed my eyes, figuring with McGlade's help I had maybe a 10 percent chance of clearing my name.

Penis farted again. I waved away the foul air.

"It's all the beans he eats. This elephant is crazy for beans. I know I shouldn't keep giving them to him, but after a while you get used to the smell. It's actually kind of aromatic." McGlade took a large sniff. "Like elephant fart incense."

Make that a 5 percent chance.

TWENTY

The Mastermind is nervous.

It will work. The math is good. The tech is solid. He's not worried about witnesses, because even if he is seen, no one will know who he is or what he's doing.

So why the dry mouth and the sweaty palms?

Perhaps it is simply a symptom of incipient genocide.

But then, it isn't really genocide. Not technically. Or, at least, not immediately.

He muses about the mouse. Talon is doing well. Better than expected. Still not close to figuring it out, but the clues are difficult.

Perhaps he'll never figure it out. Perhaps he's not good enough.

Perhaps he'll die first.

The Mastermind hopes he'll have a chance to meet with Talon. To explain himself.

He doesn't care how history judges him. He can pick the history that suits him best.

But he wants respect from his adversary. Wants him to

appreciate the breadth and scope of his genius, the depth of his determination, the brilliance of his plan.

If you play chess against yourself, you'll always be the winner.

Where's the fun in that?

He buys his ticket. Sits in his seat. Double-checks his settings; the world shrinks.

He envies Talon, in a way. The joy of discovery is such a pure pleasure. The unknown happens to everyone, but so few quest to discover it.

That fool Sata never understood that simple point. Debont whored it for wealth.

As he looks down over humanity, he recalls a poem by T. S. Eliot.

Do I dare disturb the universe?

Yes. I dare.

I dare in a big fucking way.

TWENTY-ONE

The fence was beaten to hell by weather, neglect, and mistreatment. Made of steel mesh, it stood about twenty feet high, and stretched off in either direction, cordoning off the street. Someone had stuck a large, plastic sheet on the fence, and graffiti announced:

DISSYTOWN
HOME OF THE
DISENFRANCHIZED
DISINTERESTED
DISILLUSIONED
DISMISSED
DISSERTED
DISTROYED

"Abandon all hope, youse who enter here," McGlade said.

We'd taken McGlade's biofuel bike, me riding bitch, and he'd chained it to the fence. Every major metropolitan area had a dissytown. These were the people who didn't pay taxes, and were kicked out. The abolition of welfare was one of the reasons, though welfare was replaced with workfare programs that allowed those of lesser means and with disabilities to continue being taxpaying utopeons and upstanding members of society.

Bleeding hearts and human rights crusaders bemoaned the slum-like conditions in many dissytowns. They made frequent trips inside, trying to persuade folks to join regular society, trying to show the children born there that an alternative to poverty and crime existed. And crime did exist. In the absence of police, timecasting, and ID chips, crime not only existed, but it flourished in dissytown. But no taxes meant no votes, no representation, no acknowledgment, so the crimes didn't actually exist in the eyes of the government.

My personal feelings were a bit right-wing, but years of experience hunting for runaways in Chicago's dissytown had forged me into a cynic. These weren't people whom society had given up on. These were people who had given up on society. If you want a nice place to live, be willing to work for it and follow the rules. If you don't want to work, or follow rules, a place like this was where you ended up.

McGlade and I were dressed for the part. He lent me a ratty old T-shirt and some stained camouflage khakis. His disguise was a holey sweatshirt that reeked of body odor, and some jeans with rips from the crotch to the cuffs.

But then, that might have been McGlade's normal ensemble.

"I don't get it," I said. We hadn't even crossed the border yet and already the garbage smell had gotten to me. "Who would choose to live here?"

He shrugged. "Freedom is just another word for nothing left to lose."

That was too much insight for McGlade. "Who said that?"

"Some dead singer. Janis somebody. Got a nude poster of her."

We stood at the entrance. Not a door or a gate. Just a

rusty, jagged hole in the fence. I heard rancid music coming from beyond it. Someone yelling. Someone crying.

"They should close all the dissytowns and force these people to get jobs," I said, fingering some rust off the fence and rubbing it onto my chin.

McGlade spit a loogie into his hand and messed up one side of his wavy brown hair. "The authority of any governing institution must stop at its citizens' skin."

"Who said that?"

"Some dead feminist. Gloria somebody. She had a nice rack. I have a poster of her in a Playboy Bunny outfit. Feminists are hot."

And after imparting that nugget of wisdom, we strolled into dissytown.

It wasn't exactly like stepping through the looking glass, but it was close. We left the clean, green, orderly world behind, and traded it for ugly chaos and anarchy. This used to be the south part of town, part residential, part business, now 100 percent awful.

There was a shocking lack of plants, and an even more shocking pileup of trash littering the streets. No recycling, no garbage pickup, so people left refuse everywhere.

The apartment buildings looked like they'd been bombed, not a single window intact. Storefronts had been converted into hovels. The sidewalks and streets were ripped up to shit, but no one had vehicles because there was no fuel.

There were a few people wandering about when we walked in. The stares were either suspicious or hostile. They wore dirty, ripped clothes. The bleeding hearts insisted water mains remain open, so stinky shirts and greasy hair were by choice. Other utilities—phone, electric, gas—were shut off, but like many bigger dissytowns, this one somehow provided electricity for itself. Probably a combination of solar and hydroelectric, as Tesla was beyond their technology and traditional power plants required fuel sources they didn't have.

"Untuck your shirt," McGlade said. "Your belt is like a badge, announcing you're a cop."

I complied. "Will we need duckets?"

"I brought some. I'll add it to your bill."

"What's the exchange rate?"

"Whatever I decide."

Because dissys had no ID chips or bank accounts, currency in towns like this was still paper-based. That meant a lot of predators, trolling for cash. Luckily, Tasers and firearms were either useless here or sold off decades ago, so the only weapons available were of the cutting and bludgeoning type. While this kept me on my toes, at least I would see it coming, unlike a projectile.

"Watch out for arrows," McGlade said. "They make them out of femur bones."

So much for no projectiles.

I took in my surroundings, which were both dangerous and depressing, and wondered about the lack of people. I saw a few figures disappear behind doorways, a few heads duck beneath broken windows. Who would want to live in fear like this? Who could think this was freedom?

A clearly out-of-whack dissy paraded in front of us, holding up a plastic sign that read, REPENT NOW.

"Repent?" McGlade said. "I never pented in the first place."

The dissy sneered. "God is watching you."

"Sounds like he needs a better hobby," McGlade answered.

Finally, we had our first approach. Weaselly looking guy standing on the corner. White, twenties, clothing and face so dirty it looked like he had recently been mining coal. He came up with his palms raised—a dissy gesture that showed he wasn't holding a weapon.

"Got food? Duckets? I'll suck you off for two duckets."

"Tempting as that sounds," McGlade said, "we're looking for information. Know a guy named Rocket Corbitz?"

His eyes went from McGlade to me to McGlade to me, like he was watching a hypertennis match. "I know a lot of people. Whatcha paying?"

"Whatcha know?"

"Roider. Biggest in town. Got the rage."

"Know where he is?" McGlade asked.

"How much?"

"Ten duckets. Five when you tell us. Five when we get there and you point him out."

"Y'all are fuct. I'm not bringing you to Rocket. He'll rip off my arms and shove 'em up my ass."

"Okay," McGlade said. "Eleven duckets."

"No way in hell."

Didn't hear the term *hell* used much anymore. But where there was desperation, there was religion, and dissytown had plenty of both.

"Maybe we're friends of Rocket's." I tried on a smile. "Maybe we want to give him some roids, make his biceps bigger."

"His biceps can't get bigger. And you don't look like no dealer."

"Four to point us in the right direction," McGlade said.

"Five."

"Three."

I raised an eyebrow at McGlade, wondering if he understood the concept of haggling.

"Not worth it for less than five, man."

"Three forty-nine," McGlade said.

"Give him the damn five, McGlade."

He shrugged and dug a wrinkled bill from his pocket.

The dissy looked around, apparently worried that Rocket would jump out and give him an arm enema. "Try Rosie's."

McGlade forked over the five and the weaselly man scurried away.

"You know where Rosie's is?" I asked.

"That's what you're paying me for, hoss." We set off walking. "You didn't tell me Rocket was a roider."

"News to me."

I stepped on something, saw it was a syringe. Didn't these idiots know that everything these days was available in pill form?

"Some of those guys can get pretty big," McGlade said.

"I watch *Mr. Hyperuniverse*. I know."

"Seeing it on your projector is one thing. You ever see a roider in person?"

"Haven't had the pleasure."

"It's sort of like the cyborg in *Terminator 39*. But bigger."

I glanced at him. "You scared, McGlade?"

"I don't get scared."

"Really?"

"Really. Before situations get scary, I run away."

I didn't buy it. Not the scared part. The running part. McGlade's fastest speed was turtle, as evidenced by the way he lingered several steps behind me.

As we were cutting through an alley someone else approached us. A woman. I looked for hidden bows and arrows, but her tight outfit didn't give her room to conceal anything. The bodysuit was neon green, made of shiny latex. It matched her hair color, which hung down to her waist. The fact that she wasn't filthy made her stand out. So did the fact that her body was incredible.

"Dibs," McGlade said.

"I thought you liked natural hair color."

"I like anything with two tits and a pulse. And even the two tits are negotiable."

She stopped a few feet in front of us. I noticed she was Asian, that her bodysuit extended to stiletto boots, and that it was so tight you could see her nipples.

"Nice," McGlade said out of the corner of his mouth. "And proof that God doesn't exist."

"How so?"

"Because if God really existed, all women would be this hot."

He had a point.

McGlade smacked his lips. "Anime chick. And I bet she's a BHV."

The woman did indeed look like a Japanese cartoon character come to life. But I wasn't sure about her being a BHV. I would bet this one had better things to do with her time.

When she spoke, her voice oozed like honey. "Would you gentlemen like to talk about the opportunities available to leave dissytown and becoming upstanding citizens?"

Son of a bitch. A bleeding heart volunteer. McGlade was right.

"I'd be happy to sit down with you and discuss it," McGlade said. "Or lie down."

I shook my head. "Sorry, lady. We've got an appointment."

I tried to walk past, but she stepped in front of me. Then she ran her tongue across her upper lip—also painted green—and gave me a stare that would make pudding hard. "I'm Yummi. I work for Operation Second Chance. We recruit dissys and offer them housing and jobs." She lightly chewed her lower lip, then said, "I can think of several positions you'd be perfect for."

"And slots for me to fill?" I asked.

Yummi nodded.

"I can fill slots, too," McGlade said.

"Aren't you worried someone in this rough neighborhood will take advantage of a pretty lady like you?" I asked.

"The only people who take advantage are the ones I allow. The rest . . ."

Yummi's perfect leg shot out, extending to its full length at a 115-degree angle to her body, the sharp tip of her stiletto heel an inch from McGlade's throat.

"I just ejaculated," McGlade said.

Yummi lowered her leg, keeping her eyes on me. "So what's your name?"

"Not interested."

She took a quick step toward me, putting her hand directly on my crotch.

"It doesn't feel like you're not interested."

"Step on me," McGlade said. "I'll give you five hundred duckets if you step on me."

I sighed. Another place, another time, this would be amusing. But I had more pressing issues. "Do men ever say no to you, Yummi?"

She batted her eyelashes. "Not men or women. I have the best dissy recovery record in OSC."

"Then I'm proud to be the first."

I gave her a polite but firm shove out of my personal space, grabbed McGlade by the collar, and walked past.

"Are you nuts?" McGlade said. "Do you know how long it's been since I got some strange without paying for it?"

"Never?"

"Yeah. Never. And I—*Shit!*"

The same moment McGlade swore, I felt myself flipping over. I landed hard on the asphalt, the breath knocked out of me, hearing the squeak of latex against my cheeks as Yummi's thighs straddled my face and she sat on my chest, her eyes full of rage.

TWENTY-TWO

Scratch that. Her eyes weren't filled with rage.

They were filled with lust.

"No means no," I said when I caught my breath.

"No means try harder."

With one hand, she ran her thumb across my lips. The other snaked behind her and managed to work itself inside my pants.

"This is so hot," McGlade said, staring from a few inches away.

Her fingers wrapped around me, and Yummi made a sound that was somewhere between a squeal and a gasp.

"You're so big," she said, her voice dropping an octave.

Now, I'm all for women taking the lead sexually. And I'm open-minded enough to have married an SLP. But even though Vicki had sex with a lot of men (I didn't want to know how many) I could honestly say I'd never been with another woman since we'd exchanged our vows. Whenever we argued about her profession, Vicki encouraged me to go out and have affairs. But I had an old-fashioned streak in me that always refused, and I limited my sexual escapades to my time with her, and my time alone in the shower.

That didn't mean that I didn't want to take Yummi right then and there. Or that the thing she was doing with her hand wasn't driving me out of my mind.

She rubbed her crotch against my chin, and then her body tensed, and shuddered. I'd seen enough women coming to know Yummi just had.

"Holy shit!" McGlade said. "Women can have orgasms?"

Her hips moved faster, apparently going for seconds, and I slapped her ass and pushed her up over my head and off of me. I rolled onto all fours—or in my case, all fives—and saw Yummi had assumed a similar position. She crawled around me like a panther ready to pounce.

"Don't make me hurt you," I said.

"Please," she breathed. "Hurt me."

I tried to back up, and Yummi launched herself at me, surprisingly strong for her size. She managed to slip underneath me, her arms locking around my waist. I tipped onto my side as Yummi's thighs wrapped around my head and she ground herself against my face. Her moan made my hair curl.

I looked around for McGlade, hoping for some help. He was standing next to an overflowing Dumpster.

"McGlade! Put your pants back on or I'll kick your ass!"

Yummi came three or four more times, and then she worked my dick out through my fly and took me in her mouth.

Vicki was amazing at oral sex. Yummi came very close to matching her expertise. I gasped, and a little voice inside my head said this wasn't cheating. Technically, this was rape.

As her head bobbed up and down, and she worked her tongue and throat, that little voice became a big, loud voice.

But good as it physically felt, it didn't feel good in my heart. Call me a sappy romantic. Call me a fucking idiot.

But I wasn't going to be with any woman other than Vicki. I wouldn't respect myself if I did.

I tried to hoist Yummi off, but she had a lip-lock on me that couldn't be broken without the aid of a crowbar. So I went on the offensive.

Reaching up my left hand, I found the seam where her latex pants began and forced my way inside.

Yummi screamed around my cock, which felt pretty incredible. I penetrated her with one, then two fingers, while my thumb worked her clit. Yummi released me, sitting straight up like someone had shoved a rod into her spine, making a sound that was so overwhelmingly sexual I should have won some sort of award.

I increased the speed, thrusting my fingers in and out while slowly easing out from under her. Yummi's moans became higher and higher pitched, until the only things that could hear her were dogs.

I changed the tempo, deliberately teasing her, making her follow my fingers as I disentangled our bodies. When I was free and clear, I did a trick Vicki had taught me, a movement with my thumb that made Yummi's entire body stiffen up.

She went off like a volcano. I shoved her away and retrieved my hand, leaving her curled up on the ground, twitching and moaning. Then I zipped myself back up and grabbed McGlade.

"Time to go."

"You're a fucking idiot," he said.

"I know. Now let's go to Rosie's."

"But we can't leave her like that. Look at her." McGlade pointed at Yummi. The girl was shuddering, her eyes rolled up in her head and a line of drool dripping down her cheek. "She's in a sexual frenzy. The poor thing doesn't even know where she is."

"She'll be fine." I continued to pull him away.

"You should let me stay with her. So she doesn't get hurt."

"No."

"I just need two minutes to ensure her safety."

"No."

"One minute. I'll give you a thousand credits."

I put my hands on McGlade's shoulders and stared at him, hard. "You can come back for her some other time. My life is on the line here, old buddy. We need to get to Rosie's. This is hugely important. Do you understand?"

He nodded slowly. "Yeah."

"Are you sure?"

"Yeah."

"And you're going to help me?"

"Absolutely."

I let him go, and he went running toward Yummi. I caught him by his hair and wasn't gentle in dragging him away. He might have cried for a little while, but eventually he manned up and was able to lead us through the decimated town to Rosie's.

As we got deeper into dissytown, more people hung out on the streets. Whores and peddlers, sk8terz and zonerz, even a few kids. I wondered if Yummi had tried to recruit them, and hoped she used a less aggressive but more effective approach.

Rosie's, it turned out, was a P&P bar. I had no idea where dissys got their pot and pills, but I could smell the weed long before we walked through the front doors.

There was music, an old guy at an out-of-tune piano growling the blues. The joint was full, around fifty people dope-smoking and pill-popping. Apparently dissytown had no rules against public fornication, because several folks were going at it. Some hetero. Some same sex. Some solo. I tried not to look. My boys were blue, and I had no desire to add to the ache.

The place had an air of danger about it that I was

ashamed to admit I got a charge out of. These scumbags
were the reason I became a peace officer. I had an urgent,
irrational desire to arrest everybody.

"What now?" I asked McGlade.

He ignored me, his nose a few inches away from some
girl-on-girl action. I gave him a punch in the arm.

"What?"

"Do you have a contact here? Or are we supposed to try
to shake down four dozen people?"

McGlade had taken out his DT and was shooting video.
Without looking at me he said, "Guy behind the counter.
Name is Lewis. He's got a mustache."

"You want to give me an intro?"

"Not really. Ladies? Can you do that thingy again? I
didn't have it zoomed in."

I left him to his voyeurism and pushed my way through
the crowd. The guy behind the counter had a clipped black
mustache, the kind favored by Adolf Hitler. It comple-
mented the swastika tattoo on his head, done in a lumines-
cent ink that blinked red and blue light.

"You Lewis?"

"Who the fuck wants to know?"

"I'm looking for Rocket Corbitz."

He folded his arms. "So?"

I grabbed him by his Hitler 'stache and pulled him up
over the top of the bar. "So tell him I want to see him.
Please."

Though we weren't technically allowed to use them, at
the peace academy we learned there were several compli-
ance points on the human body. Pinching a suspect in the
armpit, kidney, balls, or upper lip caused instant pain and
total obedience. Lewis made a half-assed attempt to raise a
fist, but I squeezed even harder, making his eyes go glassy.

When I released him, he immediately ran off.

Some skank came up to me, the scowl on her face making her look like someone was holding a turd under her

nose. A large joint burned in the corner of her mouth. Apparently dissys abused pot the old-fashioned way.

"What the fuck's your problem with Lewis?"

"I hate Illinois Nazis."

"Well, you're really gonna hate this one."

She took a deep drag off the weed and glanced at something high over my shoulder. I turned around.

It took me a second to realize I was looking at a man, and not a shaved grizzly bear. He had to go seven feet tall, and damn near as wide. All of it was muscle. Freakishly overdeveloped muscle. Every striation, every vein, every tendon was visible through his tan skin. I knew a few bodybuilders, but this guy looked like he ate Mr. Hyperuniverse, along with the four runners-up.

His biceps had to go forty inches across. His chest was so thick I didn't know how he could fit through doorways, even sideways. Even his fingers had definition.

And on the top of his shaved head, blinking red and white, was a glowing swastika tattoo.

"I'm Rocket," he said, he voice too low for a human being.

This guy wasn't just a roider. He was the King of the Roiders. I could have thrown a saddle on him and won the Kentucky HyperDerby.

"Hi, buddy," I said, trying to smile. My bladder felt like a tire with a slow leak. "I just wanted to ask—"

His massive paw shot out and grabbed my shirt. With seemingly no effort, he lifted me into the air.

"You! You're the SMF that killed my aunt Zelda! I saw you on the news!"

Then he reared back his other hand, his fist bigger than my whole head, and I realized with absolute certainty that I was going to die.

TWENTY-THREE

"Beat the shit out of him, Rocket," said the chick with the joint.

Rocket looked at her, cockeyed. "That's what I'm doin', Camilla."

I swiped at Camilla's face, snagging her burning doobie and mashing the hot ash into Rocket's knuckles. He dropped me and jerked his hand back, and I let loose with a hard left to the roider's kidney. It was like punching a giant pile of sandbags.

Rocket threw a roundhouse, much too fast for a guy so big. I managed to pull away from the brunt of it, but he caught the very tip of my chin. The blow spun me, and I dropped to my hands and knees, trying to discern up from down. My eyes gravitated to the counter. In one spring, Rocket leapt on top of it. His combat boots were almost as long as my arm.

I crawled in the opposite direction, feeling the vibration as he jumped to the floor. Moving as fast as I could, I scurried under a heavy faux-wood table, and tried to remember where the front door was. From under the table it was tough to judge.

Several people laughed, and I realized I was the source of their amusement. This wasn't the first time Rocket had put on a show for them.

The table suddenly disappeared. It reappeared on the other side of the room, crashing into the wall forty feet away. I stared up and saw Rocket looming over me.

I twisted onto my back and thrust my foot at the one place I knew he didn't have muscles, right in the balls. My kick bounced off, harmlessly. Then Rocket raised a size thirty-eight shoe of his own. I could picture my rib cage and pelvis being crushed, and didn't much care for that picture, so I tucked in my arms and rolled sideways.

His stomp made the floor shake. After a few revolutions I got on my hands and knees and stood to face him.

Rocket had a smile on his face, obviously enjoying himself.

"This is the part where you beg me not to kill you," he said.

"Does it help?"

"No. I'll kill you anyway."

He stepped closer. I stepped away. I tried to run left. He got in front of me. I feinted right, then left, but he blocked each attempt, gradually boxing me in. It took less than thirty seconds for him to herd me into a corner of the room. Nowhere to hide. Nowhere to run.

"You gonna beg?" he asked, his expression playful.

"Please don't beat me to death."

"That's not very good."

"Pretty please, with pink sugar on top." I didn't have to fake the cowering at all; my knees were knocking together.

"I saw what you did with my aunt. Twisted her head around. That's what I'm gonna do with you. But first I'm gonna do it to your arms and legs."

He threw an easy jab. I took it on the shoulder, and it

knocked me back into the wall. The impact made my eyes water.

"I twisted this one guy's arm around eight times. You know what happened then? It came off. Like a fried chicken leg."

Another jab. I brought my arms up to block, and it felt like I'd tried to stop a bus. Rocket was just playing with me, like a deranged child who pulled the wings from butterflies. I was nothing more than a toy for his amusement. Something harmless, to be used and then forgotten about.

That pissed me off.

I latched onto the anger, using it to push back some of the fear. Rocket lobbed another jab my way, but this time I sidestepped it, grabbed his shirt, and rammed the top of my head up under his chin.

The roider staggered back. When he regained his balance, he jammed two giant fingers into his mouth. He pulled something small and bloody out from between his lips, then looked at me, amazed.

"You knocked out my—"

I repeated the maneuver, cracking my head against his jaw so hard I saw stars.

Rocket yelped—probably the first time he'd ever made a sound like that—and then spat two more teeth onto the floor.

I gave him another swift punt between the legs, got no reaction, and dove past him as he snapped off a haymaker, his fist burying itself in the wall with an explosion of plaster dust.

Beelining for the exit, I ran right into Lewis and two of his Nazi pals. Lewis had an aluminum bat. I made my fingers stiff, got inside his swing, and poked him in the throat hard enough to break cartilage.

One of his friends hit me in the shoulder, but compared to Rocket it was just a love tap. I started a war between my elbow and his nose, bringing them together three times in rapid succession. His nose lost.

The third guy punched me in the gut, then screamed

when he noticed something behind me. I doubled over just as Rocket's fist missed my head, instead connecting with the Nazi. His upper body snapped backward with a nauseating *crack*. He crumpled to the floor, never to goose-step again.

"Fucking shit monkeys! It's Roidzilla!"

McGlade had apparently taken his nose out of the girl-on-girl action long enough to see what was going on. I tugged the folding knife off of my utility belt, opening it up. I doubted the three-inch blade would do much, but it was better than nothing.

"Shoot him!" I screamed at McGlade.

"With what?"

"Your Taser!"

"No Tesla service in dissytown, partner."

Rocket darted in close. His chin and shirt were soaked with blood. I jabbed with the knife, driving it into his stomach. With amazing speed he swatted my hand away. The knife remained lodged in his abs, looking tiny among the striations. He flicked it away.

"Use your Magnum, McGlade!"

"I didn't bring it."

"Why the fuck not?"

"I didn't want it to get stolen. Have you seen how dangerous this place is?"

McGlade was an asshole, but he did have a point.

Rocket spread out his arms, trying for the bear hug. I didn't want my insides to squeeze up out of my mouth like a tube of toothpaste, so I stepped away and kicked him in the groin again, which he ignored.

"He's a roider," McGlade said. "His balls are the size of peas. If he even has any left."

I dropped to my knees and crawled through Rocket's legs just before his arms closed around me. Then I did a quick spin and worked his kidneys, left right left right, like I was whaling on a heavy bag at the gym.

Rocket grunted, and caught me with a backhand that connected with such force I was actually lifted off the ground. I landed on a torn-up pool table, fell behind it, and lay there for a second, waiting for the world to stop spinning. Before it did, Rocket was stomping over, kicking chairs and tables out of the way. His earlier, playful look had been replaced by something dark and scary.

McGlade called out, "You seem to have the situation under control here, buddy, and everyone else is leaving, so I think I'm gonna hit the road."

"You're an asshole, McGlade."

"Pretty much."

He ran out with the rest of the crowd.

I looked around, and noticed Lewis on the floor next to me, clawing at his broken trachea and turning a shade of purple normally reserved for plums. I grabbed his dropped baseball bat, then got unsteadily to my feet, ready to hit a home run.

Rocket hesitated when he saw the bat. He stopped, his pecs twitching, his forty-inch biceps flexing. I couldn't get over how huge he was. A basketball had only a thirty-inch circumference. This guy's arm was thicker than McGlade's pudgy waist.

The roider feinted a grab. I swung and missed. He rushed me. This time, my swing connected. I aimed at his elbow, putting all of my hundred and ninety pounds behind it, the impact making the handle vibrate in my hands.

Rocket howled, and I aimed the next one at his head. He shifted, the bat bouncing off his overdeveloped trapezius. I was rearing back for another swing when his enormous hand grasped my face, cutting off my air. Then he began to squeeze.

Talk about tension headaches.

Before he could pop my skull like a grape, I switched my grip on the bat, thrusting blindly in the direction of his head. I connected with his chin and he released me. I advanced, swinging wildly. He was so big that I didn't know if I was damaging him, but I did manage to back him up against the wall. Seven, eight, nine times I struck him, my hands stinging with each impact. He kept his head covered pretty good, so I worked the body, worked the arms, figuring something inside him had to break eventually.

Then Rocket managed to catch the aluminum bat between his side and his arm, ripping it from my grasp. He held it out in front of him—

—and bent it in half.

Then he screamed. Not a scream of pain. Not a scream of fear. This was closer to a lion's roar—the sound of an angry predator, asserting its dominance.

One of the reasons I didn't use steroids, other than possible shrinkage of my masculine parts, was because I'd seen the dangers of roid rage on the job. Before timecasting, a good number of assaults involved roiders. Too much testosterone led to temporary—and in some cases permanent—insanity. During rages, some people were even immune to Taser shocks. I'd witnessed roiders bust out of flex-cuffs and break through brick walls. Any trace of humanity, logic, or common sense was lost in a roid rage. You might as well have been dealing with a mad bull.

That was how Rocket looked—like he'd abandoned his humanity. Bending a bat was nothing for him. He could go way beyond that.

Which was why it didn't really surprise me when he picked up that pool table.

What did surprise me was how far he was able to throw it.

As soon as he pressed it to his chest I ran in the opposite direction, getting a good thirty feet away before looking around for a weapon. I figured the table—slate and metal—weighed at least twice as much as Rocket did. He wouldn't be able to chuck an eight-hundred-pound table more than thirty feet. No way.

Then I heard the crash and saw the pool table skidding

across the floor at a high speed, plowing through over-turned chairs, smashing Lewis's head open like a dropped pumpkin, and finally banging into me.

I rode the pool table another ten feet, and then it slammed me against the wall.

Amazingly, I didn't seem to be injured. It hurt, sure, and I'd be pretty bruised up, but nothing seemed broken or crushed.

The panic set in when I tried to move.

I couldn't. The table had me pinned against the wall.

I was trapped. And Rocket was heading my way.

TWENTY-FOUR

There are stories that, when confronted with frightening or emotionally overwhelming situations, human beings can exert feats of strength disproportionate to their size. Mothers lifting cars to save their children trapped underneath was an oft-told example.

Those stories were complete bullshit. I couldn't budge that pool table a single inch, no matter how hard I strained against it, and I'd never been more frightened or overwhelmed in my life. The only disproportionate thing in my entire body was my bladder, which felt enormous and clenched tighter and tighter each step closer Rocket got to me.

The only time I'd ever been this frightened, other than the skydiving fiasco, was years ago, back when being a timecaster meant catching crooks instead of visiting grammar schools. Someone had been planting bombs in nursing homes, and following the perp's trail led me to a cache of plastic explosives hidden under a snack table during a geriatric polka night. The six seconds ticking down on the bomb's timer had paralyzed me with fear. There wasn't time to get the elderly out of there, or even time for me to take cover, so my only choice was to try to defuse it.

Looking at that bomb, I had known I was going to die. I knew it the same way I knew I'd hit the octeract point while timecasting. It was a whole-body feeling, as real and as sure as any tactile experience.

Dying was something I desperately didn't want to happen, so I'd waited until the last possible moment to take the long shot and disconnect one of the wires. Blue or red. Blue or red. I knew one would save me, and the other would kill me. Luckily, the wire I pulled was the right one.

But now I didn't have any wires to choose from. I felt the same overwhelming sense of my own demise. Death was counting down for me, and there was nothing I could do about it.

When Rocket finally reached the pool table, he cocked his head to the side, licked his bloody lips, and stared, as if studying a bug on a pin and finding it sexually arousing. Exhibiting superhuman self-control, I managed not to piss myself, and instead used my only remaining weapon. Truth.

"I didn't kill your aunt. I didn't even know who she was. Your cousin Neil hired me to find her because she'd gone missing."

Some of the rage melted off his face, replaced by confusion. "Neil?"

"Do you know your aunt used to be a man?"

"Yeah. He invented the intranet."

Actually, he'd only invented the search engine the intranet used, but I saw no need to correct Rocket on that point. He raised a fist, ready to pound me into the wall.

"That means"—I spoke quickly, flinching away and squeezing my eyes shut—"now that your aunt is dead, you're a billionaire . . ."

The blow didn't come. I peeked open one eye. Rocket had his hand in the air, but he wasn't throwing the punch.

"I'm rich?"

"Your aunt is dead. You and Neil are her only surviving relatives. You inherit all of her money and possessions. And there's a lot."

He lowered his fist. "Who's Neil?"

"Your cousin."

"Don't have no cousin. My mom only had one brother— Aunt Zelda. I'm really rich?"

"You could hire Donald Trump the Third to be your cabana boy."

Rocket didn't look enraged anymore. If anything, he appeared pensive. Maybe I'd actually have a chance to—

"I'll save you, Talon!"

McGlade came running up behind Rocket. He had my tiny folding knife raised up over his head.

"McGlade! Don't!"

"Die, you enormous son of a bitch!"

McGlade stabbed Rocket in the left ass cheek. To my trained eye, it didn't seem to be a killing blow.

Rocket snarled, then stared down at McGlade. McGlade grabbed the knife's handle and yanked on it.

The knife wouldn't budge. It was lodged to the hilt in the roider's rock-hard gluteus maximus, and I doubted nothing less than a block and tackle would be able to remove it. McGlade grunted with effort for a few seconds, trying both overhand and underhand grips. He even tried bracing his foot against Rocket's leg. Eventually, he gave up.

"You got a really strong ass, buddy," McGlade said, out of breath. He wiped his brow with his sleeve, then gave the knife handle a baby pat. "You should keep it there. Makes you look tough."

"You're dead," Rocket told him.

"Kinda figured."

Then McGlade took stupid to the next level. He reared back and kicked the knife blade.

Rocket's eyes practically shot out of his head. He

howled, the roid rage once again taking control, and back-handed McGlade so hard it could be heard in neighboring states. Then he turned his fury on me. Shoving the pool table to the side as if it weighed nothing, he grabbed my shirt and lifted me up over his head.

I'd felt trapped before. Now I felt helpless, which was even worse.

He tossed me, visions of broken bones and organ failure swirling through my head as I spun through the air.

Incredibly, miraculously, I landed on something soft.

"You broke my fall," I said, amazed.

"You broke my ribs," McGlade groaned underneath me.

I disentangled myself from McGlade and picked up an overturned metal chair. Rocket rushed at me, fists clenched. I kept him at bay like a lion tamer, poking at him without letting him grab the chair and pull it away. He still had my knife in his buttocks, but I didn't think asking for it back was a smart idea.

"You're rich now," I said, as we circled each other. "You don't want to go to jail for murder."

"I'll hire a good lawyer."

"Bust the chair over his Nazi head, Talon," McGlade said from the floor. "This fucknut gets that kind of money, he'll start the Fourth Reich."

Rocket turned to McGlade, snarling. I busted the chair over his Nazi head. The roider stumbled, falling to his knees. I reared back to hit him again, and he kicked out one of his enormous legs, sweeping my feet out from under me. I dropped the chair and slammed onto my back.

McGlade screamed. I watched. Rocket had his arm. The giant snapped it in half, like it was a breadstick. I saw McGlade's knuckles touch his elbow. He saw it, too, and lost consciousness in midscream. Then Rocket gave me his full attention.

"No fun when they pass out," he said. "You gonna pass out on me?"

I felt like passing out right then.

I've had some experience with violence. While timecasting discouraged most inappropriate behavior, there were still instances of two people coming to blows because they were both convinced they were right.

Usually, violent acts were fast and ugly. Two or three quick hits, someone going down, and a hasty retreat. People didn't like to linger. Dwelling on the violence you've committed, even if it was justified, was never a satisfying, wholesome experience.

Fights—outside of a televised hyperboxing match—rarely lasted more than thirty seconds. A fight that traversed the entire length and width of a dissy P&P bar, complete with smashed furniture, bent bats, tossed pool tables, broken bones, lost teeth, stab wounds, and several deaths . . . It was unheard of.

So when I forced myself to look at Rocket, it was eight kinds of surreal. This shouldn't be happening. Not to me. Not at this moment. Not in this country.

I'd spent most of my adult life making sure things like this didn't happen.

I felt overwhelmed. And tired. So tired.

There might not be dignity in surrender. But there is finality. The willingness to give up, just so it could be over, was a powerfully tantalizing feeling. With one direct punch, Rocket could end my life. My pain would end along with it. My worries would be gone. If victory was impossible, why keep fighting?

I took a deep breath, let it out slow, and realized I already knew the answer.

This battle wasn't with Rocket. There was no contest. I couldn't beat him.

So it wasn't about winning.

The battle was with myself. The measure of a man's worth was all about what finally made him give up.

Rocket laughed. "You gonna pass—"

I clenched my hands and raised them.

"Just shut the fuck up and fight, bitch."

For a fraction of a second, Rocket appeared uncertain. Then he came at me.

He swung. I ducked. He feinted. I dodged. I swung. I connected. No effect. I kicked. I connected. No effect. He kicked. I jumped away. He punched. I dodged. I punched. I connected. No effect. I punched. I connected. No effect. He punched—

—catapulting me off my feet, flipping me end over end until I came to rest on my belly, sucking air and exhaling pain, my cold hands and shaking legs the first symptoms of going into shock.

Rocket towered over me. He was going to reach down, grab my arm, and start twisting until things snapped. Bone, muscle, tendons, ligaments, veins, arteries, flesh, skin. To think that a human being would want to tear off another's arm was disturbing. To think it was about to happen to me was unfathomable.

Rocket reached down. He took my wrist.

I scissor-kicked the bastard in the nose, hard as I could, elated when it burst like a Fourth of July firework, showering me with streams of blood.

Then I got to my feet, again, to face him, again. This was my fate. To trade blows with this monstrosity, this grotesque parody of a human being, until he beat me to death.

"Come on," I said, raising my fists. "Let's go."

And then I saw something on Rocket's face I never expected to see.

I saw fear.

But before I could be empowered by it, and take the initiative, and make him feel what he'd undoubtedly made many men feel before he killed them, Rocket reached behind him and grabbed something in his belt.

When he brought his hand forward, I questioned my own senses. He wasn't holding anything. All I saw was his empty fist.

Then he shifted, and out of nowhere, it appeared.

He shifted again. It was gone.

Again. It was back.

I realized what was going on. I could see it sideways, but not straight on.

"Oh . . . no . . ."

Rocket had a Nife.

TWENTY-FIVE

Rocket with a Nife was so redundant I almost laughed at it. Sort of like giving a shark a machine gun. Nifes were for total psychos, so it wasn't a stretch that he owned one. But the thought of facing an assailant with a Nife made me want to vomit.

To reinforce my feelings on the matter, Rocket swung the Nife at the overturned pool table. He sliced off the corner, the thin blade cutting through the slate like it was a watermelon.

I was dead. The thought was both depressing and liberating. The only thing left for me to decide was how I wanted to go out.

The decision didn't take long.

I wanted to go out swinging.

Rocket sauntered over, taking his time. His face was a bloody mess, making his smile all the creepier.

"You know what this is?" he asked, waving the Nife in front of him.

I scanned the floor around me for weapons, then realized it didn't matter. The Nife would make easy work of a thrown chair or a plastic table leg. If I had a chain saw, it would make easy work of that as well.

I considered my utility belt. The supplication collar needed a Tesla field to work. The wax bullets in my Glock would sting, but not much else. I had some flex-cuffs, but they weren't big enough to get around Rocket's wrists even if I could get close enough. My nanotube reel was empty. I didn't see what good my flashlight or various tools would do, and my folding knife was still stuck in the roider's ass.

I was fuct.

"It's a Nife," Rocket said. "I'm going to use it to slice off your eyelids, so you can't look away while I skin you alive."

I thought of something tough and flippant to say back, but I didn't trust my voice not to quiver.

Rocket strolled toward me, taking his time. He waved the Nife in front of him, knowing I couldn't take my eyes off of it, knowing I was imagining how it would feel when it cut me. According to all accounts, being sliced with a Nife didn't hurt at first. Being only a few nanometers thin, it was so sharp a person didn't feel it going in. It was only after the body part dropped off that the pain began.

Escape was impossible. Rocket was between me and the exit. I moved left. He mirrored it. I moved right. He mirrored it. Even if I ran for it and tried to dive past him, all he had to do was extend his arm and the Nife blade would open me up like a zipper.

"I need more fucking drugs!"

McGlade was awake again. With his good hand, he was shoving pills into his mouth like they were M&M'S. If the pills were morphine, it was enough to make an entire frat house OD.

Rocket moved in closer, wiggling the Nife at me. Like before, he was backing me into a corner. I held up my hands, pictured all of my fingers being lopped off, then kept them at my sides. The only chance I had, if it could even be called that, was grabbing his wrist when he lunged. I'd have to time it perfectly.

All too soon my heels hit the wall. I couldn't retreat any farther.

"Okay, you win," I managed to say. "I surrender."

Rocket barked a laugh. I watched his eyes. His eyes would telegraph his move a millisecond before the blade flashed.

I waited, zoning out a bit while also maintaining full concentration. It was a bit like timecasting. Letting instinct guide me, tell me when he was going to—

His pupils widened, his hand blurring. I dodged left, slapping my hand on top of his wrist as the Nife cut empty air.

I tried to execute an arm bar, getting my other hand under his armpit and pushing him forward, using his elbow as leverage against him. But in this case, it was like putting a judo hold on an oak tree. He ignored the attempted joint lock, lifting up his arm and me along with it, shaking me off. I landed on my back, my head bouncing off the floor.

I didn't know I'd been nicked with the Nife until I saw the blood seeping out of my knuckles. The same knuckles McGlade had just repaired with the living stitches. I made a fist, saw my white bones peek through the split in the skin.

Then the pain hit, accompanied by a slow, sickening roil in my stomach. The roil became a full-blown tsunami when Rocket straddled me and sat on my legs.

"Which eye first?" Rocket said. "Left or right?"

I stared at him, unable to speak.

"Hello? Can you hear me?" Rocket cackled, and the Nife flashed alongside my head. Rocket reached down, then held something next to his mouth.

Shit. He's got my ear.

"Can you hear me now?" he said, into my severed ear.

Ironically, now that my ear was detached from my head, it was actually harder to hear him. I did hear McGlade when he screamed, "The eyes! Do the eyes!"

Asshole. Why did I ever befriend that bastard?

"Shoot his fucking eyes out, Talon!"

I reached for my Glock, my brain making the connection before McGlade explained it. Wax bullets stung, but weren't fatal, and without the Tesla lightning, I'd disregarded using them. But McGlade was right—a shot in the eyes would blind somebody. And with Rocket on top of me, I couldn't miss.

I jammed my gun up to his face, pulling the trigger as fast as I could. Had Rocket been expecting it, he could have cut my gun in half before I fired the third round. But he did what anyone else would have done if someone fired a gun into his face, point-blank; Rocket flinched and tried to get away, raising his hands to protect himself.

I fired until I was empty, and managed to get up onto my butt. Rocket was on his knees, hands clutching his face. He'd dropped the Nife. He'd also dropped my ear. I searched the floor for both of them, and managed to find my ear. I holstered my gun and reached for it, surprised how small it looked.

"My eyes!" Rocket moaned. "My fucking eyes!"

I tenderly picked up my ear and tucked it into my shirt pocket. I was tempted to crawl around, try to find the Nife, but I was afraid I'd cut off my fingers or my knees if I accidentally brushed against it.

Turned out I didn't have to find it. Someone else already had.

"McGlade! Put down the Nife!"

McGlade had it in his good hand. He was coming up behind Rocket. "I got this, Talon."

"Murder is against the law, McGlade."

"Chill out. I'm not killing him. I'm just making sure he's disarmed."

He swung the Nife twice. Both of Rocket's severed arms fell to the ground. McGlade thought this was hilarious, and laughed like a hyena.

Rocket, eyes bleeding, said, "What happened? I can't feel my arms!"

"They're right in front of you," McGlade said. "You just need to pick them up."

The blood was impressive. Rocket bled out in about sixty seconds. Prior to his messy death, he did actually try to reach down and grab his severed arms with the small stumps still attached to his shoulders.

"You need a hand?" McGlade asked him before he flopped over, dead.

"Dammit, McGlade. I wanted to question him."

"You still can." McGlade held up the Nife. "You want me to get him to open up for you?"

"Give me that."

I grabbed his wrist, then carefully took the Nife away. Rocket's Nife sheath, also made of carbon nanotubes, was on the back of his pants. I took it, slipping the Nife inside and hooking it to my belt.

"This isn't right." Stoned out of his brainpan, McGlade was flapping his hand in front of his face, twirling the broken part like a propeller.

"McGlade, stop that. You need to throw up or you're going to overdose on morphine."

"I'm fine, Talon. I feel fine. Look." McGlade help up his arm, and his fingers touched his elbow. "It's just a minor fracture."

"That's great, buddy. But what's that over there?"

I pointed up. He looked. I made a fist and belted him in the solar plexus. He doubled over and puked pills all over his shoes.

"Shit, Talon! WTF? Oh, look. Someone dropped morphine."

He tried to pick up the slimy pills, but he was using his bad hand, and all he was doing was sweeping them back and forth across the floor. I helped him to his feet, and together we staggered out of the P&P.

"You're hurt!"

I glanced in the direction of the voice. It was Yummi.

She ran over, but I was pretty sure I didn't hold the same sex appeal with a missing ear and a hand squirting blood, so I didn't get on my guard.

"What happened? Where's your ear?"

"In my pocket."

"I got something in my pocket, too, baby," McGlade said. He absently reached for his fly with his broken arm, and thankfully wasn't able to grab his zipper.

"I live nearby," Yummi said. Her cheeks were still flushed from our previous encounter.

"We need to get to a hospital," I told her. "And I don't think I'm up for sex right now."

"I am," McGlade said. "I'm up for it."

"He took some morphine," I explained.

McGlade smiled. "My arm is broken." He waved it at her, and it flopped back and forth.

"I can see that. I have a medical doctorate."

"Can you fix his arm?"

"Yes. And reattach your ear. Is anything else hurt?"

"My balls," McGlade said. "I need you to take special care of my balls."

"How much morphine did he take?" Yummi asked.

"All of it," McGlade said. He grinned, his smile as wide as a zebra's ass.

"I'm four blocks away from dissytown. Can you both make it?"

I looked at my knuckles, then thought about my ear. I needed a hospital. Health care was free, even to dissys, but it still meant a report. I may not have had a chip anymore, but it was likely someone could recognize me.

"I don't think we have a choice," I said. "Thanks."

"You'll pay me back." She smiled, her eyes flashing challenge. "And I know the perfect way how."

TWENTY-SIX

The Mastermind is awed by his own power.
   He didn't expect it to feel like this.
   Is it possible for God to amaze Himself?
   Unequivocally: yes.
   But he plays it cool. Aloof.
   The recognition will come later. Or maybe it won't.
That depends on the mouse.
   In the meantime, he plays the game and wears his mask.
   He's actually a good actor. The role of the concerned
friend. The shocked utopeon. The interested scientist. The
outraged citizen.
   People play so many roles in their lives. Most of the
fools stick with the part they were given, never even con-
sidering something greater.
   The Mastermind is sickened by mankind's predictabil-
ity. A species should have some concern for its own evolu-
tion. Bacteria don't get complacent. There are no fat and
lazy fungi.
   What began as tech and discovery has become too good

for the human race. Pure science has been replaced by vendetta.

Yes, it is amusing. Why did God create life if not to be amused by death?

But now it is so much more than mere amusement.

Humanity needs a wake-up call.

It just got a big one.

And by the time the Mastermind is finished, there won't be anyone left to wake up.

TWENTY-SEVEN

Like most BHVs, Yummi was a communist. Not in the political sense of opposing democracy or capitalism, but in the literal sense that she was part of a commune. The same urge to help others often lent itself to living with a like-minded group of people who shared the workload and ownership of everything within their community. In Yummi's case, it was a parking farm called Eden.

"Fifteen men and fifteen women live there," she said. Earlier she'd called ahead, and told them to prep the infirmary for our arrival. "We're very discriminating on who we allow to join. They have to meet our high ideological and physical standards. The sex is fab. I'm bi, and so are the other girls. We swap partners all the time. I'm highly orgasmic, so it's a perfect lifestyle for me."

"I love you," McGlade said. "I've never loved anyone more."

We'd exited dissytown without anyone else trying to kill us, leaving McGlade's bike chained to the fence, and eventually arrived at her building. It was multilevel parking garage, retrofitted for foliage farming.

"We sit on an acre of land, but we have nine floors, so we can harvest nine acres, eighteen if we include the vines on the ceilings. It's mostly fruits and veggies. We only eat a small portion of it. The rest is donated to the dissys, or sold to the local supermarket."

"Do you make enough to support yourselves?"

She snorted. "Of course not. Everyone in Eden is an SLP."

"I have money," McGlade said.

Yummi flipped her green hair back. "The infirmary is on the second floor."

Instead of taking the stairs, we walked up the gradual incline. Like its biblical namesake, the garden was expansive and impressive. Plants of all types grew in a seemingly haphazard way, different species intermingling on every square inch of space. Even the pathways were clover.

"Looks natural, doesn't it? Our horticulturalist, Barry, believes plants grow better when they compete with other species. So instead of having all the tomatoes, or watermelons, grouped together, we plant them in different locations."

"It's so pretty," McGlade said. "Pretty pretty pretty."

"Do you have any narcotic antagonists?" I asked.

"We have everything. It's right through here."

We veered off the path, heading for a door. I touched my head where my ear used to be. The bleeding had slowed to a trickle, but it still stung like crazy.

"We'll fix you up," Yummi said, giving me a pat on the ass. "Don't worry."

McGlade stopped walking. He was staring at a monarch butterfly, which had landed on his chest.

"Hello, little guy. Aren't you beautiful?" He tried to pet the insect, and smeared it all over his shirt. Then he picked off a crumpled wing and released it into the air. "Go on. Fly free, little butterfly."

I took McGlade under the arm and led him into the infirmary. The white room was a stark contrast to all the green outside. We sat McGlade up on one of the three examination tables, and a naked woman walked in.

"Awesome," McGlade said.

Like Yummi, she also had dyed hair. Hers was pink. And like Yummi, her body was pretty close to being flawless. The two women gave each other a quick French kiss.

"Are these the two you mentioned earlier?" the new arrival asked, winking at me.

"Yes." Yummi rubbed my shoulder. "And this is the one I told you about."

"I'm Tasty," the pinkette said, running her hand over her breast.

"I'll bet you are," McGlade said. "I have a butterfly. See?" He pointed to the spot on his shirt.

"Tasty, can you give that one some Narcon?" Yummi said.

"Opiate overdose?"

"Yes. Be ready with the sevo, too."

"Sure. Can I do his arm?"

Yummi looked at me. "Tasty's in school, studying for her MD. Is it okay if she works on your friend?"

"I'm sure he'd like that."

"I love you, Tasty," McGlade said. "I've never loved anyone more."

Tasty handed McGlade a pill. He swallowed it, then asked, "What was that?"

"A narcotic antagonist. It reverses the effect of opiates."

McGlade smiled; then his face contorted in agony. "FUCK! MY FUCKING ARM!"

Tasty slapped a gas mask to his face and turned on the sevoflurane. McGlade took a breath and then flopped over. Tasty secured his forehead, chest, and legs to the table, using straps.

Yummi put me on a table as well, and had me lie down.

"You don't mind if I take this off, do you? In Eden, we all prefer going around naked."

"If you insist."

Yummi peeled off her latex outfit, looking as amazing as I'd expected her to look without clothes. She removed something from a drawer. I winced when I saw what it was. *Living skin.* I steeled myself, not willing to scream in front of two beautiful, naked women. But Yummi spared me any such indignity, giving my knuckles a spray of topical anesthetic before applying the skin.

"Take this," she said, handing me a pill I didn't recognize.

"What is it?"

"Anticoagulant. It will help with the reattachment. May I have your ear?"

I swallowed the pill and handed her my ear. She had me put my head down, applying more anesthetic. Then she picked up an eyedropper and a different type of living skin—one that was gel-based.

"You can't move," she said. "If I don't get this right, your haircut will look crooked."

"Well, we don't want that."

She put a strap over my forehead, and two more across my chest and legs, securing me to the examination table. I stayed perfectly still while she adjusted my ear. As the bacteria did their work, I felt my ear get hot. The warmth spread to my head, and down my neck, my chest, my stomach, eventually reaching my . . .

"That wasn't an anticoagulant, was it?" I asked.

"Hypererection pill." Yummi glanced at my groin. "Seems to be working, I see."

She lazily trailed her fingers over my belly and then seized me through my pants.

"I'm married," I told her as she worked her hand up and down.

"Does your prenup have a fidelity clause?"

"No. But I still prefer to remain faithful."

Yummi licked her lower lip. "Sex is a normal, healthy biological need."

"You sound like my wife."

She freed me through my fly and began to stroke me harder. "It's selfish not to share something this beautiful with others."

I cleared my throat, then said, "I'm a selfish guy."

Yummi took a two-handed grip, provoking a sublime sensation that gave me chills. "Your wife is lucky to have such a devoted husband. What does she do?"

"She's . . . an SLP."

"Then as long as I don't kiss you, she won't mind."

"That's . . . that's not the point." I swallowed and closed my eyes. "I mind."

"So you'd like me to stop?"

Just say it. "Yes."

"What about if I did this?" Yummi hopped onto the table and straddled me. Staring deep into my eyes, she slowly impaled herself on my cock. Then she worked her pelvic muscles in a way that could only be described as astonishing.

My breath caught in my throat.

"Still want me to stop?" Yummi said.

"Uhhnnnn . . . yes."

"I've never had a man reject me before," Yummi said. "That makes me horny."

I doubted there were many things that didn't make Yummi horny, but I didn't say anything. No point in being mean to the woman who saved my ear.

She increased her tempo and began to moan. I concentrated on not moving my hips, not matching her thrusts. I reached up to try to unstrap my head, but it was no good—the straps were locked down. Yummi grabbed my hands and placed them on her breasts, grunting as she did. Then she did more than grunt. She began to moan and, ultimately, scream.

I glanced sideways at McGlade. Tasty had straightened out his arm and was injecting nanotubes into his bones. She saw me watching and winked at me.

"I'm almost done here. I'll be right over, handsome."

Just what I needed.

I thought about Vicki, wondering if she'd made it to Sata's. I wanted to call both of them, but I didn't think anyone would be able to hear me over Yummi's cries.

After her eighth or ninth orgasm, she eased herself off me. I thought she'd finally had enough. Or perhaps decided to respect my wishes.

I was wrong on both counts. She simply wanted to change positions, and began to ride me backward.

For my own part, I was holding out pretty well. While I didn't have the size or the endurance to make the Olympic hyperfucking team, I had pretty good staying power. So I was able to control myself, even when confronted with Yummi's overdeveloped Kegels.

Then Tasty walked over. She ran a finger across my lips and asked, "Is this seat taken?"

Without waiting for an answer, she climbed onto the table, spreading herself open over my mouth. She was already soaking wet.

"Please use your tongue on me," she breathed. *"Please."*

Not wanting to be rude, I used my tongue on her. When someone sits on your face, it's impolite not to.

"Aw . . . come on." McGlade was awake again, looking visibly annoyed. "In what universe is this fair?"

I tried to answer, but couldn't talk with my mouth full. It didn't take long before Tasty climaxed, coming very close to breaking my jaw. Whereas some women were very sensitive after an orgasm, Tasty became more aggressive. There was actually a very real possibility of suffocation. And oddly, the lack of air was making Yummi's movements feel even more incredible.

"All right! This is more like it!" I followed McGlade's line of sight and saw another naked woman walk into the infirmary. Purple hair, in long pigtails. She too was devastatingly beautiful, but her perfect breasts were a bit larger than I preferred.

"Is this the killer?" she asked.

Tasty writhed on top of my face, then groaned, "Yes. The one on the news."

"I never fuct a killer before. Is it hot?"

"Real hot!" Yummi screamed.

"You know what else is hot?" McGlade said. "Fucking a killer's best friend."

I made noise until Tasty gave me some breathing room. "So you ladies know who I am?"

The purplette gave Tasty a deep kiss, then stroked my hair. "We know. We saw you murder that poor old lady." Her eyes got wide and she shuddered. "It was horrible."

"Are you going to turn me in?"

"Of course we're going to turn you in. You're a danger to society." She stuck her finger into her mouth, then began to touch herself. "But first, we're going to hump you until you're dry."

"Come on!" McGlade yelled. "Why can't you hump me dry and turn me in?"

Purplette sneered at McGlade. "He's a killer. A real bad boy. You're flabby and gross."

"I'm a killer!" McGlade said. "I killed a roider in dissytown!"

"Sure you did."

McGlade strained against his bonds. "I'll prove it! Let me go and I'll kill somebody else for you!"

I also strained against the straps, which seemed to excite Yummi and Tasty even further. BHVs were law-abiding do-gooders, so it was ironic that violence and death turned them on. But everyone had their kinks, I guess.

"Okay, switch," Tasty said. Yummi climbed off, Tasty sat on my dick, and the new girl took Tasty's place on my mouth.

"Either fuck me or knock me out," McGlade pleaded.

Yummi frowned at him, then pulled the curtain between the tables, cutting McGlade off from us.

"Hey! Don't do that! Aw, come on!"

After a dozen more orgasms, and two dozen more complaints from McGlade, everyone changed positions again. I still hadn't come, but it didn't matter even if I did—erection pills would keep me hard as long as there was stimulation. How many women were in this commune? Fifteen? I could be there for hours.

"I call next."

I followed the new voice, staring at the naked man who had entered the room.

I needed to put a stop to this and get out of there. Right now.

I considered reaching for the Nife on my belt, but it would be too easy to accidentally cut these women to pieces. Or cut off a part of my anatomy that I'd grown quite fond of over my lifetime. But maybe, if I timed it right . . .

"At least let me watch," McGlade wailed.

I closed my eyes, picturing the Nife sheath. My right arm was still injured from Sata's blow. I'd have to grab it lefty, bring the blade up to my head without being able to see it, and cut the strap, all before someone tried to stop me. If I did wing one of the women, at least we were already in an infirmary. Maybe they could reattach whatever I cut off.

"Okay, switch."

The woman got up, and I made my move, pulling out the Nife and holding the flat of the blade against my head—this was the scary part—slicing the strap before a new set of thighs closed around me, lifting my head after the restraint broke and freed me, not waiting to see if I'd slit my own throat or cut off my ear again, quickly making work of the chest strap, cutting away from my body, shoving some naked girl to the side but spending a fraction of a second admiring her finely sculpted butt, then hacking the strap around my legs and getting to my feet, holding the Nife sideways so everyone could see it.

"The orgy is over. Anyone comes near me, they'll get hurt."

"You are so hot," the naked guy said.

"Thanks." I tucked myself back inside my pants, then drew the curtain back. McGlade also had his hands in his pants, but I was pretty sure he wasn't tucking himself in.

"A little privacy here," he said.

"We're leaving." I sliced through his straps and carefully sheathed the Nife. "We need to—"

One of the women screamed. But it wasn't the kind of scream I'd gotten used to hearing. This one was a scream of fear.

I spun around, just as four shots rang out and four naked people flopped to the floor, trailing Tesla lightning.

"Found ya, you fucker," Teague said, pointing his Glock at my chest from only a few feet away.

TWENTY-EIGHT

I didn't think. I reacted. Taser rounds would put me down, so I needed to get something between me and the gun.

Teague fired three times, each one hitting McGlade as I held him in front of me like a shield. With McGlade held rigid by the electricity, I took three quick steps and shoved him at Teague, toppling them both like hyperbowling pins and then running past.

Once through the door I expected to be greeted by the entire Chicago Peace Department. But the garden was empty, confirming my suspicions that Teague had played a part in setting me up. Why else wouldn't he have called for backup?

I sprinted through Eden, hauling ass down the clover path, passing up two more naked women, one with blue hair and the other, incongruously, brunette. I'd never really considered the communist lifestyle, but it certainly had several points in its favor.

I reached the street level slightly winded. Teague's car, like mine, was trashed. But there was a police biofuel scooter parked in front of the parking farm. Bad form on Teague's part, leaving it in the open. I cut off the handlebars with one sweep of the Nife, then cautiously tucked it away again.

My next course of action was to lose Teague. I had too much stuff I needed to figure out, and I wouldn't be able to do that with him sticking to my ass like dirty underwear. So I used my DT to find the nearest train.

Tracking a subject on foot with a TEV was time consuming, but relatively simple. You simply kept the lens on the subject and followed him. Tracking while on a vehicle was harder. Teague had tailed me to McGlade's, but he also could have guessed I'd visit McGlade, since Teague had access to my complete background.

But tracking with a TEV was impossible on heliplanes, and very hard to do on trains. To tune in to the fabric of spacetime, a timecaster had to occupy the same space as the subject, and be moving at the same speed, or else he would overshoot or undershoot him. In the case of trains, unless Teague got on the exact same train I did, the space would be different. The speed might also be slightly different, if only by a few inches per second, which was enough to really mess up a trail. The TEV's internal program compensated for rotation of the earth and the orbit around the sun because those were constants and were mathematically predictable. But with subjects in vehicles, a timecaster needed to constantly adjust the tuning and his own speed and location as the subject moved through spacetime, making it very hard to focus.

I couldn't get on passenger trains, not without a chip. So I'd have to hobo a cargo train. I didn't have appropriate hobo gear, but I figured I could throw something together. How hard could it be?

My DT led me to the nearest hardware store. I picked up a hundred meters of jelly rope, some molecular bond glue, goggles, a square-foot sheet of heat-resistant aluminum, two iron stakes, a metal-shaft hammer, and gecko tape. Then I watched the four cashiers to see who was paying

the least amount of attention. I picked a teenager whose
lips were moving; he was on a headphone call.

I got into line; he rang up my items; I waved my wrist
over the pay bar, then walked briskly away before he realized my chip hadn't scanned. By the time he said, "Hey!" I
was out the door just as it autolocked behind me, sprinting
out into the street.

According to uffsee (thanks kindly, Aunt Zelda) the
nearest southbound was the Baton Rouge line. Fifty cars,
averaging eighty miles per hour, hauling corn. I jogged ten
blocks to the track and checked my time. Four minutes
until the Hawkeye arrived.

First I pounded the metal stakes into the ground, leaving three inches of each sticking out. I folded the sheet
of aluminum in half, slipping it inside my belt. Then I
wrapped the jelly rope around my shoulders and chest,
bandolier-style. Knots in jelly rope were notoriously slip-
pery, because they stretched, so I used the molly glue to
fuse it closed.

The ground began to rumble. Train a-comin'. I wound
the gecko tape around my knees and hands, making sure
the setae were lined up the right way. Then I attached the
handle of the hammer to the other end of the jelly rope, and
soaked the entire hammer with glue.

I eyed the train, bracing my feet against the stakes, trying to envision success and push away the catastrophic
failure that kept running though my head. I'd talked with
hobos before, and they'd said the key was the release. If you
went too soon, the jelly rope didn't maximize its potential
energy, and you'd be dragged to a horrible death. If you
went too late, you'd hit the train traveling too fast, and splat
against it like a bug on a windshield.

I did the equation on my DT after checking the speed of
the train with the built-in laser. Factoring in my weight, my
surface area, and the length and diameter of the jelly rope,
I should dig in for 5.19009 seconds before letting myself

go. If I were off by .6 seconds either way, it wouldn't end well.

I readied my timer, gripped the rope under the hammer, and began to twirl it.

The ground rumbled harder, and I could hear the train now, a gathering storm of pounding engines and steel wheels.

Of the two ways to screw up, I disliked dragging more. Might be smart to keep the Nife in mind to cut the rope if my head started bouncing off of railroad ties.

But then, smacking hard into the train, bouncing off unconscious, and then being dragged to death was potentially worse than being dragged from the get-go.

Or hitting so hard it shattered my bones, then sticking there on the train for ninety minutes until it reached Chicago, every bump and vibration absolute agony.

I remember Teague playing a video in our office a few months ago called *Extreme Hobo Deaths 7.* This one guy somehow got his legs cut off, an inch at a time, as he slowly slipped under the wheels. Another one hit upside down and his face was erased, pressing against the rail. He lived, and now spends his days alternating between being fed mush through a tube and screaming for someone to kill him.

This was really a bad idea. WTF was I thinking?

Then the train was upon me, and I thought about Vicki, thought about never seeing her again because I was killed in prison, and I threw the hammer.

It clanged against one of the grain cars, the glue forming an instant mollybond. I braced myself, tensing my feet, leaning slightly back as the jelly rope played out—

—and that was when I realized I'd forgotten to hit my timer.

Panic spiked my adrenaline even higher. How much time had already passed? Half a second? A full second?

Assume a second and count, dammit!

"One one thousand . . ."

The jelly rope was uncoiling like a tornado, half of it gone.

"Two one thousand . . ."

Now the rope had all played out, tugging on my chest lightly as it began to go taut.

"Three one thousand . . ."

I leaned back as the rope stretched, going from a slight pull to a serious yank, almost pulling me off my feet.

"Four one thousand . . ."

I leaned back at a forty-degree angle, my heels digging into the dirt, gritting my teeth as I strained against the tremendous force.

"Five one thousand . . ."

I jumped, springing ten feet into the air, rocketing at the train extremely fast.

Too fast.

The potential energy in the elastic had become kinetic energy, hurtling me toward the train much faster than it could speed away. I was within fifty yards of it and accelerating, traveling in an imperceptible arc, pinwheeling my arms in an effort to slow down.

I wondered if the train had its rear cameras on, and if I'd make the cover of *Extreme Hobo Deaths 8*.

Twenty-five yards to impact and I was still going too fast. When I hit, I'd fragment like a snowball.

Ten yards away, and I began to rapidly slow down. As my speed came closer to matching the speed of the train, it seemed like everything was taking a lot longer to happen. The wind, screaming in my ears and drowning out the roar of the engine, was countering my momentum.

In a fraction of a second I went from worrying about splattering to worrying I wasn't going to reach the train at all.

I tucked my knees up and my elbows in, streamlining my body, trying to cut down the wind resistance for the last few yards, getting slower and slower until it seemed like both the train and I had come to a complete stop. I reached out, floating gently though the air, and finally touched the side of the grain car, gently as kissing a lover.

I slapped my hands against it, the millions of setae on the gecko tape forming van der Waals adhesion and sticking me to the aluminum. Unlike a mollybond, which combined molecules into solid compounds, the gecko tape induced dipole forces. The result was very sticky and incredibly strong, but easy to remove by peeling the material away from the angle of incidence.

While the scientific principle was simple enough, trying to climb up the side of a train speeding at eighty miles per hour was anything but. The wind and the speed made me feel like I weighed three hundred pounds. Plus the dipole on the gecko tape shifted, making it tricky to break the adhesion. I placed a hand onto the roof of the train, trying to pull myself on top, and felt a sharp tug.

Immediately, I was a flag flapping in the breeze, only one hand still on the train. I turned around, trying to figure out what had a hold of me, and saw my jelly rope stretching off into the distance.

It had snagged a tree.

I breathed a sigh of relief for my misaligned dipole—had I put the tape on correctly, I'd be wrapped around the tree right now.

My relief was short-lived. Van der Waals's forces would rip my arm from my body before the gecko tape detached from the train. Since it had already pulled taut enough to yank my other three limbs away, I figured I had less than two seconds before I lost the arm.

I frantically reached for my Nife with my bad right hand, missed the sheath, and my palm stuck to my side.

The jelly rope pulled so tight I no longer worried about losing my arm.

That was because I realized it would crush my chest first.

TWENTY-NINE

It was hard enough to breathe with the wind slapping me in the face and blowing my cheeks wide open, turning my tongue into a dried-out piece of beef jerky. But with the jelly rope constricting my chest like an anaconda, breathing was impossible. Not that I'd be short of breath for long. In just a few nanoseconds my rib cage would be only slightly wider than my spine.

Seeing red, I yanked my stuck hand, hard as I could. The gecko tape stayed attached to my shirt, but the shirt ripped away, allowing me to unsheathe the Nife.

I slashed blindly behind me, hoping I'd nick the rope. Then, suddenly, I was free, my lungs greedily sucking in air, the terrible stretching/crushing feeling replaced by wonderful freedom.

Elation became fear as the slingshot effect once again threw me into the air, my hand peeling off the roof of the train as I sailed several feet over the top.

I bent into a pike, trying to grab the speeding train below me, knowing the last car was coming up fast and soon there wouldn't be anything to grab. My Nife trailed across the roof, digging a trench in the aluminum, and then I'd flown too far, staring down at the ground rushing past, realizing that would be the last thing I ever saw.

I jerked to a sudden stop, the gecko tape on my knee catching on the train, slapping me against the side, facing upside down. I wasn't sure whether to laugh or sob, so I laughed.

My laughter died abruptly when I saw the viaduct coming up. There was very little space between the concrete support pillars and the moving train. When we reached it, it would scrape me off like a bug on a windshield.

I had ten seconds, tops.

I put the Nife handle in my teeth and placed my palms on the side of the train, pushing myself sideways, heading for the car ahead of me a few feet away. If I could crawl in between the cars before hitting the viaduct, I'd be safe. But it was easier said than done. The wind was insane, whipping by so fast it caught my goggles and yanked them off. My muscles had nothing left to give. I inched forward, hand . . . knee . . . hand . . . knee . . . not daring to see how much time I had left.

Incredibly, I reached the link between the cars with a few seconds to spare. But, like the rest of this train ride, my happiness was short-lived. To cut down on wind resistance, the cars had a rubber screen between them, shielding the link.

I removed the Nife from my aching jaws and slashed the divider—

The viaduct almost on me—

Slipping through the slit in the rubber—

No time left—

The tip of my shoe whacked against the stone support column as we rocketed past.

I took a deep breath and waited for the tornado to hit, pick up the train, and hurl it into the sun.

There was no tornado. For the moment, I was safe.

The space between the cars was dark and quiet compared

to the outside. I stood on the coupling, sheathed the Nife, and then pressed my earlobe.

"Call Vicki. Adjust sound filter for clarity."

When she picked up, we both said, "Are you okay?" at the same time.

"You first," I told her.

"I'm at Sata's. I just got here."

"Problems with the cops?"

"They questioned me for a while. I told the truth."

"Good. There's nothing to lie about. Nothing to hide. Was Teague there?"

"For a little bit. He left when he caught your trail. But there's something else. The cops . . . they found something."

"What?"

"Bugs."

"You mean listening devices? Could they track them?"

"I assume they're trying to."

I wondered who would bug my house, and why. It might not have been related to me at all. For all I knew, one of Vicki's clients liked to eavesdrop on her.

"Where were they? Your bedroom?"

"There were four. One was in my bedroom. One was in our bedroom. One in the kitchen, and one on the roof."

Curiouser and curiouser.

"Where are you now?" Vicki asked.

I adjusted my footing. "I just caught a train."

"Where?"

"I can't say, Vicki. They could be monitoring our head-phones. I just wanted to make sure you're safe, and to tell you I love you."

"I love you, too. How are we going to get out of this, Talon?"

"I'm working on it."

"Wait a second. You're on the TV. Some naked woman with green hair is talking about you."

"Yeah. About her. She's a BHV, and she helped me out."

"Now there's that disgusting friend of yours. Harry somebody."

"McGlade." I could only imagine what McGlade was telling reporters. Rather than imagine it, I dug out my DT and flipped to CNN.

"So I'm tied down, vulnerable, and he's having sex."

Thanks a lot, McGlade.

"You had sex with this woman?" Vicki said.

"It's complicated, Vicki."

"And then two other women joined in," McGlade said.

"You're on the run and you had time for sex with three women?" Vicki said.

Her tone put me on the defensive. "Didn't you say it didn't matter who I slept with?"

"It's not the sex, Talon. It's that I've been worried sick about you—"

"I've been worried about you, too, hon."

"—and apparently you took time out for a gangbang."

"Technically, they gangbanged me. And it wasn't consensual."

"You're incredible." She didn't say it in a nice way.

"He was like a fucking stallion," McGlade said, *"going at it for at least an hour."*

I muted him.

"An hour?" Vicki asked.

"What's the problem here? Are you jealous?"

"Of course not. Sex is a natural—"

"Biological function. I know. She said the same thing. Are you guys taught to say that when you test for your licenses?"

"These women were SLPs?"

"Yes. And they acted like consummate professionals. No kissing at all."

"So you *paid* for this?"

"No. I was tied to a table. And I owed them because they saved my ear. And you have no right to be jealous."

"I'm not jealous, Talon."

"Are you sure?"

Vicki didn't answer.

"Look, Vicki, I need to call Sata and find out if he made—"

"Talon—"

"—any headway with . . . What, Vicki?"

"Talon . . . did you do this?"

"Do what?"

I looked at the DT. The graphic read, *Boise, Idaho*, and showed an empty crater that had to be ten miles wide.

The next graphic read, *Death toll estimated at 500,000*. It was followed by a video of me—well, the alter-me—standing on a hill overlooking the city, some sort of device in his/my hand.

"Bye-bye, Boise," Alter-Talon said.

Then he pressed a button, and the city—

Well, it just . . . *imploded.*

Within two seconds, everything that used to be there got sucked into itself, stretching and shrinking and eventually disappearing into a singularity. There wasn't a trace of anything left. Only a giant crater.

It was the most horrible thing I've ever seen. Half a million people, murdered in an instant. I couldn't wrap my head around it. Couldn't comprehend death on such a huge scale. The number was staggering.

If someone read a list of the names of the dead, it would take an entire month to finish if the person didn't stop to sleep or eat. And each of those names represented a life. A person. Mothers. Fathers. Children. Brothers and sisters and cousins and friends and neighbors. Half a million of them, snuffed out of existence.

It was the biggest tragedy of this century.

And for what purpose? Why would someone do that? What could the motive possibly be for something so monstrous?

"Oh, Talon . . ." Vicki was whispering.

"I . . . I didn't do this, Vicki."

"Don't you remember talking about Boise this morning?"

"I talked about moving there. Not destroying it."

"But . . ."

"Vicki, I have to call Sata. That wasn't me. I'll call you soon."

"Talon, I—"

I cut her off. "Hang up. Call Michio Sata."

A moment later, Sata came on the headphone.

"Talon?"

Freaked-out as I was, it was a relief to hear his voice. "What's going on, sensei?"

"Where are you now, Talon?"

"I'm not near Boise, if that's what you mean. What the fuck happened to it?"

Sata paused. I could picture him, forehead bunched up in thought. "Watching the video, it looked like it was sucked into a black hole. Do you remember the media backlash when some scientists postulated that timecasting could create micro black holes?"

"Yeah."

"Well, timecasting *does* create micro black holes. So do Large Hadron Colliders, and, believe it or not, commercial manufacturing of feminine deodorant spray. But there's no danger. There are already micro black holes all around us, billions of them, left over from the big bang. Their mass is so minute, they're harmless."

I stared at the DT. "This one doesn't look harmless."

"I know. Apparently, someone has figured out how to make micro black holes bigger."

"So why does it look like I'm the one destroying Boise and killing half a million people?"

"That's because," Sata said, "you're the one that did it."

THIRTY

I wasn't sure I heard him correctly.

"Sata-san, I didn't destroy Boise. And I didn't kill Aunt Zelda."

"Actually, Talon, you did."

"Even if you don't believe me, I have people that can account for me for the last several hours. Not only that, if you timecast my location all day, you'll see I never went anywhere near Idaho."

"Yes, you did."

I let out a deep breath. "No, I didn't. And you're starting to piss me off."

"Talon, are you aware of the many-worlds interpretation of quantum mechanics?"

Crap. Science talk. "You mean parallel universes? Just what I remember from theoretical physics class in grammar school. We're on a membrane in the eleventh dimension, right?"

Sata's voice took on a condescending tone, like he was speaking to a child. "We're not *on* a membrane. Our universe, and its associated laws of physics, are *part* of the 'brane. But we aren't the only 'brane. There are infinite 'branes in the multiverse, made up of infinite other universes, with infinite other—"

"Earths," I interrupted. "I know this. There are other earths where Columbus never discovered America, or where Texas won the second Civil War, or where I had eggs for breakfast this morning instead of oatmeal. Every possible variable that can exist, does exist."

"Including a parallel earth where you destroyed Boise, Idaho."

Just like in grammar school theoretical physics class, I felt a headache coming on. I rubbed my eyes, the gecko tape sticking to my cheek. I peeled it off carefully so I didn't lose any skin.

"In the transmission of the alter-me killing Aunt Zelda, I had different hair. The color was off."

"In that universe, on that parallel world, the spectrum of light is different because the laws of physics are slightly different."

"So I really did kill her. And I really did kill half a million people in Idaho. But not in this universe."

"Correct."

It still didn't make sense. "But Aunt Zelda is dead in this universe. And Boise is gone on our world, in our 'brane. Is an alternate version of me committing atrocities in a parallel universe, but the effects are being felt in this one?"

"I don't think so. I think someone killed the old lady, and destroyed Boise, in this universe. And then this person blamed you for it by releasing transmissions of you doing it in a parallel universe."

"But that's impossible. We can only timecast in our universe. We don't have the ability, or the tech, to timecast in the multiverse."

"Apparently someone has figured out how."

I rested my forehead against the side of the train. I could feel the vibration in my teeth as the engine hummed and we sped over tracks. It was solid. Real.

Certainly more real than being framed by some sort of multidimensional murderer.

"This reeks of bullshit," I decided.

"Science often starts out as bullshit ideas. But the equations back this up."

"So was it actually me that did this?"

"Think of it as a person similar to you. Same DNA. Perhaps many of the same life experiences. But you aren't privy to this person's thoughts, and don't control his actions. It's you if you grew up in an alternate universe."

"And somehow, I'm getting blamed for his crimes. Terrific."

"I know this is tragic for you, Talon-*kun*, but from a scientific standpoint, this is extraordinary. The unlimited possibilities boggle the mind. If we can communicate with beings in alternate realities, think about what we might be able to learn."

Extraordinary wasn't the word I'd use to describe it. "Can we prove this? Can we prove to the authorities it wasn't me?"

"Doubtful. Maybe we could make the numbers support it. But in order to prove your innocence you'll need to find out who framed you, and how. Showing a judge the mathematical plausibility that you may be innocent isn't as compelling as the evidence that shows you're guilty."

The headache arrived, full force. Jumping down biorecycle chutes and hoboing moving trains was child's play compared to understanding this multiverse nonsense. Why not just say it was all the master plan of alien space bats? That made about as much sense.

"How do I find this person?" I asked.

"I don't know. But whatever you do, it had better be

quick. Right now you're the most wanted man in America. Possibly the world."

Great. "Thanks, Sata. Take care of Vicki for me."

"I will."

"Hang up."

I rubbed my temples, and the gecko tape stuck to my nose. I removed my hand carefully, trying to plot my next move. I figured there were two choices.

First, I could visit Neil over at Aunt Zelda's, assuming he was still there. Teague was on my trail, but my hobo act would lose him. He might stake out Zelda's home as an obvious place to wait for me, knowing I'd come back. It might also be crawling with peace officers, but I doubted it. AFAIK, Zelda's name hadn't gone public yet, and no one knew who she was.

Had Teague deliberately withheld information?

Teague had shown up solo at Eden. If he was indeed the mastermind behind this plot, he might not want the CPD to know what he was doing.

I had doubts, though. Teague was a lot of things, but a brilliant physicist wasn't one of them. I didn't believe he could orchestrate all of this. At least, not alone.

My second alternative was to bring a TEV over to my house and see if I could find out who put the bugs there. It was too much of a coincidence that I mentioned Boise earlier today while arguing with Vicki, and then Boise got annihilated nine hours later. But even that stretched credulity. Someone heard me mention a town, then somehow searched an infinite number of galaxies and found a parallel universe where I destroyed the same town?

Then again, none of what was happening seemed possible. And I was currently without a TEV—mine was back at police headquarters, either still being examined or in the evidence locker. There was no way I'd be able to get it.

But maybe I didn't have to. After all, there was another TEV unit in Chicago.

Teague's. I could take his.

Facing Teague would also give me the chance to question him, see how involved he was in all of this.

Once I reached that decision, I wanted to kick myself for hoboing the train. I'd almost died trying to get away from Teague, and now I needed him to find me.

Which meant now I had to prepare for him.

He'd be armed. And he'd be cautious. For all of our differences, Teague was a very good cop when he wanted to be. I respected his abilities, which were on par with mine. So how could I get the drop on someone with a TEV, a Taser, and the training to anticipate anything I might try?

I took one last look at the crater where Boise used to be, then tucked away my DT and removed the square foot of sheet aluminum I'd bought. A minute with the Nife and the molly glue, and I was ready.

I pushed through the rubber partition. The wind slapped my face and stung my eyes. My right arm was still numb, my toe hurt from when it hit the viaduct, and the copious amounts of unfulfilled sex I'd had made me feel tender in my masculine parts. The cherry on top would be jumping off a speeding train.

Luckily, hoboing off a train was easier than hoboing onto one. It took me a little while to climb behind the last train car, and it took a fair bit of guts to drop my aluminum-covered shoes onto the train track and skitch behind the train at eighty miles an hour. It reminded me of my teenage years, grinding railings on my hyperblades. My shoes threw a cascade of sparks that would make any hobo proud, and I let go of the train and skidded to a gradual stop without losing my balance and killing myself.

Like most of Illinois, and the other fifty-three states of America, the land that wasn't residential was used for farming. I found myself in the middle of a vast, multitier cornfield that stretched on for miles in either direction. It would work out well for what I had planned.

I pinched my earlobe and said, "Call Teague."

He picked up on the second beep.

"Boise, Talon? WTF?"

"We need to talk, Teague. Face-to-face."

"Half a million people, you psycho. I can't believe it."

Was he playing me? I checked my coordinates on the DT and read them to Teague. "Come alone, or I'm ghost."

"What happened to you, man?"

I wondered the same thing about him. Instead of answering, I pinched off the call.

Now for the hard part.

The sun was close to setting, which would make it easier for me to hide. If Teague called in the cavalry, chances were slim I'd be able to escape. But he'd followed me to Eden alone, and I assumed he'd do the same here.

The multitier was four stalks high—taller than my house. Instead of using soil, which made crops difficult to irrigate and cultivate, this farm used carbon netting. Seeds were planted in the crisscross of netting material, which was hollow and provided their root system with a steady stream of water, insect repellent, and nutrients, along with a heating element so they could grow during winter. Then they were stacked one on top of another, tethered to mirrored poles that held them up. Other mirrors were also strategically angled, to make sure each plant received adequate sunlight. Harvesting was a snap—the nets were simply reeled in.

I took a deep breath of the oxygen-rich environment, then walked for a hundred yards, zigzagging the railroad track, giving Teague an easy trail to find. From there, it was into the corn net. I followed one of the mirrored rows, squinting against the glare. The sun was close to setting, but under all the corn it was bright as a cloudless high noon. It would stay bright all night; the solar panels in the mirrors had absorbed enough energy during the day to power the net's lighting system.

Fifty steps down the row I stopped, my foot in midair. I remained perfectly still for eight seconds, then carefully walked backward in my own footsteps. After ten steps back, I ran forward another ten. Then I sat down and waited.

Teague couldn't track my chip, because I'd stuffed it down a raccoon's throat. But I could track Teague's chip. Even though the cops had suspended my electric account, I was still able to access the CPD GPS system, thanks to the good old Freedom of Information Act. A person's location wasn't considered private. Anyone could find anyone, as long as they were chipped.

I punched in Teague's ID number, plotting him on the map, and waited for him to come. Then I watched CNN. Relatives of those who died in Boise pleaded for information leading to my capture. The president spoke, calling the massacre the biggest tragedy of our era. He vowed to find me and bring me to justice. Scientists were interviewed, postulating that it must have been a black hole that sucked up the city. The implosion footage, with Alter-Talon pressing the button, was shown over and over and over.

I gave up wiping the tears off my face and just let them flow. I was numb, devastated, shocked, upset, and confused all at the same time. But most of all, I was angry. Like the rest of the country, I wanted to get that son of a bitch who did this.

Unlike the rest of the country, I was the only one who truly knew that son of a bitch wasn't me. Even with Sata and Vicki believing in my innocence, I'd never felt so alone in my life.

My DT beeped. I checked the GPS.

Teague had arrived.

I stood up, gripped my Nife, and hoped this plan was going to work. If it didn't, I'd get caught. And then I'd die. There were more than a hundred thousand cops after me. And the president wanted to call a special session of Congress, and have them vote to repeal the Twenty-ninth Amendment.

Because of me, he wanted to bring back the death penalty.

THIRTY-ONE

I waited and watched, figuring I had a fifty-fifty chance of this working. If the same trick was pulled on me, I might fall for it. Or I might not.

It took ten minutes before Teague appeared. He was playing it very cautious, moving slow. His left hand was on the TEV. His right held his Taser. His eyes flitted between the monitor and the corn around him, including the net overhead.

When he passed under me he looked up, and I swear his eyes met mine. I didn't move, didn't breathe, hoping the corn leaves I'd glued to my body were enough camouflage in the strong lighting.

Then, on the monitor, I began to walk backward. Teague studied it for a moment, following my movements with the lens. Then he set down the TEV and holstered his gun.

I shifted left and dropped through the slit in the netting, right on top of him, aiming my knee at his collarbone.

His reaction was instantaneous. Before I connected, Teague rolled sideways. I landed on his legs, slipping off due to momentum and the aluminum sheets still glued to

the bottoms of my shoes. I landed on my side, reaching for
Teague's holster at the same time he did.

He got there first, drawing his Glock. I lifted my foot
as he fired. The wax bullet hit the aluminum on my sole, a
Tesla bolt throwing sparks and bouncing off into the corn. I
kicked out my other foot, connecting with the gun, sending
it flying. Teague replied with a kick of his own, catching
my chin, snapping my head back. Then he scrambled on top
of me, thumbs digging into my neck. He quickly found the
carotid, and applied pressure. The edges of my vision got dark.

I brought my knee up, connecting with Teague's balls.
Unlike Rocket, his were average-sized, and he grunted and
pulled away. I rolled onto all fours, getting up in a crouch
as Teague did the same. His face was flushed, and there
was sweat on his forehead.

"You walked backward," he said, pain in his voice.
"Made me think the TEV was glitching and had switched
to rewind mode. So, like a dummy, I holstered my gun to
tune the dial. Mistake on my part."

I felt my chin. My fingers came back bloody. "I probably
would have done the same thing. Did you see me hobo the
train?"

Teague got to his feet. "Missed that. I did see you kill
half a million people, though."

"You know that wasn't me, Teague." I raised my fists
and took a step toward him. "Did you set all this up?"

"WTF are you talking about?"

He looked truthful. But he'd also looked truthful when
he swore he was over Vicki, when later I saw her, topless,
as a screen saver on his DT. That resulted in another fist-
fight that left each of us with various broken extremities.

I stepped forward, feinting with my right, jabbing with
the left, and pounding him on the side of the head. He staggered. I followed it up with a tight spin-kick, connecting
with his chest, knocking him down.

Pressing my momentary advantage, I rushed at Teague,

swatting away his kicking legs, joining the fight on the ground by grabbing him under his right armpit and around the neck in a reverse half nelson. Teague and I were even when trading punches, but I was a better grappler. I dug my feet in, pushing him over, trying to jam his face into the dirt path. If I could force him onto his belly, get his arm into a hammerlock, I could hyperextend his elbow or pop out his shoulder.

Teague arched his back, resisting the move. I squeezed his throat with my hand, but it was like squeezing steel cable. Then, surprisingly, he grabbed my shoulder and wrenched me out of position, clenching me in a bear hug. I felt his chest muscles flex and realized I'd made a mistake.

"I'm gonna break you in half, bro."

Teague was on steroids.

It seemed that everyone these days but me was taking roids. Teague was bigger, and much stronger, than the last time we'd tussled. Instead of ignoring him at work, I should have been paying closer attention. Based on the size of his chest, he'd gained at least fifty pounds of muscle mass.

And I'd stupidly brought the fight to the ground.

I went low, reached for his balls. He twisted he pelvis away from my hand, crushing my chest even harder. I couldn't inhale, and the oxygen still in my lungs was getting squeezed out like a tire pump. Bright motes popped up in my vision, a precursor to unconsciousness. I grabbed Teague's side, digging my fingers into his oblique muscle, fighting the striations to pinch his kidney.

Teague grunted. I pinched harder, the motes swimming around and beginning to fade into darkness. Finally, he moaned and shoved me away. I rolled several body lengths from him, sucking in air. I managed to get to my feet, but I was wobbly, like I'd taken too many whiskey pills.

"Why'd you do it, bro?" Teague had his hand pressed to his side, but I knew he wasn't asking me about his kidney.

"I didn't. And you know I didn't. Or else you would have brought the cops with you."

Teague spat over his shoulder. "Maybe I had another reason for not bringing the cops."

I followed the line of thought. "You want to kill me, Teague? Is that it?"

He didn't say anything.

"Vicki already rejected you. It doesn't matter if I'm in the picture or not. You still won't get her."

Teague snarled, launching himself at me. I blocked two wild punches and then hit him in the kidney. He flinched, and I followed up with a right cross to the jaw, my numb hand not feeling the contact. He countered with a right jab, popping me in the solar plexus, driving me to my knees.

"This isn't about Vicki," he said, towering over me. "This is about you betraying me. You knew I loved her, and you went behind my back."

"So you're going to kill me because I chose a woman over our friendship?"

"I'm not going to kill you, bro. I'm going to bring you in, and let the system take care of you."

I held up my palms. "I didn't murder that old woman, Teague. And I didn't destroy Boise."

"Then you have nothing to fear. I'm sure the truth will prevail in court."

He threw a roundhouse that would have knocked my head off if I hadn't ducked. I tucked and rolled to the left. On my feet again, I took a running jump at Teague. He covered up, but rather than attack I snagged the corn net over my head. When the kick didn't come, Teague dropped his hands. That was when I kicked him, hard as I could, in the side of the head. He spun a hundred and eighty degrees, and I dropped onto his back. I locked my fingers around his chin, dug my knee into his spine, and yanked with everything I had.

I heard the *crack* of his neck snapping, and we both fell to the ground, Teague onto his face, me onto my ass. I flipped Teague onto his back and checked his pulse. Weak, but there. Then I found some ammonium salts on my utility belt and held them under his nose.

"WTF? Bro? I can't move. I can't fucking move!"

"I broke your neck," I said, sitting next to him and digging out my DT. "Don't try to call anyone, or I'll put your supplication collar on you and leave you here."

"Asshole."

"You know what this is, Teague?" I unsheathed my Nife and held it in front of his eyes.

He squinted at me. "I knew you were a psycho, Talon. Only psychos carry Nifes."

"I agree. But my current situation has forced me to compromise some of my beliefs. Now I need to ask you some questions. If you refuse to answer, I'm going to cut off your fingers and take them with me."

I let him process this. No one wanted donor fingers. As miraculous as modern medicine was, replacing a limb from a cadaver wasn't even close to being perfect. Muscle and nerve problems left it less than fully functional, and the immunosuppressant drugs had some pretty nasty side effects, and were required to be taken for life. If they even worked in the first place.

Plus, biting someone else's fingernails was just plain gross.

"What questions, psycho?"

I turned on the voice-stress analyzer and said, "First me. Right now I'm recording a baseline."

I showed Teague the screen and said, "I did not kill Aunt Zelda." Then I double-checked to make sure it said *Truth*. I turned to toward him again and said, "I did not destroy Boise, Idaho."

"You could have tampered with the program," Teague said.

"You know I didn't. Just like you know I didn't kill anybody. I've never killed anybody, Teague. Now state your name."

Teague didn't say anything. I picked up his hand and showed it to him. Then I set down the DT and used the Nife to shave off the very tip of his index finger.

"Fine! Fuck, bro!"

I picked up the DT. "Go ahead."

He sighed. "Joshua Teague VanCamp."

"Did you set me up?"

"No."

Truth.

"Do you know who murdered Aunt Zelda?"

"Yes."

Truth.

"Who did it, Teague?"

"You did, bro."

Truth. Son of a bitch. He still believed it was me.

"Do you know anything about timecasting parallel worlds?"

"What? Fuck, no."

Truth.

"Did you set up a fake timecast at Aunt Zelda's place?"

"I don't even know who Aunt Zelda is."

Truth.

"Are you working with Neil Winston?"

"Neil who?"

Truth. Teague had nothing to do with this frame. He was just being his normal, asshole self.

"Do you still love Vicki?"

"No."

Untruth.

I showed him the screen, then tucked the DT away. "You need to get over her, old buddy. It's not healthy."

His eyes went hard. "You're giving me advice? You're in the center of a shit storm, bro. You'll be dead by the end of the day."

I stared at him, feeling very sad all of a sudden. "What happened to us, Teague? We were like brothers."

"You chose a woman over your brother. There's no bigger sin than that."

I didn't want to argue with him, and truth be told, I don't know that I disagreed.

"I need to borrow your TEV. And your shoes. You won't be walking out of here anyway."

I pulled the boots off his feet. Teague was a half size bigger than me, but it was better than stomping around with aluminum soles.

"You're going down, Talon. Going down hard."

"Don't come after me, or I'll break your neck again. And next time I'll twist it off, so the ER can't fix it. Just like Zelda."

"Fuck you."

I bent down and pinched his ear.

Teague said, "Call 911. Officer down."

I sheathed my Nife and left Teague to his headphone call. Then I grabbed his TEV and got out of there.

My next destination would be heavily guarded. I had no idea how I was going to pull it off.

But I didn't have a choice. Teague was right. Unless I proved my innocence, and fast, I'd be dead by the end of the day.

And the day didn't have that many hours left in it.

THIRTY-TWO

I couldn't start Teague's biofuel scooter without a chip, so I cut away the override switch with my Nife and did an old-fashioned hot-wire. I was really getting to like the Nife, though I was sure my opinion would change when I got careless and accidentally sliced off my pelvis.

Once on the bike, I followed the railroad tracks to the nearest street, and then headed south, toward home. Using Teague's TEV, I wanted to timecast my house to see who'd planted the listening devices. I had a hunch the perp picked Boise based on my morning conversation with Vicki. If I could catch his trail, I'd know who my adversary was. I was both disappointed and relieved Teague hadn't played a part in this, but with him no longer a suspect I had no clue who could have set me up.

I pressed my earlobe and said, "Block all calls." I hated to miss it if Vicki or Sata tried to contact me, but if they were being monitored, it was too easy for the authorities to triangulate my position once a call connected. Headphone silence was safest.

Once I left the corn farm and entered an industrial stretch

of Illinois, lighting became poorer. I knew the cops would be covering the main highways, so I'd have to deal with less-traveled routes, and remain as inconspicuous as possible.

I pulled over and took out my all-vision contact lens from the case on my belt. Though my Tesla account had been closed, the AVCL had a full battery charge that would last for hours. I put the lens in my eye, then closed my lid and tapped it three times to activate the night vision. Closing my left eye, the world was bathed in a soft, green glow. I killed my headlight and motored through backyards, alleys, and side streets. It took me two hours to travel the forty miles to home, and I doubled back a few times to confuse Teague, who I'm sure would be on my trail again once they reattached his nerve endings.

I parked in an alley a block from my house, then did a quick reconnaissance. Two cops were circling the perimeter. I tapped my eyelid once, going to infrared, and saw four more cops inside. Two on the first floor, two on the second. Then I checked my neighbor's house. The only one home was that dick Chomsky. Sitting in front of his projector, probably watching animal pr0n.

I hefted the TEV to my back using the shoulder strap. Then I put some fresh gecko tape on my hands and knees, snuck around the opposite side of Chomsky's house, and scaled the wall.

It was difficult, especially since my right arm had been growing considerably weaker since leaving the cornfield. When I reached his green roof I took some amphetamines and some aspirin to improve the blood flow, and spent a minute trying to catch my breath. Then I looked around for Chomsky's atomizer.

Like most folks, Chomsky grew a lot of hemp. And like most folks, Chomsky often got stoned off his own supply. Smoking weed died out around the same time as smoking tobacco, due to various health risks. Some used a home pilling machine to make their own hash tablets. But the easier, and less expensive, way to get high was with an atomizer. Weed went in one end. Pure THC came out the other. It could be inhaled in a health-conscious, noncarcinogenic way.

I'd seen Chomsky puffing on his atomizer many times. You might have thought it would mellow him out, but you'd be wrong. Even wasted, Chomsky was still a dick.

I found his atomizer next to his lawn chair. It was roughly the size of a miniature dachshund, and in fact was painted to look like one. You put the pot in the dog's mouth, then sucked on his ass.

Boy, was this guy a dick.

I also found a plastic garbage bag filled with marijuana buds. I sniffed one. White rhino strain. Good shit. I put the atomizer in the bag and slung it over my shoulder. Then I stared over at my roof.

I was tired. Beyond tired. There was no way I could make the jump between our houses. Especially with a Santa Claus sack full of weed. But I wasn't sure I had the energy to scale my wall, either. I could picture myself halfway up, just hanging there, exhausted, and the cops walking up and seeing me. It would be an inglorious end to my supposed crime wave.

So I settled for jumping, once again. I tapped my eyelid, checking the cops' position. They'd just reached the front of the house, which gave me about twenty seconds. Then I shoved the top of the bag into my belt, set my jaw, and sprinted for the edge of the roof.

I jumped.

I soared through the air.

And once again, I realized I was going to come up short. Really short.

I didn't even make the edge of my roof. I missed it by about a foot, slapping into the side of my building, sticking there by my hands and knees as the gecko tape performed as advertised.

Then I felt the garbage bag begin to slip. I peeled a hand off the wall and stretched down to grab it. The act jostled the TEV on my back, and the strap came off. It fell on top of the garbage bag, the strap catching on its circumference.

I lifted it up, my fingers digging into the thin plastic, stretching it, and then breaking through. The bag began to tear, and I was in real danger of losing it, and the TEV. The buds would survive the fall. The TEV likely wouldn't.

Which was when the cops rounded the corner, heading my way.

I was hanging about ten feet over the walkway. The bag was maybe eight feet above the ground, but the plastic was stretching thin, descending about an inch per second. With all the cool things science and technology have brought mankind, why couldn't they invent a tear-proof garbage bag?

It was dark, but not so dark the cops wouldn't notice a man dangling over their heads. Especially a man dropping dope.

They took their time, strolling slowly, locked in a deep conversation that luckily precluded them paying attention to their surroundings.

"What would you do if you got the reward?"

"I'm a public servant. I couldn't collect."

They stopped directly under me. I tried to lift up the bag, but it was stretching faster than I could raise it.

"The president said anyone can collect."

"No shit? Well, with ten million credits, I'd buy property. Serious property. Maybe even this house here."

He tapped the wall with his monadnock baton, and it gave off a little spark. I felt my sphincter squeeze closed.

"It's a nice place. Probably pays a fortune in biodiesel tax, though. And you meet his neighbor?"

"I did. What a dick."

"I wonder if the wife comes with the house. She's worth the ten mil, easy. Real redhead, I hear."

I managed to lift the bag up to my mouth. I held the plastic in my teeth, then reached lower for a better grip and watched in horror as a bud slipped out and began to fall. Without thinking, I peeled away my right hand and reached for the bud. I snagged it and wound up kneeling on the wall at a perfect ninety-degree angle. My legs, abs, and glutes burned like they'd been set on fire. I couldn't hold this position for more than a few seconds.

"I hear she's an SLP. Maybe you can get on her waiting list."

"Chick like that? Couldn't afford her."

"Maybe you should save your money, stop giving it all to El Stop Linda."

"Don't knock El Stop Linda. She may not be much to look at, but she's got the vibrating tongue implant."

"She looks like a guy."

"You wouldn't care, once she starts licking."

Gravity began to beat me down, my upper body starting to sink. Getting caught wasn't the only threat anymore. If my ass touched my heels, I had no idea how I'd ever get back up.

"You know who she looks like?" The voices were fading. They were finally walking away.

"Who?"

"Stan, in accounting. Except El Stop Linda has more facial hair."

"I'd call them about even. Stan's got bigger boobs, though."

I watched them round the corner. Then I dropped the bud, adjusted the TEV strap, and grunted in agony sitting up into a vertical position again. I couldn't hold the bag anymore, so I tossed it onto my roof, hoping no one would hear. Then I painfully climbed the two more feet to the edge, hooking my arms over the top, dragging myself onto my lawn.

If I lived through this, I was going to buy a ladder for the side of my house.

After half a minute of rest and recuperation, I fished out my DT and did a quick calculation figuring out the air volume of my home and the parts per million of atomized THC needed to get someone high.

I crawled over to one of my hemp plants and began harvesting buds. When I finished the plant, Chomsky's garbage bag was full. I dug out the atomizer and moved in a crouch over to my air-conditioning unit, the fan humming. I didn't bother with unscrewing the top, instead using the Nife to remove the outer housing and hepafilter. Then I placed the ass end of the atomizer above the spinning fan and began feeding it marijuana.

It took fifteen minutes to empty the bag. I waited another five, cutting the hepafilter to mask size and taping it over my mouth and nose. I tapped my eyelid and viewed the infrared. The four cops were still in my house. They all appeared to be sitting down or reclining, two in the upstairs living room, and two in the downstairs den. Hopefully, the pot had put them to sleep, or at least made them so loopy they'd forgotten why they were there.

I slid open my patio door and crept inside, powering up the TEV, which was still set to Teague's Tesla account. Vicki said a listening device had been found in the kitchen, so I set the lens for a wide angle and got started. It took only a few seconds to tune in to the eighth membrane and less than a minute to find the octeract point and pet the bunny. Once I had a decent image on the monitor, I did a speedy rewind and watched, viewing back in time from an hour ago.

I saw cops, lots of cops, moving in reverse. I went further back, before they arrived, and I saw the skinny, elderly face of Barney the dentist, one of Vicki's clients, sticking his nose in my refrigerator. I slowed it down, got a close-up. He was eating an apple, the same smug/satisfied look on his face every man wore after being with my wife. I highly doubted he was the one who had set me up, but I followed his movements anyway to see if he planted any bugs. I trailed him, in reverse, out of the kitchen, down the hallway.

I paused, hearing a noise coming from the living room. Peeking around the corner, I saw two cops slouching on my sofa. My projector was on. The cops looked dead, except every few seconds one of them would giggle. I looked at the wall to see what they were watching.

Extreme Hobo Deaths 11.

I snuck past, peeling the gecko tape off my hands and knees as I tiptoed to my wife's bedroom. I never went in her bedroom. It was her place of business, and none of my business. But a bug had been found in her bedroom as well, and I needed to see if it was one of her clients who had planted it. I opened the door.

Then I whirled around, hearing someone behind me, and stared right down the barrel of a Glock Taser.

THIRTY-THREE

The cop holding the Taser had droopy eyes, the whites completely bloodshot.

"Dude," he said. "You got any chips?"

I cleared my throat. "In the kitchen. Cabinet next to the refrigerator."

"Thanks, man."

"You want me to hold your gun for you?"

"Sure. Thanks."

He handed it over, giggled, and stumbled off. That was some good weed.

My eyes dropped to the monitor and I followed Barney into my wife's bedroom.

Vicki was standing next to the bed, taking her clothes off in reverse. I paused it, wondering if I should continue. Vicki was entitled to privacy. And I really didn't want to see her making love to another man. I should just skip past this, and keep searching for bugs.

But I didn't. The TEV still paused, I zoomed in on Vicki's face. She appeared businesslike, perhaps even a bit bored. Not flushed or smiling, like she did after we had sex.

How did I feel about that? Should I even be feeling anything? Vicki had been telling me, for years, that jealousy was a useless emotion, and that I acted like a caveman whenever I brought up her job. Just because I married her didn't mean I owned her body, or could dictate what she could do with it.

But it wasn't like that. I didn't want to fully possess Vicki. Nor did I look down on her profession, or think less of her because of it.

So what was my problem?

My problem was I had an emotional connection with sex, and I didn't want her to have that emotional connection with anyone else.

Looking at her face, it didn't appear she had any emotional connection at all to skinny old Barney the dentist. It was just business. It wasn't intimacy.

I unbunched my shoulders, feeling like a great burden had been lifted off my back. All of my petty jealousy vanished. Earlier, I'd had sex with three women, with zero attachment to any of them. Apparently, it was the same with Vicki. Like she said, this was no more personal than a massage.

Sighing with relief, I let the TEV play in reverse, watching as Vicki and skinny old Barney undressed, watching as they climbed into bed, watching as they switched to doggy-style, then standing up, then her on top, then him on top, then sideways . . .

Skinny old Barney was a stallion. He was also a few inches bigger than me in an area that mattered.

I paused again, zooming in on Vicki's face as she was getting fuct silly. She was flushed, sweating, her mouth open in a scream.

It didn't seem businesslike at all. Not one little bit.

I kept rewinding, and Barney kept humping. When he put my wife's legs up over her head and executed a pr0n-star position called the *brass clown*, I had to turn it off or else smash the TEV against the wall. Then I left, resolving to never go into my wife's bedroom again.

"Dude! Thanks, man!"

The cops were shoving chips into their mouths, missing at least half of their attempts. They both waved at me. I walked into the kitchen and tuned in to spacetime once again, starting over.

Once I pet the bunny, I adjusted the speed and buzzed past the argument I'd had earlier with Vicki. I stopped and let it play out, syncing the sound to my headphone.

"If you love me, you'd quit," I said. I looked angry when I said it.

"I shouldn't have brought anyone here while you were home." Vicki also looked angry.

"You could have gone to his place."

"You don't let me go to my clients' homes. You don't trust any of them."

"And why would that be? Maybe because they're nailing my wife?"

"It's my job, Talon. Nothing more. I can't believe we're having this conversation. You promised you'd stop doing this."

I paused, zooming in on her face.

Her eyes were tearing up. I'd been so into winning the argument I hadn't even noticed.

Okay, so I was an asshat. In a way, that was good, because being angry at myself overrode any feelings of jealousy I had. I loved her. She loved me. We'd make it work. In fact, once we got through all of this, I would actually mention my issues to my therapist. Vicki was right. I was acting like a Luddite. Jealousy was so twentieth century.

"Got any dip?"

I glanced at the cop, and pointed to the fridge. Then I continued rewinding.

I stopped at four days ago, seeing a man in the kitchen next to the stove.

Barney again. And he was bending Vicki over the stove, his flabby old hips a blur, gripping her waist and driving into her like a jackrabbit.

I glanced at the stove—the stove where I made my eggs every morning—and seriously wanted to kill this old bastard.

"Dude! You got Jell-O! You mind, man?"

"Help yourself," I told him.

He took the bean dip and the Jell-O mold. Two steps away from the fridge, he fell onto his face. I pulled his head out of the Jell-O so he didn't drown, and decided I'd try planting some white rhino next season. Maybe, if I atomized enough of it, I'd be able to forget the image of Barney the Fucking Machine, which was now permanently burned into my cerebellum.

More rewinding. Vicki making breakfast. Me cooking dinner. Coming and going, going and coming. I slowed down whenever I saw one of Vicki's clients, but none of them planted any bugs, and thankfully none of them bent her over the stove.

As time raced backward, I was getting close to the two-week cutoff. The TEV couldn't go more than two weeks into the past. If the listening devices were older than that, this was a dead end.

But then, at thirteen days and seven hours ago, I got lucky. Neil, my old friend who led me to Aunt Zelda's and started this whole mess, opened up the utensil drawer, but didn't take anything out. He followed that up by opening the cabinet under the sink, sticking his head inside, and then standing back up, hands empty.

I checked the utensil drawer, finding nothing but sporks and knives. Then I ducked under the sink, tapping my eyelid three times for night vision. Besides the dishwashing detergent, plunger, and various cleaning chemicals, I spotted something round and metallic, roughly the size of a hyperbaseball, under a box of sponges. I brought up my DT and took a picture of it, then ran the picture through uffsee.

I got zero hits.

"Hey, man, don't hoard all the Jell-O."

Another cop stumbled over, snagging the bowl. He brought it to his lips and slurped.

I ignored him, studying the object. It obviously wasn't a listening device, because the cops would have found it when they did their transmitter sweep. A bomb?

I flipped the air sensor on my DT, letting it have a digital sniff. It analyzed the air around the object, finding standard atmospheric gases, traces of cleaning agents, and a decent amount of atomized marijuana. But nothing caustic, flammable, or potentially explosive.

So what was this thing?

Then I scanned it, revealing the interior guts. Circuits and servos, unrecognizable to me.

I threw caution to the wind and picked the ball up. It was smooth, heavy for its size, and in the light of the kitchen it appeared to be many colors all at once, like an oscillating prism. I turned it over in my palm and noticed a panel, along with a button. Next to the button were the engraved words PRESS ME.

That didn't seem like the wisest idea. Especially after watching Boise implode. This didn't look like the device Alter-Talon had used, but I wasn't taking any chances.

"Cool! Hyperbaseball!"

The cop snatched the ball from my hand. I reached for it, slipping on green Jell-O, falling onto my face.

"Hey! A button!"

Before I could yell, "Don't press it, you fool—you'll kill us all!" he pressed the button.

It didn't kill us all.

In fact, it didn't do anything. The cop stared at it, puzzled, and then looked at me. "You got any cereal?"

"Last cabinet on the left. Milk's in the fridge."

"Thanks. Trippy ball, man."

He tossed it to me. I caught it. While the ball looked

exactly the same, I noticed the prism effect had sped up. There was also a very faint buzzing noise coming from inside. But other than that, it didn't seem to be doing anything.

I went to my TEV, and saw Vicki boffing somebody on the kitchen table. Where I ate my eggs every morning. I really needed to tell her to keep her clientele in her bedroom.

I got ready to fast-forward to see where Neil had gone, when I noticed Vicki had a black eye and was sobbing uncontrollably. The sex was violent, and hardly looked consensual.

I clenched my jaw, panning left to see the face of the son of a bitch doing this to her.

The son of a bitch turned out to be me.

THIRTY-FOUR

The Mastermind listens as Talon watches the timecast. The incompetent cops hadn't found all of the bugs. He wishes he could see Talon's face, wishes he'd used video cameras instead of listening devices.

Watching half a million people disappear with the press of a button was a heady experience. But they weren't real to him. They were numbers. Statistics. The first hash mark of many.

But Talon . . .

The mouse is personal. Being able to see him suffer will be a treat for the Mastermind.

Not now. But soon.

The Mastermind is interrupted by a knock at his door. The cops? Did they know?

No. It's reporters. They want him to comment. He declines with a smile.

Later, when they realize how close they were to the real Butcher of Boise, they'll want to hang themselves.

If they aren't already dead by then.

He resumes listening to Talon. It has taken the mouse longer than expected, but he's followed the trail of crumbs.

Soon the trail will end. And the cat and mouse will meet.

Watching half a million vanish from a distance won't be nearly as much fun as watching one man die up close.

THIRTY-FIVE

I stared in disbelief as Alter-Talon violated my wife. He had one hand on her throat, squeezing hard, a sick grin on his face as he pumped away. I'd been angry before, many times. But seeing this filled me with such absolute rage I would have killed the guy if he were in the room.

And he had been in the room. Almost two weeks ago, according to the TEV. But how? And why hadn't Vicki told me?

I tried to remember two weeks back. Had she seemed upset? Had she covered up her black eye with makeup? Why hadn't she said anything?

I paused the scene and rechecked the date. It couldn't be right. Two weeks ago, I had the house to myself. Vicki was visiting her mother in New Los Angeles. She wasn't home when this took place.

So how . . . ?

My eyes drifted to the prism ball, the button still depressed. I thumbed it off.

The TEV monitor went fuzzy, and then showed an empty kitchen.

I pressed the on button.

The monitor showed Vicki being assaulted.

That was when I figured it out. This hadn't happened to the Vicki I was married to. It had happened to an alter-Vicki, in a parallel universe. Somehow this prism ball made a TEV tune in to past events in an alternate universe.

I flipped the ball off. Had Neil created this thing? Had he been the mastermind all along?

No. This tech seemed way beyond Neil. And he'd passed the voice-stress detector. Neil was involved, but he wasn't the mastermind. I thought about following him backward, letting him lead me to the person who gave him the prism ball, but the TEV was at its limit and couldn't go back any further.

Then I realized the obvious. If this prism forced a time-cast in a parallel world, then there had to be a prism at Aunt Zelda's apartment that made me pick up the transmission of Alter-Talon killing her.

I put the prism ball in a pouch on my belt, then tapped my eyelid for infrared. The two cops on the first level were still in the den, lying next to each other on the floor. It looked like they were spooning. I checked the perimeter of the house, and the chatty duo walking the route was passing by the front door.

Time to go.

I snuck downstairs and outside, happy to take the hepa-filter off my face and breathe some fresh air. I barely took two steps before I heard a whistle.

It was my dick neighbor, Chomsky, out for a stroll with his genipet—some sort of mini alpaca or llama. He had his fingers in his mouth, producing a loud, shrill tone that could be heard across Lake Michigan and all the way to New Detroit.

"It's Talon Avalon! The fugitive!"

He whistled again, and his miniature critter seemed to be getting agitated by the sound. It bumped Chomsky with its head, then spit on him.

"Barack O'Llama!" Chomsky chastised, slapping his pet on the snout. "Behave!"

I saw the two cops hauling ass around the corner, Tasers drawn, so I didn't have a chance to break Chomsky's nose, like the dick deserved. I began to run.

Chomsky whistled again. "He's going that way!"

Barack bit him in the nards. I always liked Barack.

I beat feet through the alley, hopping on Teague's bio-fuel scooter. My biggest concern was a satellite spotting me. I wasn't sure if the old Tesla Taser satellites were still in operation, since violent crime was pretty much eliminated in Chicago. They worked like giant, orbiting versions of my Glock Taser, sending lightning from the Tesla field and zapping targets on earth. But unlike a handheld version, TTSs were computer controlled and not subject to human error. If you were moving less than five miles per hour, and a TTS locked onto you, it rarely missed.

Zipping up the street, I heard Chomsky scream as his llama gnawed away. Then I was immediately intercepted by three peace officer scooters. Teague's bike was also CPD issue, so I aimed the kill switch laser in their direction and gave them a rapid-fire burst. It cut their engines, but they still coasted toward me, shooting their Tasers. I swerved left, merging into traffic, and found six more cops on my tail. Like Teague, they were also equipped with kill switches. And if they killed my bike, I'd be easy pickings for the TTSs.

I weaved through the sea of motorists, listening to the sirens behind me, and then hit my siren and pulled into the frog lane. The kermits freaked out, jumping out of the way, some of them falling over and eating pavement. I tailgated one, very close to running him over, but he saw me in his headband rearview mirror and jumped backward, completely over me, clearing my bike by at least five feet. It would have been a lot cooler if he didn't look so goofy doing it.

The CPD bikes followed me into the lane. I hadn't been on scooter patrol in more than a decade, but I remembered kill switches had a range of about twenty meters, so as long as I had a sixty-foot lead, they wouldn't be able to—

My engine died. Apparently the range had gotten better in the last decade.

I coasted, turning into an alley, smacking right into a powerbocker who was taking a leak in a biorecycle toilet, the opening thirty inches higher than the pedestrian version to accommodate the frog leggers. He toppled, and I jumped off the scooter, mostly to dodge the urine stream. I skidded onto the greentop, coming to rest on my stomach.

"WTF!?" The kermit was on his back. He'd been unable to stop his flow, and an arc of pee splashed onto his chest and drenched his Green Bay Packers shirt, which was not what the Packers deserved.

I got to my knees, trying to decide which way to bolt, when two CPD scooters pulled in, Tasers blazing.

I ducked behind my fallen bike, wax bullets exploding around me, Tesla bolts raining down everywhere. Piss Boy got hit twice, his fountain of urine sparking up and zinging his ding-a-ling in a way that could only be described as extremely uncomfortable. I scrambled to my feet and launched myself at the nearest cop, shots whizzing past my head, hitting him with a body tackle and taking him off the bike and into a lovely hydrangea bush. I landed on him, my knee in his solar plexus, then grabbed his gun hand and pressed his finger on the trigger, firing at his partner, making him dance to the million-volt boogie.

His partner flopped off his scooter, and I ran for it, ready to speed off into the street, when three more cops entered the alley from the other side, heading right for me.

A bike chase was a no-win proposition for me. They could go wherever I went, and they were armed.

I glanced at the kermit. He'd managed to stop peeing, and steam was rising from his wet chest. Without thinking I knelt next to him, hitting the release button on his left knee, the clamps of the frog leg automatically opening up.

Before I could second-guess myself, the spring stilts were on my own legs, automatically snugging themselves to a perfect fit.

Frog legs worked on two simple principles. Longer legs meant longer strides, and springs transferred energy. They were made of reinforced carbon slats, which curved backward in half-moon shapes. This allowed them to bend. Extra height plus extra bounce meant higher speed. I'd heard some folks could reach fifty miles per hour on them, which was faster than biofuel scooters.

But how in the heck did you get up once they were on?

The legs were lightweight but cumbersome. The added height made it impossible for me to stand because my knees were too high. I crawled to the alley wall and had to pull myself up on the ivy. Once erect, balancing was awkward, and I had no idea how anyone could walk in these things, let alone run.

The cops got within Taser range. I pushed myself off the wall, took three staggering steps, and then realized that the frog legs changed my center of gravity. Leaning forward corrected this issue. Head down, I sprinted at the scooters.

The rate of acceleration was surprising, blowing my hair back, the world blurring past me on either side. Each stride covered ten or twelve feet, and the bouncing—though it looked silly to an observer—actually felt steady and controlled. It was like regular running, only enhanced.

Time to try a jump.

The cops swerved out of my way, probably thinking I was just another kermit. Then one of them IDed me and raised his weapon, coming at me fast.

I bounced on my right leg and leapt up, clearing his bike easily. But my exhilaration was short-lived, because I actually kept going higher, as if gravity no longer had a hold on me, and when I looked down I was twenty feet in the air. If I landed wrong, it would break me, or possibly kill me.

After a momentary adrenaline surge of pure panic, I

brought both legs together and leaned forward in a crouching position, clenching my teeth, ready to absorb the shock of impact.

I hit the ground hard, slamming into the greentop with incredible speed and force—

—and didn't feel the impact at all.

The frog legs absorbed the kinetic energy, then released it, launching me into the air again. The relief that surged through me was fleeting; I was leaping into oncoming traffic.

I shifted my body in the air, trying to control my trajectory, even flapping my arms like a pigeon to prevent me from landing on top of a motorist. I managed to squeeze between two scooters, hopping on one leg, bending my knee so the next bounce wouldn't be as high. My left stilt clipped a commuter's helmet, throwing me off balance, and I did a bizarre pirouette, landed on both legs, and then did splits in the air like a freestyle skier, leapfrogging another two bikes and heading straight for a bus.

I had déjà vu of the train incident earlier, except this time I didn't have gecko tape, and the bus was coming at me rather than moving in the same direction. I bent into a pike, managing to get my legs out in front of me, my ass brushing against the vehicle's green roof as I barely cleared the top. My stilts dug two trenches in the flowers, then caught on the internal irrigation system. My body continued its forward motion, my knees bent, and I bounced off the roof, just as a gigantic bolt of Tesla lightning split the night and struck the bus less than a foot behind me.

The TTS had locked on.

THIRTY-SIX

I wasn't a fan of heights, so seeing the ground whir by thirty feet below me made my stomach do flip-flops. The frog legs had amazing stabilizers and shock suppressors, but all I could think of as I plummeted to earth was, *I'm on a one-way trip to Pancake Town.*

I brought my ankles together, feeling the impact this time—a bone-jarring shock that made me bite my tongue. But I managed to keep my balance, and the spring stilts performed as advertised, once again bouncing me skyward.

Another Tesla bolt singed some poor sap in my wake. I managed to get the next bounce under control, and hopped into the frog lane, spitting some blood over my shoulder, heading for Wacker Drive. My bouncing gradually became manageable and I began to run once again, weaving through other kermits.

I easily outsped the CPD bikes, which were stuck in congestion, but not without personal cost. Though quick, the frog legs required a lot more exertion than simple running, and after two blocks I was a gasping, sweaty wreck. Every time I slowed my pace, the TTS threw a Tesla bolt at me, each one closer than the last. I needed to find some shelter and catch my breath.

I darted through more powerbockers, several of whom got zapped in my stead, then ducked into an office building. It was a typical Chicago skyscraper—a green lobby, a security island, about two dozen utopeons milling about amid the chrome, mirrors, and ficus trees.

"Hey! No frog legs!"

The security guard's only weapons were a harsh tone and a stern glance, neither of which cowed me. I sighted the escalator and bounded toward it, relaxing a bit; TTSs didn't work indoors.

"I'm talking to you, buddy."

The guard waddled over to intercept me, perhaps driven by an inner desire to keep his paycheck. I tried to go around him, but he cut me off.

"We don't allow kermits inside. Lose the legs or—"

The Tesla bolt hit him in the mouth, which must have stung like crazy. He flopped to the ground, and I ran to the right, searching for cops.

No cops. Which meant—

The Taser zap hit me in the stilt, making me fall over. I wasn't stunned, at least not in the physical sense. The frog leg acted like a lightning rod, drawing the charge away from me. But color me shocked that TTS tech had advanced to the point where it now worked indoors.

Scooting backward on my butt, I reached the marble security counter and hoisted myself back up. Then I sprinted for the escalator, another lightning strike missing my nose by inches, so close I could smell the ozone.

The bottoms of the frog legs had rubber grips, about half the length of my feet. But I misjudged the moving stairs and began to topple on the first step. I grabbed the person ahead of me for balance. She swore, giving me a shove, pushing me out of the way as a Taser bolt struck her.

I fell onto my butt, then crawled like mad on all fours,

over to the elevator. A dozen or so people in the lobby gave me a wide berth.

"Hold the elevator!" I yelled.

No one in the elevator made any sort of move to indicate they heard me.

Another zap in the frog leg. I was fifteen feet away from the elevator, and doubted I'd make it.

That was when ten cops poured into the lobby. They sighted me and began to fire their Tasers.

I put my palms on the floor, kept my legs straight, and then walked backward on my hands until I looked like an upside down *V*. Then I bent my knees and pushed forward, as if diving into a pool. In three quick steps I was on my feet, then back on my belly, sliding into the elevator as the doors began to close, a Tesla bullet hitting me in the back. I fought the pain, my muscles bunching up, until the elevator climbed out of range and the current cut out.

I caught my breath, wiped away a few errant tears, and said, "Fifty-second floor, please."

Someone pressed the button for me, but no one offered to help me up.

After a minute of rest, I crawled out onto my floor, wondering what to do next. This was the top of the building. Any second now, cops would be surrounding me. I could ditch the frog legs, take my chances on the stairs, but they'd be covering those as well.

I took a quick look around, and saw a door at the end of the hallway that had ROOF ACCESS stenciled on it, which gave me a really stupid idea. I got to my feet doing the upside-down *V* trick, and hauled ass over there. It was locked, but nothing my Nife couldn't handle.

The two flights of stairs weren't easy to climb. I balanced by palming the walls. When I reached the top I dealt with another locked door, and then I was on the roof. The greentop was regular grass, and hemp bushes competed for space with bamboo. The wind was fast and strong, changing

direction randomly. Following a path in the lawn, I walked
to the edge of the roof. The city was all lit up, spectacular,
the famous Chicago skyline a marvel to behold.

I looked ahead, to the neighboring skyscraper. One story
shorter, and perhaps ten yards away. Then I looked down and
felt my stomach clench. This was way too high for me. There
was no way I'd pull this off. I was better off surrendering.

A bolt of Tesla lightning hit me in the stilt. I staggered
backward, then turned around and took five giant steps. I
turned again, eyeing the edge of the roof, feeling like I had
to vomit.

*Just do it. The next building is only thirty feet away.
You've jumped farther than thirty feet.*

"Not in this wind," I said to myself. "Not at this height."

Noise, to my right. The cops flooding onto the roof.

I sprinted toward the building's ledge.

I kept my eyes on my mark. I'd hit the edge with both
feet, then spring out into the empty air. No problem.

My first two steps felt pretty good.

On my third step, I remembered a video I'd seen Teague
watching, called *Insane Kermit Deaths 17*, which featured
some idiot trying to jump from one building to another. He
missed, and when he hit the ground his head came off his
body and bounced several yards away.

I changed my mind at my fourth step, realizing this was
the king of very bad ideas, but I'd already committed to it
now, do or die. Or, more likely, do *and* die.

I hit the edge of the roof with both feet, bending my
knees, screaming into the wind as I launched off the building with every last ounce of my strength.

In a day filled with some really scary shit, this was the
worst. The terrifying and unnatural experience of no longer
being tethered to the earth. I knew I shouldn't look down,
but I did anyway. A horrible, helpless feeling overcame me,
quickly replaced by a wave of anger that I'd do something
this monumentally stupid.

I looked ahead. The next skyscraper was fifteen feet away. But the wind gusted against me, pushing me, slowing me, and gravity took its cheap shot as well, mocking my attempt, dragging me down.

Halfway there I knew I wasn't going to make it.

I thought about Vicki, about her seeing my splattered remains on the news. Would she always wonder if I was really guilty? Would she know my very last thought was of her?

Then the wind changed, an updraft that pushed me from behind, and I piked my feet in front of me, surprised, amazed, that I was actually going to survive.

I hit the roof, legs together, laughing aloud as my stilts kissed the lawn.

In hindsight, I should have landed on my belly or knees.

Once my feet hit, the frog legs bent and launched me into the air again. A huge hop, bouncing me way up over the top of the building, toward the opposite edge.

I was going too far. I'd miss the ledge by a few feet and fall to my death.

I pinwheeled my arms, trying to turn around in midair, and managed to face backward, watching the ledge disappear beneath me. I stretched out, my fingertips brushing the edge of the skyscraper, catching it for a moment, a moment that lasted long enough for me to have some hope.

Then my grip slipped.

I fell, hugging the side of the building, seeing my own terrified image reflected back at me in the pristine windows.

Insane Kermit Deaths 18, *here I come.*

This time my last thought wasn't of Vicki. It wasn't cursing my own stupidity, either. The only thing in my brain was raw, screaming, animalistic terror. The last few seconds of my life would also be the worst few seconds.

Then my chest smashed into something, followed by my chin. I spread out my arms instinctively, trying to grab whatever I had crashed into. My upper body had caught on some kind of platform, my legs swinging wildly in open air. I looked around and saw I was hanging on an automatic window washer. It slid up and down the side of the building on tracks, using a motorized spray and squeegee. The whole thing was no more than two feet wide and five feet long.

It was almost enough to make me start believing in a deity.

Capitalizing on my luck, I kept a death grip on the squeegee arm with my left hand, and used my weaker right to fumble for my Nife. The shoulder strap attached to Teague's TEV picked that moment to slip off, falling down the length of my forearm. I curled my wrist and caught the strap, and the wind caught the machine, making it—and me—sway back and forth.

Which was when I started to lose my grip on the squeegee.

It made me understand why organized religion failed; ten seconds after I'd begun believing in God, I cursed his name.

The simple solution was to drop the TEV. But it was probably the only unit left in Illinois, and if I lost it, I'd have no chance at clearing my name.

I grunted as the swinging got worse, rocking my lower body back and forth. Using the momentum, I waited for the pendulum to reach its apex, then continued the motion, throwing the TEV up onto the cleaning platform.

Unfortunately, the effort made me lose the little balance I had left. I stretched my bad right arm, trying to find some sort of handhold, but my lower body rocked too far to the side, and then I was in midair again, my body parallel to the street below.

My hand was yanked from the platform.

I might have whimpered, but I was too busy throwing up inside my mouth. I stared at the platform, only a few inches away but impossible to reach, and then that old bastard gravity gave me a bitch-slap, and once again I began to fall.

If I were a cat, I'd have used up my nine lives hours ago. But I wasn't a cat, and the green ripper wasn't ready to claim me just yet. I had a death grip on the TEV strap, and it must have snagged on something, because I swung beneath the platform and banged against the window.

I swallowed bile, amazed I'd made it this far. With my right hand I fumbled for my Nife, and managed to unsheathe it. I made a quick square in the reinforced window I was facing, the glass falling inward. Then I tossed the Nife into the building and swung through the opening I'd made.

When I hit the floor I rolled over and kissed the carpet. It tasted sweeter than anything I'd ever eaten in my life.

The office I'd entered into was dark, empty. After a few seconds wrangling my nerves back into working order, I tapped my eyelid for night vision, and found my Nife. Chances were high I'd lost the cops, but did I lose the TTS?

I didn't want to stand still long enough to find out. I pulled off the frog legs, found the stairs, and took it up a floor. I found the office directly above the one I'd swung into, and used the Nife to open the door and the window, retrieving the TEV from the window-washing platform.

Once inside the elevator, I cleaned myself up, patting the dirt off my clothes, tucking in my shirt. When I reached the lobby I walked out casually, like I belonged there. Then I merged into pedestrian traffic, walked north for two blocks, then ducked down an alley and relieved a kindly young lady of her biofuel scooter by pulling her off by her waist.

"OMG! You're that guy! The one from the news!" She seemed more excited than scared. "You are soooo hot."

She whipped out her DT and took a picture. I waved good-bye and hopped onto the scooter, heading north.

Half an hour later, I was back at Aunt Zelda's. The adrenaline had all worn off, and I felt like a wad of gum that had been chewed for a week straight. Every muscle in my body was cramped and hurting. Competing for gold in the Pain Decathalon was a killer headache. I dry-swallowed two aspirin and an amphetamine, ditched the bike, and then took the elevator up to Aunt Zelda's apartment.

I was about to get some much-needed answers.

THIRTY-SEVEN

The door was unlocked, as I'd left it. Neil was sitting at the kitchen table, eating a bag of chips. Apparently he hadn't figured out that my Tesla account had been suspended, and that ergo his supplication collar no longer worked. If I'd been in a reflective mood, I might have quipped something about how the biggest boundaries people had to face were the ones they didn't test. But I wasn't feeling reflective. I was feeling tired and sore and mean.

Neil's eyes bugged out when he saw me, and he made a choking sound.

"You . . . you . . ."

"Yes, Neil. I'm me. But the question is, who are you?"

"You killed half a million people."

I sat down next to him, taking the TEV off my shoulder and setting it on the floor.

"So you know half a million and one is no big deal for me." I tugged out my DT, put on the voice-stress analyzer. "State your full name, or I'll do something horrible to you."

"Neil Anders Winston," he quickly said.

"Is Zelda your aunt, Neil? Tell the truth this time."

"Yes."

Untruth.

I took out my Nife, let him see the blade, then drove it through the table we were sitting at. He jumped about a foot. When I pulled the Nife toward me, cutting the table-top in half, Neil lost all color in his face.

"No, she's not my real aunt. Someone told me to tell you that."

Truth.

"Who?"

"I don't know. He never told me his name. He called me up, out of the blue."

Truth.

"Do you normally follow orders from strangers?"

"No."

"Did he have something on you? Blackmail? Extortion?"

"No."

"Did he offer you credits?"

"No."

"What did he offer you, Neil?"

Neil studied his lap. "He said he had a way to get you into trouble."

"Why would you want to get me into trouble?"

"He said you'd go to prison. Then I could have Vicki for myself."

My anger was tempered with a healthy dose of pity, so I didn't smack him. Yet.

"Tell me everything he told you."

Neil talked through the headphone call with the mystery man. He'd fixed it so Neil could get into the apartment using his chip. He made Neil type and memorize everything he needed to say, which Neil had done. He sent Neil the prism ball via UPS, no return address, along with several bugs, and told him to plant them in my house.

"Did you get the impression this man knew you?" I

asked. I was looking at Neil's DT, studying the instructions the mystery man had given him.

"Yes. But not because I knew him. He said he'd been spying on me for a while. Knew how I felt about Vicki. Wanted us to be together."

"Did he say anything about himself?"

"Nothing."

"What was his voice like?" I raised an eyebrow. "Did he sound like me?"

"He used a voice scrambler. He called me four times. Each time he sounded different."

"Do you know what this is, Neil?" I took the prism ball from the pouch on my belt.

"No."

"You don't know, but you still hid it in my house?"

"He assured me it was safe."

"The nameless, faceless stranger assured you it was safe? What if it wasn't safe? What if it was a bomb?"

"I'm not an idiot, Talon. I scanned it, made sure it wasn't explosive or poisonous. It's just a bunch of electronics."

I raised my fist. Neil cowered.

"Please don't hurt me. Please."

I was going to hurt him, all right. He'd lied to me, planted bugs in my house, and endangered my wife. But I wasn't going to risk breaking my knuckles on his thick head.

I held up my DT, showing Neil it was recording. "You see this, asshole? I'm playing this for Vicki. After she hears it, she's never going to speak to you again. And that's the very least of what you deserve."

Neil started to blubber. I left him to his pain and began to search the apartment. There had to be another prism ball in here, one that made me timecast the parallel earth where Alter-Talon killed Aunt Zelda. I assumed the balls had a limited range, which was why Alter-Talon disappeared near the elevator—it didn't broadcast that far. That meant the ball had to be close.

There were hundreds of places a small object could hide. I began in the kitchen, going through the cabinets and drawers, opening containers. I also checked the refrigerator. Zelda's backward head stared back at me, accusatory. Her open eyes had frosted over, becoming a dull white. Even more disconcerting was Zelda's jaw, hanging wide open like she was about to eat me.

I snapped on a pair of latex gloves I keep in my utility belt for occasions such as this one, and reluctantly patted her down, feeling ghoulish. I flinched when I felt a lump under her dress, near her middle. I used the Nife to carefully cut away her clothing, and then paused.

The ball wasn't on her stomach.

It was *in* her stomach.

I frowned. At least it explained the open jaw. The killer had stuffed the ball into her mouth. I momentarily wondered why that hadn't been in the timecast transmission, then remembered the transmission was from a completely different murder. I hadn't seen this Aunt Zelda killed.

Yet.

I stared at the bulge, knowing what needed to be done, not wanting to be the one to do it. Maybe I could have forced Neil to, but his caterwauling was so intense I feared he'd slit his own throat if I gave him the Nife.

Rather than dwell on the task, I went straight to it. A quick stroke of the Nife blade across the bump split the skin. The prism sphere pushed up through the viscera like a giant eye opening, congealed blood and bits of gore sticking to the surface. I plucked the ball out, got hit with the acrid stench of gastric juices bubbling up from the stomach, and quickly slammed the refrigerator door.

Neil had watched the spectacle, and had traded wailing for covering up his mouth with both hands. He'd gotten some color back, but unfortunately for him the color was sickly green.

I studied the sphere, which was identical to the one

from my house. It was buzzing softly, the prism oscillating on the surface beneath the cold, gelatinous blood. This one had no PRESS ME inscription, but there was a button. I touched it, and the noise ceased.

I set the ball on the counter, stripped off my gloves, and washed my hands in the sink even though I hadn't gotten any blood on them. I also splashed some water on my face. When I finished, I was energized. It was finally time to see who set me up.

I turned on Teague's TEV and closed my eyes, allowing instinct to take over. My breathing slowed. My mind opened. I both focused and spaced out, quickly locating the eighth dimension. Once I did, it took only a minute to tune in to the octeract point. I mentally pet the bunny, giving the fabric of spacetime a little tickle between the ears, and then stared at the monitor. This time, the colors were correct. I was timecasting in our universe.

I panned around the kitchen, but the room was empty. A close-up of the countertop found it free of bloodstains, so I must have tuned in to before the murder. I began to wander the house, searching for Aunt Zelda. No one was home. I fast-forwarded, keeping the lens on the front door, letting it play normally when it opened.

Aunt Zelda came in, carrying a bag of groceries. She closed the door behind her, then glanced in the hallway mirror and checked her hair. It was such a candid, human gesture that I felt my heart sink. All I knew about this woman was that she used to be the man who invented uffsee, and she had a psychotic dissy nephew. Seeing her as a person was disconcerting, especially since I knew what was coming up.

She brought the bag to the kitchen, and loaded some fruit into the refrigerator. Then she opened the kitchen closet and a man stepped out and grabbed her throat.

The move was so sudden, so unexpected and violent, both Aunt Zelda and I gasped. The man was dressed head to toe in black, including gloves. Medium height, heavy build. His face was hidden behind a celebrity veil. These were a result of the Paparazzi Massacre of 2054, when a cadre of celebrities allegedly hired a hit squad to wipe out forty-seven known photographer-stalkers. The violence ended when an inventor released celebrity veils—one-way fabric that attached to a hat and draped over the face, completely obscuring identity. Celebrity invasion of privacy dwindled to zero, as paparazzi had no way of proving who was in their photos.

The celebrity veil this killer wore had a yellow circle on it, with an emoticon smiley :) printed on the fabric. There was no way to see his face.

I watched as he pulled Aunt Zelda to the sink, easily overpowering her. The rest of the scene played out as it had in the alternate universe. Aunt Zelda's head was slammed into the sink three times, then twisted around 180 degrees.

I paused the action, noting that Neil was watching over my shoulder.

"I told you I didn't do it," I said.

He sniffled. "That's you in a mask."

I switched to electromagnetic radiation resolution, and zoomed in on the killer's arm to read his chip ID.

His chip wasn't there. Instead, there was a round black disk.

"WTF?"

He was hiding his chip somehow. Which was impossible. There was no technology able to do that.

But then, there was no technology able to allow timecasting in parallel universes, either.

I fast-forwarded, wincing as he jammed a prism ball down Aunt Zelda's throat, cut out and nuked her chip, and stuffed her in the fridge. Then he did something odd. He took another celebrity veil out of his pocket and placed it on top of the refrigerator.

I paused the transmission and reached for the veil. It had an emoticon frowny face :(on the front. Why leave it there? I did a quick scan of it with my DT. No fingerprints.

No DNA. It was just a normal mask. I shoved it into my utility belt.

I unpaused the TEV and followed the killer to the front door, where he rigged the lock mechanism, allowing Neil's chip to open it. Then I tagged along as he walked into the hallway and caught the elevator. This time, he didn't vanish into thin air. He hopped into the lift and went down.

I rewound, going back two hours, and found him when he arrived, still wearing the celebrity veil. I let it play, watching him walk to Aunt Zelda's door, open it with a smart magnet, and then hide in the kitchen closet.

I had two courses of action. I could follow him to see where he went next, or I could follow him backward and see where he came from. He'd have to take off the veil eventually.

The problem was, I might have to track him for hours in either direction before he revealed his face.

I yawned, fatigue catching up with me. I needed food, and sleep. Much as I wanted to chase this bastard right now, my body was close to shutting down. I padded back into the apartment, and found my way into the bathroom. I located some sleeping pills in the medicine cabinet. I dumped three onto my hand, plus three Valium, some THC, and, just for fun, three Estrolux pills. The Estrolux temporarily increased breast size.

Neil was still in the kitchen, eyeing me like a cat when a dog came into the room. I walked past him, reaching into the cabinet, taking Aunt Zelda's bottle of contraband rum.

I located a glass and filled it halfway. It smelled like biodiesel.

Without hesitating, I poured it down my throat.

It tasted awful, like some kind of antique medicine, and burned my throat going down. I'd never tried real liquor before, and couldn't understand why anyone would do so willingly. Yuck. And people used to drink so much of this stuff it destroyed their livers? What the heck was wrong with them?

I spat into the sink, then turned to Neil.

"I need to sleep," I said. "But I don't trust you not to murder me. So I need you to take some pills."

"I don't want to take any pills."

I unsheathed my Nife. "These are getting in your stomach, one way or another. Which way do you want to go?"

"Actually, some pills would hit the spot right about now."

I handed them over, and he poured a glass of water and obediently swallowed the whole bunch. I made him open his mouth to show he wasn't cheeking them, and sent him to go sleep on the sofa.

Then I sat down at the kitchen table and called my wife.

She didn't answer her headphone, and I had an overwhelming feeling something was very wrong.

THIRTY-EIGHT

There were many good reasons why Vicki wouldn't answer, but I would have thought with me on the run she'd make an extra effort to be available. I disconnected and called Sata. He picked up on the first ring.

"Is Vicki okay?"

"She's in the guest room, sleeping. She went to bed an hour ago, Talon-*kun*. She's pretty wiped out. Would you like me to wake her?"

"Yes. Wait. No. Could you just . . . check on her? See if she's okay?"

"Sure, Talon."

After a moment I heard a soft knock, and then a door opening.

"She's asleep?" I asked.

"Yes. I can disturb her, if you wish. But she's had a hard day. Spent the last few hours crying."

That's just what I needed. Guilt on top of everything else.

"Let her sleep, Sata-*san*. I'll call her later." I got my

mind back in the game. "Have you found out anything about the technology used to timecast in the multiverse?"

"I've been doing some research. It's theoretically possible to change the frequency of a timecast transmission, which would force a Van Damme to tune to a parallel universe on another 'brane. But there would have to be some sort of jamming device that overrode this 'brane."

"I found one of those. Two of them, actually."

I ran down the events of the past few hours for Sata, ending with my current location.

"Can you bring me one of these prism spheres to study?"

I yawned. Everything seemed a bit warmer, calmer. I recognized the alcohol buzz, which had a similar effect to alcohol pills. But this was fuzzier, and actually more pleasant. I stood up and poured myself another glass of rum, sipping it this time.

"I can do that tomorrow. But I can send you a scan now."

"Please."

I took pictures from various angles, both the exterior and a computed tomography scan of the interior, using my DT.

"Fascinating," Sata said when he received the pics. "This technology is quite extraordinary. It's both a jammer and a broadcaster. There also appears to be a tuning mechanism on it, similar to the ones used on tachyon emission visualizers."

"Yeah. Fascinating," I said, yawning again. I took another sip of rum. The liquid still burned, but the taste was growing on me.

"When can you deliver this to me, Talon?"

"Tomorrow morning. First I have to follow the SMF who killed Aunt Zelda. Have you ever heard of chip-blocking tech?"

"No. But I haven't heard of timecast-jamming tech, either."

"I thought the same thing."

"If that black round disk on the killer's arm uses the same tech as your prism spheres, perhaps it also jams reception somehow. You're aware that infinite parallel universes exist less than one millimeter away from us. They're closer to us than the clothes we're wearing. If some hypergenius was able to tune in to a different 'brane, he'd be able to mask our 'brane by . . ."

I tuned Sata out. Even if I'd been completely lucid, I would have had trouble following him. Call it a 'brane deficit on my part. After thirty seconds of technobabble, I cut him off.

"Sata-*san*, I have to get some rest. I'll bring you the sphere in the morning."

"Yes. Of course, Talon. See you soon. Good night."

He hung up. I noticed my glass was empty again, and I filled it once more. The rum not only improved my mood, but it mellowed me in a way I'd never quite felt before. It was quite superior to the synth pills. I wondered what other natural products were better than their synthetic counterparts. Maybe I'd have to give Harry McGlade a call, buy some denim jeans from him. Or more liquor. I was pretty sure he dealt in alcohol as well as paper and cotton clothing.

I checked Aunt Zelda's cabinets, found a bag of genetically modified potatoes. They were bacon-and-cheese-flavored. I preferred the roast beef variety, but these weren't bad. I ate two raw. I followed them up with a genmod apple, which tasted like pie à la mode. Delicious, and nutritious, fortified with every essential micronutrient.

Sadly, the rum bottle was almost empty. I took it with me to the living room, where I checked on Neil. He was snoring on the couch, and his breasts had already doubled in size. By morning, he'd be a D-cup. Served the little bastard right.

Then I weaved into Aunt Zelda's bedroom, collapsing on her bed, feeling it form-fit to the contours of my body.

I was tired. Too tired to even take off Teague's boots.

I drained the rest of the rum in one gulp, then shut my eyes, spinning into sleep.

A noise woke me up.

I looked around, unsure of where I was. Light was peeking in through the bedroom blinds, so it was morning. Aunt Zelda, and Neil, and the fix I was in all came rushing back to me. I sat up, listened for whatever had awoken me. I heard the air-conditioning hum. Neil's footsteps, creaking outside my doorway. Snoring, from the living room.

My adrenal glands kicked into overdrive. *If Neil was snoring, how could he be walking outside my door?*

I went on the offensive, leaping out of bed, ducking through the door, running into—

"Teague. Son of a bitch. How'd you get in?"

"Smart magnet."

Teague trained his Glock on my chest, but made no immediate effort to shoot. He had a neck brace on, the healing disk humming. Other than that, he looked the picture of health.

"You track me?" I asked, noting he had a new TEV unit on my shoulder.

He set it down and shook his head. "When you mentioned the name Neil, I remembered the wimpy guy who came to the office, talking about his aunt being murdered. She the one on TV?"

"She's in the fridge."

"That's cold, bro."

"About forty-five degrees."

We stared at each other.

"I didn't kill her, Teague. I didn't destroy Boise, either."

"Maybe you did; maybe you didn't. Frankly, I don't care."

"So what do you want?"

"Who's there?" muttered Neil from the other room. "Holy shit! I have tits!"

Teague said, "Ever since we were kids, we've always competed with one another."

"You won most of the time."

"You won the girl. That beats everything else."

"She wasn't a prize to be won, Teague. She made her own choice."

"WTF?" Neil said. "They're real!"

Teague put the gun in its holster, and for a brief moment I hoped we were actually going to reconcile. It surprised me how good the idea of it felt.

My elation slipped away when he raised his fists.

"I'm better than you, Talon. And I'm going to prove it."

I put up my dukes as well. "Like you proved it in the cornfield?"

Teague's eyes narrowed. "I'm taking you in. No guns. No weapons. I'm going to break your neck, and leave you in front of the Cook County courthouse. And there's not a thing you can do to—"

I hit him with a jab in the nose, then followed with a right cross to the chin. My right was weak; the arm had gotten number overnight. Teague shrugged off the blows and snap-kicked me in the ribs, sending me stumbling down the hall. I fell onto my back in the living room.

Neil stood over me, his hands up his shirt. "I need some time alone," he said. "I'll be in the shower."

He still appeared groggy from the sleeping pills, so much so that he didn't even acknowledge Teague when he passed him in the hallway.

Teague advanced casually, rolling his shoulders. Besides my bad arm, I ached in about a hundred places. Unlike Teague, I hadn't had the luxury of an ER visit. He probably wasn't feeling any pain at all. Me? It even hurt to blink.

I stared up at my former friend. "You win," I told him. "You're better than me."

He seemed to consider the comment. Then he offered me his hand.

I took it. After Teague helped me up, he punched me in the gut so hard it knocked the wind out of me. I doubled over, unable to suck in any air. Teague yanked my Nife from my utility belt sheath, threw it against the wall, where it stuck, and then followed it up with a kick to the chest. I managed to twist away in time, taking the brunt of it on my bad arm, but it still knocked me onto the couch. I sat there for a moment, trying to get my diaphragm to work.

"Pathetic," Teague said.

He was right. I'd gone through all of this—all the fighting and running and searching—just to die in prison. The worst part was I'd never find out who set me up. It was like fumbling the hyperfootball on the nine-hundred-and-ninety-ninth yard line.

Teague grabbed my shirt and lifted me up off my feet, a power play that served no real purpose other than to make me feel helpless. Which it did.

"You know what, Talon? I've changed my mind. I'm not going to break your neck and let you die in jail."

Through my fear, I managed to sputter, "Th-thanks, man."

Teague brought my face to within inches of his.

"I decided I'm going to kill you myself," he said.

THIRTY-NINE

His eyes were so cold, and his face was so calm, when he said it. Had he always been this way? Could my lifelong friend somehow be a closet psychopath, and I just never realized it?

Teague's hands closed around my throat, his fingers digging in. I kicked him between the legs as hard as I could. He'd come prepared this time, wearing a jockstrap. My foot bounced harmlessly off his cup.

His thumbs found my carotid artery. If he blocked the flow, I'd pass out within seconds. Panicked, I scratched him across the eyes, then cupped my hands and clapped him on either side of the head, forcing air into his eardrums.

He howled, releasing me. I found my bearings and staggered to the Nife handle sticking out of the wall. Just as I snagged it, Teague grabbed me by my utility belt and flung me across the room, like I was a toy. I kept my hand extended, the Nife away from my body, but I dropped it on impact. The weapon went skittering into the bathroom.

I scrambled on all fours after it, seeing Neil in my peripheral vision. He was in the shower, a lopsided grin on his face, soaping up his new boobs. In fairness, they were pretty spectacular. And they would have been even more so, if he didn't have all those curly chest hairs.

Teague grabbed my ankle, and began lifting me up. While his strength wasn't that of Rocket, it was pretty impressive. He must have been hitting the roids for quite some time.

I stretched for the Nife, then stopped myself. The handle was facing the wrong way, and the only part I could reach was the blade. Grabbing a Nife by the blade was about as safe as sticking your hand in a spinning blender. But it was either that, or let Teague rip me apart.

Once I made my decision, I didn't hesitate. I aimed carefully, then slipped my left index finger under the blade, clamping my thumb on top, just as Teague jerked me upside down.

He positioned me over the ComfortMax toilet, my head inches from the bowl.

"Here's a good death for you," Teague said. "Like the piece of shit you are."

He dunked me. I held my breath, trying to judge if I still held the Nife. I could feel my fingers touching one another, and I didn't know if that was because I'd dropped it, or because the blade was microscopically thin. I turned my wrist slightly, and noticed the extra weight.

So I had the Nife. Now what?

Teague lifted me up out of the water. I gasped for air, then choked when the automatic bidet kicked on, spraying warm water in my face. I couldn't adjust the grip on the Nife using only one hand; plus I couldn't see. Working by feel was a surefire way to lose a few fingers.

"Round two," Teague said.

Before I could catch my breath, he dunked me again. I coughed, then couldn't control my lungs, which sucked in toilet water. It hurt more than just about anything that ever happened to me, burning my nose and throat, causing my diaphragm to rapidly spasm. Even worse than the pain was the panic. The need for oxygen was so primeval, so reptile-brain, that it overrode all other brain functions. I lost all rationale, all personality, and became a starving animal whose sole reason for existence was to breathe again.

Teague lifted me up once more. I vomited water, tried to take in air, gagged, choked, vomited again, and finally got some sweet, sweet O_2 into my aching lungs.

"Round three," Teague said.

Not looking, not even caring, I brought my two hands together, feeling for the handle of the Nife. Miraculously, my right hand found it, and then I was bending at the waist, reaching upward, slashing at Teague with the blade.

I was dropped, suddenly, landing on my back. While in the middle of a coughing fit I managed to get to my knees. I checked my hand. My right held the Nife. My left still had all of its fingers, though the thumb was missing the very tip.

Teague wasn't so lucky. He stared at his right arm, and the bleeding stump where his hand used to be. Then the toilet automatically flushed. We both looked, and watched his severed hand disappear down the drain.

Teague howled, sticking his left hand into the toilet, trying to rescue his right hand.

I raised the Nife, ready to gut him.

"Little privacy here," Neil said. He must have been thinking the same thing I'd been thinking earlier, because he was shaving his chest.

Neil's ridiculous, drug-addled actions brought some measure of humanity back to me, just in time. Rather than kill my old friend, I changed my course of action, sweeping my arm down and cutting off his foot.

Teague toppled. I coughed, spat, and got up on shaky feet.

"Hold still," I told him, "or you'll bleed to death."

He nodded at me, his eyes wide with fear. I carefully sheathed the Nife, then stumbled out of the bathroom, heading for Aunt Zelda's bedroom closet. I quickly found two belts and brought them back to Teague. The blood pooling around him was extensive. I pressed his earlobe, told him to call 911. As he did, I cinched the tourniquets around his stumps.

"Ambulance coming?" I asked.

Teague nodded, his whole body shivering. "My hand is gone. Flushed."

"I'm sorry about that." But I wasn't sure how sorry I really was. Practically drowning doesn't make a guy very sympathetic.

"You should kill me," Teague said.

"Not going to happen."

His teeth were chattering now. "If you don't, I'm going to chase you to the ends of the earth."

"I know."

I checked the belts, and saw I'd managed to staunch the blood flow. I dragged Teague across the floor and raised his legs, putting them on the toilet. Then I covered him with blankets.

After taping some gauze around my bleeding finger, I grabbed the TEV and kicked Teague's to pieces in case he recuperated faster than I anticipated.

Time to go.

I caught the killer's trail on the first floor, as he climbed out of the elevator. He still wore the celebrity veil. I chose to follow him going forward, rather than in reverse, because it was easier to track.

Once out in the street I paused and stepped aside as two paramedics ran into the building. They didn't give me a glance, but I realized that walking around in broad daylight when I was the most wanted man in the world would eventually lead to me getting identified. I remembered the celebrity veil the killer had left on top of the fridge. It was in my utility belt. I put it on over my head, able to see clearly, but unable to be seen.

Then I tailed the killer, going north. He kept a steady pace. No running. No sudden moves. Walking alongside him was an odd experience, sort of like walking with someone in reality. I almost expected to look over my shoulder and see him actually standing there.

After several blocks, he turned left on Adams, heading east. I anticipated him climbing onto a biofuel scooter, or hopping the El, which would complicate things. As I'd expected, we came to a bike carousel. Carousels were miniature pneumatic parking garages. You paid for a predetermined amount of time, placed your bike into the clamps, and the carousel lifted it up and held it for you until you returned. Larger models could hold fifty bikes vertically, saving valuable street space. This model held twenty.

The killer took a plastic parking chit out of his pocket—chits identified to location and row of your bike, which was necessary because Chicago had more than a hundred thousand carousels—and fed it into the meter.

If I had access to the CPD parking records, I could trace him paying for parking and get his ID. Or . . .

I got a close-up of the chit and read the drop-off time. It was parked here a few hours before Aunt Zelda's murder. I rewound the transmission, going back to that time, and then paused when I saw a familiar face.

Neil.

He'd parked the bike here. He'd been the killer all along.

FORTY

I sprinted back to Aunt Zelda's, reaching the front door just as the ambulance was pulling away. Neil had been pretty doped up while he was in the shower, so he could still be inside. But he could have been faking that. Like he'd been faking everything else. If he'd left, I'd track him.

The elevator ride seemed to take forever. I burst through Zelda's door, Nife drawn, ready for anything.

Except for maybe hearing Neil singing "You Are So Beautiful" in the shower.

This was the criminal supergenius behind this whole plot?

I rushed into the bathroom, the floor slick with Teague's blood. Neil had finished shaving his boobs, and was soaping them up, again. I liked boobs as much as the next guy, but his behavior bordered on obsessive.

Still, they were pretty spectacular.

"Out of the shower!" I yelled, flinging open the sliding door.

Neil jumped backward, covering up his chest with his hands. "Pervert!"

I grabbed him by his hair and sat him on the toilet.

"Why Boise, Neil? Aunt Zelda was enough to send me to jail. Why kill half a million people?"

He had his palms over his nipples. "WTF are you talking about?"

"I know it was you. I followed the killer to the scooter carousel. It was your bike."

"What bike?"

If he was faking being stoned, he was doing a damn good job. I held up my TEV, showed him the recording of him at the bike rack.

"That's me," Neil said, pointing to the screen and smiling.

I wondered if this would be enough to convict him. The hard part would be getting someone to listen when the entire world had already convicted me of the crime. But maybe, with Neil's confession . . .

"He told me to park the bike there."

"What?"

Neil was looking at his breasts again. "The bike was delivered to my house, with instructions. I had to park it in a carousel on Adams."

"What did you do with the chit?"

He glanced at me, cockeyed. "I flush it down the toilet. What do you do with it? Build little mushy brown sculptures?"

"The *chit*, Neil. The bike chit you got, after you parked it."

"Oh. I came here and put the chit on top of the refrigerator."

I took the TEV back into the kitchen, and tuned in to when the killer put the celebrity veil on the fridge. This time, I checked the top of the appliance while he did it. The killer had traded the mask for a bike chit, which had already been waiting there for him.

My hopes sank. I was still Public Enemy Number One.

I shuffled past the bathroom, wondering what to do next. Neil was rooting through the medicine cabinet.

"Which pills make them bigger?" he asked. "I want to go up a cup size or two."

"Antiandrogen," I said. It was a lie. Estrolux made them bigger. Antiandrogen shrunk the dick.

I left the apartment, plotting my next move. I could follow the killer in reverse, find out where he came from. Or I could follow him on the bike, and see where he went.

I chose the bike, and jogged back to the scooter carousel. As I ran, I thought about the celebrity veil and the bike chit. I also thought about the disk blocking the killer's chip. This was someone familiar with timecasting protocol, someone who thought he could beat it. But you can't beat timecasting. No matter where he ran to, I'd be able to follow him. Eventually he'd need his chip to pay for something, and I'd be there to catch him.

Which made me wonder, why all the subterfuge? He knew I'd be following him. What did he hope to accomplish?

I found out right after I picked up his tail again.

Timecasting someone on a biofuel bike wasn't easy to do solo. The timecaster's attention constantly switched between watching the perp and watching the road, all while operating the scooter one-handed. I expected the killer would know this, and make it difficult for me to follow him.

My expectations were wrong. Once he fed his chit into the carousel, he took out his DT. I zoomed in to see what he was doing. He brought up a keyboard and typed:

I'm taking 1-90 north to exit 15. You can pick me up again at the biofuel station on the northwest corner. I trust you're wearing the veil mask I left for you. See you soon, Talon.

I froze. Then I looked around, as if the killer was watching me right now. But he wasn't. He'd written this more than forty-eight hours ago.

Still, the paranoia was real. Granted, he'd specifically set me up, so he knew I'd be after him. But this had been a rough journey on my end. Why suddenly make it easy for me?

I waited for the next red light, then borrowed a scooter from an unwilling man who complained a lot, but came around to my way of thinking when I showed him my Nife. I strapped the TEV to my back and hit the gas, deciding to believe the killer was telling me the truth. The fact he left me the celebrity veil meant he wanted me to follow. This was part of his plan.

I headed toward the expressway, not liking this one bit. The more I thought about it, the more I realized how much this guy had been playing me from the start. He knew I'd be on the run. He knew I'd find the prism sphere. All the time I'd thought Teague was the one who'd leaked the transmission of Zelda's death. But it was the man in the mask.

I drew the obvious conclusion. The killer had to be a timecaster.

I hopped onto I-90, thinking about all the guys in my old Van Damme squad. There were twelve of us when the program began in Chicago, and four more in other parts of Illinois. Neighboring states also had their own teams. At the height of the program, there were more than a hundred working timecasters in the US, and easily another two hundred worldwide. Any one of them could have gone rogue.

If I narrowed it down to those who had some sort of grudge against me, it didn't eliminate too many names. Teague and I were the best on our squad, with the best records, which was why we were kept on. There had been a lot of resentment when the program was downsized.

When I exited at 15, I located the gas station and pet the bunny, quickly finding the killer. He was parked next to the air pump, waiting. I fast-forwarded, watching him sit there. Eventually he must have determined I showed up, and he started the bike and headed west. I quickly recognized the neighborhood.

This was Schaumburg. I was here yesterday, visiting Michio Sata.

The killer went the speed limit, but I went on ahead of him, sure of his destination. Even though this had happened in the past, I knew he was going to Sata's house. Sata, and Vicki, were in danger.

I called Vicki on my headphone.

No answer.

I called Sata on my headphone.

No answer.

I now understood why the killer had sent me on this wild-goose chase. He didn't want to just frame me. He wanted to destroy me. As I was running around Chicago, searching for answers, his intention all along was to hurt the two people I cared about most. He knew I'd send Vicki to stay with Sata. He just needed some time to get both of them alone.

Sata is smart, competent, and strong, I reminded myself. *He wouldn't let anyone get the better of him.*

And yet, he was an old man. An old man on roids, which weren't known for their positive effects on mental health. The killer who set all of this up would be able to deal with Sata.

I called Sata again, got his voice mail, and left him an urgent message to contact me just as I was pulling up to his house.

I ditched the bike and ran to the front door, which was yawning open. Any panic I'd ever felt in my life paled next to the raw fear coursing through me as I rushed into his house.

"Vicki! Sata!"

They didn't answer. Even though dread sat on my shoulders, and apprehension weighed down my feet, I powered through the house, aware that every time I turned a corner there was the danger of seeing my wife and my mentor dead.

The terror mounted with every room I checked.

Bedroom. Nothing.

Kitchen. Nothing.

Bath. Nothing.

Guest room. Nothing.

Guest bath. Nothing.

Living room. Nothing.

Dining room. Nothing.

And, finally, the gym.

Nothing. They were nowhere to be found.

Rather than being relieved, my panic kicked up a notch. Worry was a useless emotion, but at that moment, not knowing was worse than knowing. Had the killer come here? Or had it just been a coincidence? Maybe Sata and Vicki were safe, and the masked man had gone elsewhere.

I ran to the front door, set up the TEV, and tried to tune in to the octeract point. The bunny felt different, and when the transmission began I knew something was wrong.

I saw Sata. But this was not the Sata I knew. This Sata was fat instead of muscular, with shoulder-length white hair and a drawn, almost desperate, face. The house was different as well. Messy, haphazard, with no greenery, piles of garbage littering the corners.

An alter-Sata, from a parallel universe. Which meant there was a prism ball around here, disrupting the signal.

I walked out of the house, and had to get an acre away—completely off the property—before the normal signal returned.

I looked around for Sata and Vicki, walking the perimeter, trying to pick up their trail. Then, changing tactics, I went back forty-eight hours to see if the killer had come here. He did, right up the driveway. I expected him to walk onto the property and disappear, but instead he took out his DT again and wrote something.

Go inside and watch the projector.

Then he took another step and vanished.

I hurried into the house, running to the projector, pressing play.

The killer filled the screen. He still wore the black jumpsuit and the celebrity veil. I turned up the volume.

"I knew you'd make it this far," the killer said.

His voice was immediately recognizable.

"No . . ." I whispered.

Then he took off his celebrity veil, and I stared right at the face of my dearest friend in the world.

Michio Sata.

FORTY-ONE

The Mastermind, Dr. Michio Sata, sits patiently in the waiting area. Anyone passing by, if they bother to look, sees a calm, bemused man, with a strange case strapped to his chest that has a bizarre prism effect. They might guess he's a kindly old grandfather, awaiting his family's arrival. Or perhaps he's simply a people watcher, enjoying one of the few pleasures left in his golden years.

It's doubtful any of them will guess he's few hours away from killing them all. Them, and eight million more.

And that's only the beginning.

Sata has had enough of this world. He's decided to find another one more to his liking.

But first, he's going to wipe this one out.

The prospect delights him. But even more exciting is facing the mouse again. Talon. As close a thing to an adversary as Sata has.

It isn't much fun wiping out all life on the planet if you don't have to beat someone in order to do it.

Sata can still remember years ago, meeting Talon for the first time. His buddy Teague had done better in classes.

But Talon had something about him. Something special. Teague, though an excellent timecaster, was a rather boring, oafish personality.

Talon cares about people. He truly wants to make a difference.

Breaking him will be so much fun.

A child walks by, holding his mother's hand. He stares at Sata, offers the old man a smile.

Smile while you can, child, Sata thinks. You've got two hours left.

The ghoulish thought makes Sata smile back.

FORTY-TWO

"*Let me begin by saying you'll never find Vicki on your own,*" Sata's projection said. "*She's safe, for the moment. But you've seen what I'm capable of doing. Unless you follow my instructions, she'll die. And so will you. Your right arm has been growing steadily number, hasn't it?*"

I looked at my arm, flexing my hand. I had very little feeling left.

"*During our kendo match, I hit you above the padding with a well-aimed thrust. The tip of my* shinai *had a needle in it. You've been injected with a nanopoison. Your entire nervous system is shutting down. Unless you get the antidote, you don't have too many hours left.*"

My mind spun, and I began to get dizzy. This couldn't be happening. Sata couldn't be the one behind all of this madness. He was my mentor. My friend.

"*I'm sure you have questions. You'll find answers, and your wife, at the space elevator. Vicki already purchased your ticket, but you'll need your chip to get into the station. Our lift leaves at three. The authorities are looking for you, and will be waiting. I've left an obfuscation disk*" next to the projector. You can stick it to your arm, over your chip, and it will block GPS, and timecasting, as I'm sure you've discovered."

I glanced down at the thin round device next to the projector. It went into my utility belt pouch.

"If you miss the lift, you won't have any second chances. Vicki will die. And so will eight million others. Boise was just a warm-up. Once I reach low-earth orbit, I'm unleashing the device upon Chicago. By four p.m., the entire city will be gone."

This just kept getting better and better.

"Going to the authorities won't do any good. When you walked into my house, you activated a slate magnet. The recording on your TEV has been erased. I've also carefully hidden five prism balls on the property. You won't be able to track me, or to prove my involvement."

"Yeah? Well, what about this recording I'm watching, asshole?"

"This recording will now self-destruct. You should jump away."

I dove to the side, tucking and rolling, leaving my mouth open to equalize the sudden change in pressure as the projector exploded. It still hurt my eardrums, the blast of superheated air and flames setting my shirt on fire. I came to a rest on my back and patted out the fire on my clothes. I was shaken, upset, wondering what I was supposed to do next.

It didn't take long for me to figure it out. Sata had left me no other option. I had to go to the space elevator.

That meant getting my chip back.

I logged onto GPS using my DT and tracked my chip. It was moving, which meant my raccoon buddy hadn't evacuated it yet. I had no idea how difficult raccoons were to catch, but I guessed it would take more than me and my bare hands. To complicate matters, the raccoon was at a location I was unfortunately familiar with: Chomsky's house.

Boy, I hated that dick.

I was running low on people who could help me, so I called the only number I had left.

"Fuck you, Talon. I'm not talking to you."

"Look, McGlade, I'm sorry about the sex thing."

"It wasn't just the sex. I also got my arm broken—broken trying to save your ass, BTW. And you used me as a human shield. I hate getting Tased, Talon. It sucks the farts out of dead gerbils. And all of this was before I learned you killed half a million people. Not that I have any particular fondness for Idahoans, but *fuck*, Talon."

"I didn't kill those people. And I need your help catching who did."

"You can bite my ass after I shit myself."

"You're a poet, McGlade, you know that? I'll pay you."

"Pay me what? Promises and insurance credits I'll never see?"

"How about a thousand paper books?" I told him, thinking of Zelda's. "Lots of rare titles. Many of them hardcover."

There was a lengthy pause. I could picture him adding up the black market value in his grubby little head. "And you have these books in your possession?"

"Yes. I can bring you samples."

"What is it you need?"

"Do you have animal traps?"

"Of course I have animal traps. What size?"

"For a raccoon."

"You're telling me a raccoon blew up Boise?"

"It's a long story. I need an animal trap, some bait, a patch of living skin, and a sedative with a syringe. Also, bring your Taser. We may have to, uh, *subdue* the little guy."

"Nice. You're a class act, Talon."

"Bring your Magnum, too."

"Sit on a cactus and spin, asshole."

McGlade truly did have a way with words.

"I've got more than just the books. I've got paintings."

"Real paint-on-canvas paintings?"

"Yeah. Famous ones, too."

"What artist?"

I closed my eyes, trying to think of the name I had seen on the landscape scene in Zelda's bedroom.

"Monet," I said.

"You're fucking me with a jackhammer."

"Where do you come up with lines like that?"

"You so do not have a Monet. You know how much those are worth?"

"Bring the gun. And ammo. I'll meet you a block away from my house, on the corner of Randall and Monroe."

"Gimme three hours."

I checked the time on my DT. "You've got two hours. If you're late, no books or paintings."

"Two hours? No way. It would be easier to stuff my ass with synthetic cotton and then crap out a knitted—"

"Two hours," I said, interrupting him. Then I pressed my earlobe and hung up.

It took me ten minutes to find one of Sata's suitcases and fill it with what I needed. Then I was on the road again, heading back to Aunt Zelda's. I needed to focus, to plan, but my brain was stuck in a loop. I kept thinking of Sata's betrayal, and Vicki's safety. Would he hurt her? What could have happened to him?

I wondered if it was the steroids. Maybe they'd fried his brain.

Maybe I should have paid closer attention. I could remember the classes, the lessons, the countless kendo matches. Good, dear memories. He was like a father to me. Why didn't I make a better effort to stay in touch with him? Could I have prevented this?

Then I considered my relationships with Teague. And Vicki.

Apparently I needed to put in more work with the people who were important to me.

Five hundred thousand people. Damn.

When I arrived at Zelda's, I dumped the bike in a loading zone and headed for the elevator. Surprisingly, Neil was still in the apartment. He sat naked on the sofa, his head slumped down and his shoulders sagging. He was making a high, keening sound, somewhere between a sob and a yelp. When I walked over he looked up at me, his face glistening with tears.

"My pee-pee shrunk."

I was all out of stock in the sympathy exchange, so I ignored the incredible shrinking dick and turned my attention to Zelda's bookshelf. I picked four titles that looked particularly old and expensive. Then I went to the bedroom to take the Monet. Funny how we place value on physical things. This was a nice enough landscape, done in pastels, but worth a fortune? I pulled it off the wall, pried off the back, and ripped the canvas out of the matte. I folded it up, then put it and the books into one of Zelda's handbags. Also, on a whim, I grabbed her raccoon-fur coat.

Neil was curled up on the floor, cupping himself. I stepped over him, then grabbed a bottle of pills from the bathroom medicine cabinet.

"Will those make my willy grow back?"

"Take five of these, and it will grow back tomorrow."

I shook five into his hand. Technically, I wasn't lying to him. His manhood would bounce back to normal size tomorrow, all on its own. The pills would have nothing to do with it, because they were industrial-strength laxatives.

I made it back to my house fifteen minutes before McGlade was scheduled to arrive. While waiting for him to show up, I double-checked the location of my little raccoon buddy. He was still on that dick Chomsky's roof. But he'd apparently become a trifle more active. I didn't know much about raccoon behavior, but this one appeared to be running laps.

Time crawled by. Still no McGlade. I tried calling Vicki, and Sata, and was unsuccessful with both.

Ten minutes after the agreed-upon time, McGlade motored up on his Harley Davidson biofuel bike. Unlike the scooters prevalent throughout the city, this hog was three times the size and twenty times less fuel-efficient. But it was deafening to make up for it.

McGlade pulled up and said something, which I couldn't hear over the roar of the throttle. I gave him the universal *I can't hear you* hand signal, cupping my hand to my ear while saying, "I can't hear you."

"What?" McGlade yelled. "I can't hear you!"

Jackass.

He eventually cut the engine. "You got the stuff?"

I nodded. "Do you?"

"Yeah. Lemme see the books."

I handed them over. McGlade scowled. "Fiction? Who reads fiction these days?"

"I just grabbed a few."

"Who the heck is James Patterson? How am I supposed to sell that? Don't you have any Joe Kimball?"

"I think I have a few." I had no idea if Zelda did or not. "There are a whole bunch. Here's the Monet."

McGlade unfolded it, taking a long look. "Not his best work. You sure it's real?"

"AFAIK."

"I don't know if it's a fair trade, man. You know trapping endangered species is a major crime. I could do jail time, just for being caught with the cage. And selling real firearms . . ."

"Hundreds of books," I said, "and a few more paintings."

"Where?"

"I'll tell you after we catch the raccoon."

He raised an eyebrow. "What's this *we*, Mr. Most Wanted?"

"I need your help. The animal is at my neighbor's house, and he won't let me in."

"Can't say that I blame him." McGlade peered over my shoulder. "What's that?"

I followed his gaze to the things strapped to the back of my bike. "A raccoon coat."

"Real?"

"Yes."

He rubbed his jaw. "Never saw a real fur coat before. Tell you what, you throw in the coat, and we've got a deal."

FORTY-THREE

I hid around the corner, holding the cage while McGlade rang Chomsky's videobell.

"Who is it?"

"Animal control," McGlade said. "We heard you have a raccoon on your premises."

Chomsky made a face. "It's about time. The damn thing ate half my coca plant. It's running around like a spaz."

Just what I needed. A raccoon racing on cocaine.

"I'll take care of it for you, sir," McGlade said. "I'm a professional. I have years of varmint killing experience."

"Can I see some ID?"

My heart sank. But McGlade was on top of it.

"How's this for ID?" he asked, holding up the raccoon coat.

Chomsky opened his front door, and McGlade went inside, me behind him.

"You!" Chomsky said, pointing a finger at me. He was walking bowlegged and had an ice pack clutched to his groin. "I'm calling the cops on you right now!" He pointed at McGlade. "And you, too! Aiding and abetting! You're going to jail for the rest of—"

McGlade shot him with the Taser. When Chomsky fell over, McGlade injected him in the thigh with something.

"Your neighbor is a dick," McGlade said, putting the coat over his shoulders.

"Tell me about it. Come on."

I led him up the stairs, pausing to pat Barack O'Llama on the head. Once on the roof, I looked around for the raccoon while McGlade baited the steel-cage trap with cat food. It worked on a simple lever principle. The animal walked in to get the food; the door closed behind it.

"You see him?" he asked.

"No." I checked the GPS. He was hiding in the northwest corner. "He's over there. Okay, set the trap down here. If he runs past, grab him."

McGlade appeared dubious. "He's a wild animal. Is he safe to grab?"

"Yesterday I fed my chip to him. He's gentle as a lamb."

McGlade set down the cage, and the raccoon jumped out of the bushes and onto McGlade's chest. It hissed, teeth snapping, while McGlade fell onto his butt, screaming like a girl.

"GET IT OFF! GET IT OFF!"

"He thinks you're a raccoon," I said, pointing to the coat. "You're invading his territory."

"TELL HIM I'M NOT A RACCOON! TELL HIM I'M NOT A RACCOON!"

I picked up the cage and fit it over the raccoon, manually shutting the door. Its little hands grabbed my fingers and he tried to bite me through the steel mesh. I quickly dropped it and backed away.

"Gentle as a lamb?" McGlade said, breathing heavy. "Maybe a lamb with fucking rabies!"

"Did it bite you?"

His face twisted up. "I think he got my leg. It feels wet."

"You pissed yourself."

"Fuck. Look at that crazy little bastard."

The raccoon was shaking the cage, hissing and spitting. McGlade took out his Magnum and aimed it.

"McGlade! No!"

"It's evil, Talon. It needs to die."

"He was fine yesterday. It's probably the coke."

"Bullshit. It's Frankencoon. If we don't kill him, he'll eat the city."

The animal did seem a bit more hostile since I last saw him.

"Hit him with the sedative," I said.

"I gave it to your dick neighbor."

"Shit."

"Why don't you let me cap it? You have to cut the chip out anyway."

I shook my head. "I'm not slicing through innards and intestines trying to find the chip. He's going to give it to me in a different way."

"How? You'll ask him nicely?"

"Laxatives."

McGlade shook his head. "You're a real piece of work, Talon."

I picked up the fallen can of cat food, then pushed five laxative pills into the mush. Now it was just a matter of opening the cage.

"Okay, McGlade, I'll open the door; you put the food inside."

"Fuck you. Keep the Monet."

To say the animal seemed extremely agitated would be putting it mildly. It looked angry enough to eat a mountain lion.

"Come on. I can't do this alone."

"Did you join a dissy monastery this morning and take a

vow of stupid? There is no way I'm getting anywhere near that thing."

I thought about Chomsky's atomizer, still on my roof. That would mellow him out. Maybe I could sneak over, grab it, bring it back, atomize some marijuana . . .

"Fuck it," McGlade said.

He shot the raccoon with his Taser. A bolt of Tesla lightning zapped the little guy right between the eyes, knocking him over.

"Dammit, McGlade!"

"Had to be done. You can send me the medal."

The animal had keeled over onto its back, all four legs sticking straight up. But it still appeared to be breathing. Without hesitation I opened the cage and shoved all five pills down its throat, managing to lock him back up just as he was reviving.

"My work here is done." McGlade folded his arms. "Where are the books?"

"The Magnum first. And the living skin."

He handed them over. "I've only got those six bullets. No idea if they work or not. Now the books."

I gave him Aunt Zelda's address and said, "They're yours. But you might want to wait a few days to pick them up."

"Why?"

"Because the man I'm chasing has threatened to destroy Chicago in less than two hours."

"I hate you, Talon. I really—"

The raccoon squealed, spinning around and lifting its bushy tail. He ejected an impressive fountain of animal waste, soaking McGlade's pants. I'd seen less force come from fire hoses.

Ignoring McGlade's string of invectives, I toed through the mess and found my chip. I brought it over to Chomsky's sprinkler, rinsing it off. Then I went into the house.

In Chomsky's bathroom, I found a bottle of hydrogen peroxide under the sink. I poured a liberal dose on my arm, and on the chip. Then I set the chip on a clean towel and unsheathed my Nife.

Removing the chip had been easy—a quick gouge in my arm fueled by panic and adrenaline. To put it back in, I'd have to fillet my skin and muscle down to the nerves, and I wasn't looking forward to the experience. Chomsky had a decent assortment of painkillers in his medicine cabinet, but I didn't want to take anything that might dull my senses.

Making a fist, I held my forearm over the sink. Gripping the Nife in my bad hand, I waited for the shakes to stop. They wouldn't.

I'd just have to try my best.

I placed the flat of the blade against my skin. My fingers were numb, my control marginal at best. I took a deep breath, then got ready to—

"You need help?"

I startled, spinning around. McGlade stood in the doorway, buttoning his pants.

"Do I want to know why you're pulling up your pants?" I asked.

"The little bastard shit on me. I returned the favor."

"There's something wrong with you."

"Give me the Nife. You're gonna cut your arm off."

McGlade washed his hands, then took the blade. Unlike me, his hands were rock-steady. He opened up a U-shaped flap in my skin, deftly avoiding the major veins and arteries, while I chewed on a bath towel. Then he placed the chip back inside its nerve slot, closed the flap, and sealed it with the living skin. For my part, I only cried a little bit.

"Thanks, man. Let me know if I can ever return the favor."

He looked at me, hard. "Just stop the bad guy and save the city."

I appraised him. "You turning humanitarian on me, McGlade?"

"Fuck, no. I just don't want all the stuff you owe me to get destroyed."

He offered his hand. I took it.

Then I covered my chip with the obfuscation disk and went off to find Vicki and save Chicago.

FORTY-FOUR

Space elevators worked on the simple physics principle of centrifugal force. A large rope, made of woven carbon nanotubes, was anchored to the ground. It extended up to low-earth orbit, where it was tethered to a space station. The station acted like a yo-yo being twirled around, keeping the rope straight. In this case, the twirling was provided by the rotation of the earth.

Prior to space elevators, leaving earth's atmosphere required an incredible amount of energy. Now a simple motorized lift could climb the two hundred miles to LEO using regular old electricity, rather than the expensive and bulky liquid hydrogen used by rockets. As a result, space had become a tourist attraction.

Chicago's Arthur C. Clarke Space Elevator was one of the newest in the nation. It transported close to two million people a year to six hotels in geosynchronous orbit. Besides the spectacular view, and the novelty of zero gravity, these hotels offered an assortment of unique games and activities. They'd become one of the biggest tourist destinations in Illinois.

I ditched the bike a few blocks away from the station, and checked the time. Half an hour until Sata had told me to be there. As I dressed in the things I'd taken from Sata's house, I tried to picture how I could pull this off without getting caught.

The CPD had red-flagged my name and run it through the system. If they didn't already know Vicki had bought me an elevator ticket, they'd know it as soon as I arrived at the main gate. That meant the cops were already waiting for me on the off chance I showed up, or the place would be locked down once I got inside. I'd have to swipe my chip at check-in, and again at security.

Other than my clothing, there wasn't much I could do to prevent a full-scale takedown. I'd either make it, or I wouldn't. Dwelling on it wouldn't improve my odds.

Lugging Sata's suitcase, I walked over to the station entrance. The building was easy to find, viewable from miles away in any direction. The black nanotube tether was as thick as a skyscraper, extending up into the clouds like Jack's legendary beanstalk. Along the outside were lift cars on tracks, ten of them, simultaneously raising or lowering passengers in groups of fifty. The cars left every ten minutes, and a ticket allowed you to take any one you wanted, much like waiting in line for a roller coaster at a hyperamusement park.

I adjusted the celebrity veil over my head and strolled into the building, prepared for the worst. I wasn't immediately tackled, which I took to be a good sign.

As expected, the station was packed. The building formed a decahedron around the tether, each inner section leading to a lift car. Departures and arrivals were staggered. The wraparound section was comprised of various shops and restaurants, a waiting area, and the check-in counter. There were at least two thousand people milling about, which was to my advantage. The bigger the haystack, the harder it was to find the needle.

Above the crowd murmur, a recording announced which cars were coming and going. The three o'clock would be car number seven. I strolled past, and saw a small line. No Vicki or Sata.

I walked the perimeter, which took only fifteen minutes, eyes peeled. I passed a few cops, but was ignored. A few dozen folks had celebrity veils on. Some of them might have been real celebrities, or celebrity wannabes, but a lot of teens also treated veils as a fashion statement. The emoticon on mine probably helped me pass for young and hip.

The check-in line went quickly. I unzipped the top of Sata's bag, ready to throw on the *men* if the need arose. When it came time to scan my wrist, I peeled off the obfuscation disk, swiped it over the reader, replaced it, and waited for the alarm to sound.

There was no alarm. The turnstile opened, allowing me through.

I looked around, trying to spot anyone coming for me. Utopeons milled about, minding their own business. I wasn't rushed by cops. I wasn't surrounded by government agents. Everything seemed entirely normal.

I queued up for the security checkpoint, waiting to get my bag X-rayed. Unlike airlines, which were a cinch to get through quickly, space elevators had to have security because certain things, like aerosol cans and, oddly enough, microwave popcorn, weren't allowed in LEO. Nothing with the potential to explode was allowed up in space, though I believed the bias against popcorn had more to do with the difficulty in cleaning it up in zero gravity.

Again, I scanned for cops, or anyone who looked suspicious. But everything appeared normal. Besides the average Joes, there was a hyperspaceball team, in full gear, in the waiting area. So was a marching band, which seemed to be deep in a heated discussion of which car to take.

I was next in line when the first Taser hit me. I watched the Tesla bolt streak through the air and zap the front of my *dô*. Incongruously, it appeared to have been fired from a trombone. I managed to pull the *men*—the helmet—out of my suitcase and slap it over my head just as the bullets really began to fly.

Besides the full kendo armor I wore under my kimono, I'd also wound sheets of food preservative wrap around my arms and legs. In commercials, the plastic film boasted it was self-sealing and completely leak-proof. You couldn't puncture it, no matter how hard you tried. I'd soon see if that guarantee included Taser needles.

The people around me toppled over, wax bullets zapping them right and left. Within three steps I'd been hit with more than a hundred Tasers, lighting me up like a Fourth of July firework. Both the hyperspaceball team and the marching band had been undercover cops, and much of their equipment and instruments were really Tasers in disguise.

Though it was getting impossible to see in the blinding blue electrical haze, I hadn't actually felt a hit yet. The armor, and the food wrap, were keeping me safe, even though I was a walking Van de Graaff generator.

Then a bullet hit me in the hand—the only unprotected part of my body. Once the circuit was complete, the two hundred other Tesla bolts took the path of least resistance and entered my body through the hole. I folded like a bad poker hand, the pain spiking the meter somewhere between *excruciating* and *unbearable*. I could feel pressure in my eyeballs begin to build. The moisture in my mouth evaporated as my teeth began to glow.

I was going to die.

Unlike the many other times in the past twenty-four hours when I knew I was going to die, this one hurt the most. As I twitched on the ground, my only thought was to get it over with quickly because it was so agonizing.

Then, a moment later, all the pain was gone. The electricity had stopped.

I wondered if I'd passed out. Or died.

No—I was on my knees, still in the station. I blinked away the mote flashes and looked around. The marching band, and the sports team, were gone. So were the people in the immediate area who had dived for cover.

I heard gunfire, followed the sound, and saw four cops— this time dressed as cops—shooting in another direction. A moment later, they disappeared.

Or perhaps *imploded* would be a better term.

One errant musician—a tuba player—dropped his instrument and beelined toward the exit. He vanished in midstep.

My brain was still scrambled by the dose of electricity I'd received, but I managed to figure out what was going on.

Sata. He was here.

I managed to stand, turning around in an unsteady circle, trying to spot my mentor. I found him walking casually up to me. Strapped across his chest was something that looked like a TEV, but also different. It had a black shell, which reflected light like a prism. And there was some sort of lens in front. When Sata pressed a button, the lens flashed—

—forming a miniature black hole and sucking people into nothingness. I watched him implode a whole family— mother, father, two kids—who were hovering under a plastic table in the food court.

"Sata!"

He looked at me and smiled. Then he disappeared a group of grade-school kids.

I pulled off my helmet and ran over, or at least tried to. After two steps I fell onto my face. I tried crawling, but my limbs still weren't working right. Three hundred million volts will do that to a guy.

But I needn't have bothered going to Sata. He came to me, turning occasionally to implode anyone he passed.

"Stop," I told him.

"Stop what? This?" He pressed the button, taking out a fat man who'd been unable to quite make it around the bend.

"Enough, Sata. Please."

"But it's so much fun, Talon. When I think of all the years I wasted trying to protect these moronic, useless fools. What a colossal waste of carbon our species has become."

I got to my feet, though I was wobbly. "Is this what you did with Vicki? Sucked her into a black hole?"

"Actually, it's not a black hole. It's a wormhole. I'm not technically killing these people. These utopeons, along with the unfortunate denizens of Boise, were sent to a parallel earth on another eleventh-dimensional membrane."

"So they're not dead?"

"Not when I send them there. But I have no idea how long they'll last once they arrive. They're now on an earth where the Chicxulub asteroid never caused the Cretaceous-Paleogene extinction event and wiped out the dinosaurs sixty-five million years ago. I suspect most of the unfortunate wretches have become food for superintelligent T. rexes by now. It's quite amazing how much the dinos have evolved. They might even be smarter than us."

I didn't want to ask, but I had to. "And Vicki?"

He shook his head, slowly. "Talon, Talon, Talon. I wouldn't send her to that awful place. She's safe in Wisconsin, with someone watching her. Someone you've come to know intimately well."

"Where is she, Sata?"

Sata smiled. "She's with you, of course."

FORTY-FIVE

Words don't normally fail me. But when I processed what Sata had said, and all it implied, I was speechless.

Vicki wasn't with me. She was with that psycho Alter-Talon.

"Yes, he's here," Sata said. "Dimensional travel to parallel worlds. Extraordinary, isn't it? We're supposed to view this primitive Tower of Babel"—Sata swept his hands at the space elevator—"as mankind's crowning achievement. The pinnacle of technology and human ingenuity. And for what purpose? So people can play volleyball and hump each other in zero gravity? But with this"—he patted the TEV—"I can travel to places beyond mere space. I can access an infinite amount of worlds, with an infinite amount of variation. If it can be imagined, it exists. And I can see it all."

"How . . . could you?" I managed.

Sata frowned at me. "I assume you mean *How could you send people to the man-eating dinosaur planet?* instead of the far more compelling *How could you accomplish this miracle of modern science?* I'll answer both. If you recall timecasting class, you know one of the many unique properties of tachyons, other than their ability to travel faster than the speed of light, is they have negative mass squared. Yet even with imaginary mass, they can decay to closed strings, which, in vibrational mode, can cause instability in spacetime itself. Can you even imagine?"

I shook my head. I couldn't give two shits about the science. I just wanted him to keep talking until I was lucid enough to draw McGlade's .44 Magnum, which was wedged in my chest plate.

Sata continued, "When I developed the tachyon emission visualizer, my immediate success was focusing this instability on our 'brane, to record the past in our universe. But at the same time, the disruption of spacetime caused by the tachyons opened wormholes to infinite other membranes. I ignored them, because even though it was theoretically possible to tune in to those 'branes, I had no way of knowing which one I'd be on at a particular time. The vastness of infinity made the process entirely random. What I needed was a way to impose order on infinity. I needed . . . a search engine."

"Aunt Zelda," I said, slipping my hand inside my padding.

"Yes. Mister—or I suppose I should say Miss—Debont had perfected WYSIWYW search-engine technology with uffsee. But she had an even greater patent. One she never got to use. A way to compile relevant terms by metacrawling an infinite data source, using a geometric fractal algorithm. Anything that can happen, *does* happen, on some parallel earth. With her tech, and my tech, I could now search those infinite dimensions."

My fingers wrapped around the butt of the gun. "So you searched the infinite multiverse for a world where I killed her, and where I destroyed Boise."

"An excellent deduction. You'd think it would be an impossible task. Finding a needle in an infinite number of haystacks. But it was only impossible without a machine to help search for it. Because when there are infinite parallel earths, there are infinite parallel earths where you are a killer. With the search engine, I had a one-in-one chance of finding an earth that matched my exact criteria."

"And you brought this lunatic to our world. Why, Sata? What happened to you?"

Sata assumed a reflective pose, tapping a finger to his chin. "I've thought about that a lot, Talon-*kun*. Maybe it was my growing disdain for our race, and how we waste the opportunities handed to us. Or maybe it's because life has become so damn boring these days. Here I stand. The man that erased violent crime from humanity. And I now wish I hadn't done it, because nothing interesting has happened on this planet in years. Admit it, Talon. Didn't you get excited when you saw me murder Zelda? Didn't you feel your heart racing?"

"You're crazy," I said.

"Yes. That's the final conclusion I came to as well. My years of steroid abuse have severely compromised my judgment. But it's still such great fun. Which brings us to the next part of my plan. Our space lift awaits. I'm going to give you a chance to stop me before I turn Chicago into a giant buffet spread for talking velociraptors. Won't that be exciting? You and I, battling for the lives of eight million people? Head over to car number seven, please."

"I don't think so," I said, whipping out the .44.

I'd never killed anyone before. But unlike Sata, I was in full possession of my faculties when I squeezed the trigger, aiming a shot right at his diseased head.

The hammer rose, and fell, connecting with the bullet in the chamber.

It cartridge sparked, then fizzled, without firing.

A dud.

I pulled the trigger five more times.

Dud.

Dud.

Dud.

Dud.

And finally, a big, fat dud.

If McGlade had been nearby, I would have shoved that gun so far up his ass it would have poked out his nose.

Sata laughed, absolutely delighted by this. "Where on earth did you find a firearm?"

I thought about throwing it at him, remembered how much it was worth, then stuck it back in my shirt.

"And none of the bullets worked," Sata continued. "How marvelous."

"Fuck you." It was the best I could come up with, under the circumstances.

"If you're done playing around, we have a lift to catch. Or we could hang out here, and I could keep sending people to the land that time forgot as they disembark their cars."

"I'll go with you."

"A noble, albeit shortsighted, choice."

I walked through the metal detector and managed to palm a confiscated can of aerosol spray from the security bin. I tucked it into my *dô* as Sata prodded me forward, to the next available lift.

The tether car was about the length and width of a bus, with two rows of seats facing the gigantic front window. This lift was empty, except for the pilot, a chubby guy with wide eyes who was raising his hands up over his head.

"Please don't send me to another dimension," the chubby guy said.

"I should, because it's impolite to eavesdrop," Sata said. "These cars aren't difficult to run. It's just an up button and a down button, isn't it?"

Sata aimed the TEV at the pilot.

"Leave him alone, Sata," I warned.

"Or else what? You'll misfire again?"

"I beg you, sir," the pilot said, spreading his hands.

"My name is Hinge. Jonbar Hinge. You really can't predict the potential ramifications of your actions here. The slightest miscalculation could have far-reaching consequences that—"

"Boring." Sata activated the wormhole and imploded Jonbar. "Some lucky allosaurus will make a good meal out of that tubby."

I swung a fist at Sata, and he easily dodged the blow, rapping me on the head with his forearm, dropping me to my knees.

I stared at him, disgusted. "I used to look up to you."

"It's so sad when our heroes fail us," Sata said. "Even sadder to not even know who the heroes are. You're hated by over one billion Americans, and yet you're still fighting to save them. Why even bother, Talon? They're meaningless. Worthless. There are an infinite number of them on an infinite number of worlds. You could wipe out a trillion of them—a trillion to the trillionth power—and there would still be infinitely more. What does it hurt to have a little fun with a select few?"

"Every life counts, Sata."

"Impossible. You could never count them all. Now, strap yourself in, or you'll be allosaur dessert after he finishes with Jonbar."

I crawled into a seat and buckled my lap belt. Sata went into the control booth and barked a laugh. "I was right. Two buttons. What a predictably primitive species we are." He sat down, pressed one, and said, "Going up."

The lift raced skyward, pinning me in my chair. The car floated on a track of ceramic magnets, the same mechanism used in bullet trains, and reached 300 mph in less than twelve seconds. I stared, impotent, out the front window as we shot up.

"Take a good look at the Chicago skyline, Talon. It will be the last time you ever see it."

The ground, and even the horizon, quickly disappeared

as we entered the domain of clouds. When we reached our peak speed, my body adjusted and I unbuckled my belt.

Sata chuckled. "I'm reading that dim-witted pilot's cue card. All the little factoids he was supposed to share with his passengers. Did you know the tether is wirelessly powered by the Tesla field? During construction, six workers were blinded by Tesla lightning, which made their eyeballs boil, then burst. That's not a very family-friendly tidbit to impart, is it?"

I stood up. From the control room, I saw Sata frown.

"Sit back down, Talon, or I'll hit the emergency brake and you'll have to be scraped off the ceiling."

I sat, and rebuckled my safety belt.

"The dashboard says we're going through the Tesla field now."

On cue, the windows darkened like automatic sunglasses. The entire car filled with sparkling blue light as we shot up through the Tesla field surrounding the earth—the same field that supplied our electricity. It looked like a million lightning storms, all firing at once. I would have been impressed, but it was eerily similar to what I just saw at the station while getting shot several hundred times. I was grateful to be in the lift, and not out in that mess.

"We have some free time before reaching the space station, so allow me to tell you what I have planned. Undoubtedly, news has gotten to the security force up there. I plan on dispatching them with the TEV. Unfortunately, unless any of them are wearing space suits, they'll die immediately when they travel to a parallel earth without any space station."

Sata smiled, as if the image pleased him.

"If any are in space suits, they'll either float out into space, or orbit the earth a few times until gravity pulls them into a free fall. Hopefully their space suits will be heat-resistant, for when they reenter the atmosphere. And they'll need parachutes. Of course, on dinosaur earth, they won't have to worry about free-falling through the Tesla field. I've only done a cursory study of the life-forms, but there are several species of flying predators likely to pick them right out of the sky."

His speech was getting faster and faster, like it had been a long time since he'd talked to anyone. And that might have been the case.

"The reason we're going up here," he continued, "is the same reason snipers use a perch. From this height, I'm able to aim my device thousands of miles in any direction. Yesterday I tagged Boise from the window of my bedroom suite at the Hilton. But this time it will be different. Once I send Chicago into the wormhole, the base of the space elevator will vanish as well, and it will float away. So I've made some provisions for that."

I had a headache, and wanted more than anything for Sata to shut up. But as long as he was talking, he wasn't killing me.

"In a locker in Airlock C, near the docking station, are two atmosphere suits of my own design, retrofitted with chutes. They're insulated against cosmic rays, pressurized, and have rebreathers. They also have air jets, for getting to the earth's atmosphere. Once gravity takes over, the suits will protect against the heat of reentry and the electricity of the Tesla field—though admittedly, I've never tested them. No one has ever skydived from two hundred miles up before.

"If you're able to stop me, the suits will be unnecessary. But if you're not, the TEV has a timer on it. You'll have twenty minutes to jump out of the space station and get a safe distance away before Chicago disappears. We'll then continue our game in Milwaukee. I hope you know your geography. You can adjust your aim accordingly as you plummet. Wisconsin is just west of the state that looks like a big mitten."

Sata smiled again, obviously enjoying himself. "The

highest known free fall was from twenty miles above the earth. The world-record holder attained speeds in excess of six hundred miles per hour. I expect to beat that. Though, by next week, a world record won't matter very much, because there won't be a world left."

"What about the nanopoison?" I asked. I was feeling lighter in my chair. We'd risen higher than the mesopshere, passing the Kármán line. The blue and white of sky had been replaced by the enormous blackness of space. I knew enough about gravity to understand that weightlessness didn't happen because you were far from earth. In low-earth orbit, you weighed only 11 percent less than you did on the surface. Being weightless happened when you went into orbit around a planet, because an orbit was essentially a free fall around a curve. You could float in zero-G because you were falling at the same rate your ship was falling.

"That's wonderful, Talon. You actually have delusions of winning. Alter-Talon has the antidote, of course. If you survive this game, there will be others to play. Which brings us to our current situation. At Airlock C, I'm going to mollybond the TEV to the wall, program the angle of the wormhole beam, set the timer, and leap to safety. Your goal is to try and stop me. It's sort of like hyperfootball, with higher stakes."

"Thanks for the info dump," I said. "But what if I don't want to play your game, Sata?"

His jubilant face darkened, becoming sinister. "Then I'll call Alter-Talon, and you can listen in while he skins your pretty little wife."

FORTY-SIX

I unbuckled my seat belt and stood up, convinced Sata wasn't going to hit the brakes. He didn't go through all of this meticulous planning for me to die in the lift car. I, however, had no such compunctions. If he died in the lift car, I was fine with that.

Sata eyed me, looking curious and somewhat superior, like a cat watching a mouse. Besides his TEV, I assumed he was armed. But he was pretty gung ho about going mano a mano, so I doubted he'd use weapons.

"You're wearing *bōgu*," Sata said. "Clever of you. But it won't be enough." He set down the TEV and reached behind his neck, drawing an aluminum sword.

So much for him not using weapons.

I advanced anyway, taking small, quick steps, keeping my balance centered. I could feel my heart start to race and my palms get sweaty. Insane as Sata's motives were, he had a point about the world being unexciting these last few years. I had become a cop to protect and serve. Right here, right now, was the essence of who and what I was.

Time to kick this old fart's ass.

I ran to him, jumping into the air, aiming a flying kick at his chest. Not a regulation kendo attack, but I wasn't worried about points this time.

My foot connected, and it was like hitting a wall. Sata's feet remained firmly planted. I pushed myself away from him, landing on all fours, and checked out his footwear.

Antigrav shoes. There were magnets in the rubber soles, which adhered to the steel floors of the lift car and the space station.

In my rush to get here I'd forgotten to bring a pair for myself.

Sata walked robotically toward me, lifting and planting his feet in an awkward manner. He raised his *shinai* and swung at my head, the sword a blur. I lifted a padded forearm to block, but as soon as he hit me he pulled back and struck again, tagging me in the side.

Even with the chest plate on, it hurt like a bitch. The metal *shinai* had more weight and speed than the traditional bamboo version. I rolled to the left, bumping into a row of seats, ducking again as Sata knocked off a headrest. Then he raised the sword up in both hands, like Arthur freeing Excalibur, and drove the tip right into my gut.

I braced for it, blowing out a gust of air through my pursed lips as the sword connected with my diaphragm. Ignoring the pain, I latched onto the *shinai* with both hands. I was determined to rip it from Sata's grasp.

I heard the zap at the same time I felt it, a burning sensation that ran all the way up both of my arms. I immediately let go of the sword, somehow managing to bring up my leg and kick Sata out of range.

"My own design," Sata said, admiring his weapon. "I've infused the *shinai* with a cattle prod. Makes things more interesting."

He thrust the tip at me, ramming my hip. It was like I'd been struck with a mining pick. I cried out, smashing my forearm against the sword, knocking it away. Then I pulled

myself to my feet using a chair, rubbing my thigh furiously
to get some feeling back in my leg. I considered pulling out
the Nife, but decided to hold off for the time being. Accidentally disabling the car or cutting through the fuselage
would kill us both. Plus, based on something he'd said, I
had a feeling I'd need the Nife later. If I revealed the Nife
now, I could very well miss a last-chance opportunity.

I second-guessed my reluctance when Sata zapped me
again, this time in the shoulder. It lit up my nerve endings
like they'd been soaked in acid and then set on fire. I danced
away from the blow, did a quick spin-kick, and hit Sata
between his legs. He wore a supporter, my foot bouncing
harmlessly off. I was going to have to rethink my affinity
for the groin shot; it never seemed to work.

Sata swung the *shinai* like a hyperbaseball bat. I went
in low and got inside the arc, clipping him under the jaw
with my elbow. When his head snapped back, I chopped at
his neck with the edge of my hand. His throat was corded
with muscle, and my blow did no damage. I might have to
rethink my opinion of steroids as well. The only thing staying roid-free had gotten me was multiple beatings.

I picked up the detached headrest and backed away,
standing on the balls of my feet. Sata glanced at my make-
shift weapon and shook his head, looking disappointed.

"I expected more from you, Talon-*kun*. Back when we first
met, you showed so much promise. You reminded me of—"

"I'd rather get beaten to death than endure another one
of your endless monologues," I interrupted. "Now, shut the
fuck up and fight, old man."

He thrust the sword at me. I blocked with the headrest,
did a tight spin-kick, and knocked him upside his diseased
head. Sata staggered, pitching onto some chairs, leaving
his back exposed. If I got my arm around his neck, I could
choke off his air and end this right now. I dropped the
headrest and jumped at him, bracing myself to land on his
shoulders.

But instead of landing I sailed right over him, heading straight for the rear wall of the lift, moving in what felt like slow motion.

We'd ascended high enough to reach zero gravity.

I held my hands out in front of me, Superman-style, and soared into the wall. My fingertips brushed against it, and I bent my elbows, kissing the metal, and then pushed myself back toward Sata.

He was waiting for me, his *shinai* resting on his shoulder. I flailed my arms, trying to change my speed and/or trajectory, but I kept drifting straight at him. I was about to learn how it felt to be a slow-pitched hypersoftball.

Sata smacked me in the arm. It hurt, but before he could get his zap on I was floating away from the blow in the opposite direction. Thank you, Mr. Newton, for your Third Law of Motion.

I hadn't spent much time in zero-G, but I knew the challenges it posed from the few times I'd had space sex with Vicki. Unless we held each other tight, a single pelvic thrust would send us in flying opposite directions. Amusing at first, but it eventually got frustrating. That was why space hotel bedrooms came equipped with suction cups and bungee cords.

There were no such luxuries in the lift car. But I did remember the can I had taken from the security bin earlier. It was one of those feminine deodorant sprays, guaranteed to make your nether region smell like cherry pie. While I'm pretty sure nature never intended for women to smell like bakery goods, Vicki told me the reason these sprays were so popular was due to an ingredient that stimulated nerve endings. One spritz and sensitivity quadrupled.

But I had a different use for it. I pressed the spray button and the hissing gas functioned as an accelerant, halting my momentum. Another quick spray and I was able to spin around in midair. I rotated too far, twirled three hundred

and sixty degrees, and then slowed myself down and faced
Sata. He sniffed the air.

"Do I smell . . . pie?"

I sprayed it again, heading for the ceiling. It was just
high enough that Sata wouldn't be able to reach me, even
with his sword.

My relief didn't last long. Sata walked up the wall in his
magnetic shoes, and then clomped onto the ceiling.

I sprayed myself back down to the floor. He followed.
By then, the can was almost empty, and my mouth was
watering for cherry pie. I tucked the can into my *men* and
tied a seat belt around my leg, waiting for Sata to approach,
believing I could defend myself if I was anchored down.

Not my wisest move.

The word *piñata* came to mind as Sata let loose with
an electrically charged barrage of hits, pummeling me so
quickly that all I could do was cover up and hope he got
tired.

He didn't get tired. Luckily, the knot around my ankle
came loose and I floated away from him, a blob of blood
trailing from my mouth and floating silently through the
air in my wake.

This time, Sata didn't chase me. He drew his Glock.

My hands and head were my vulnerable spots, so I covered my face with my padded forearms, and kept my palms
on my scalp. I heard the shot, felt the impact in my chest,
and waited for the Tesla bolt to come.

It didn't come. Instead of a wax Taser bullet, Sata had
fired a mollybond round. Newly attached to my *bōgu* was
a length of jelly rope. I watched Sata reel in a bit of length,
then shoot himself in the leg.

We were now tethered together.

He grabbed the rope and tugged. It stretched, then
contracted, and we began to drift toward each other. Sata
raised his *shinai*. Once again I thought about the Nife,

wondering if it was still too soon. Sata was better at hand-to-hand combat. He could block it, and take it from me, and then Chicago would be lost. Then I thought about getting hit with the sword again, and decided to risk the chance.

I reached around, grabbing for the blade—

—and Sata kicked his leg back, pulling the jelly rope like a rubber band. I flew at him at a quick clip as he drew back his *shinai*.

My face versus Sata's sword.

His sword won, connecting with my cheek. I spun on my axis, lines of blood spilling from my lips and twirling around me like a DNA helix. I pulled in my arms to reach the Nife and spun even faster, the world blurring around me, unable to focus on anything. But I kept my head, closing my eyes to ignore the rotation, feeling around the back of my utility belt, wrapping my fingers around the handle of the Nife and unsheathing it.

Time to give this son of a bitch a bunch of new orifices.

That was when the lift stopped and bounced me off the ceiling, making me drop the Nife.

The impact slowed my spin, but I still had no idea which way was up. Though I suppose in zero-G there was no up. I blinked a few times, and peripherally noticed the lift doors open. I hit the floor, focusing on the door, wondering what was going to happen next.

The cab filled with light as our welcoming party of cops unleashed a torrent of Taser fire.

That lasted half a second before Sata imploded them, flying bullets and all.

"It's cold out there," he said. His voice was wistful as he glanced out the lift window into the blackness of space. "Only three degrees above absolute zero. I hope they were wearing warm socks."

I tried to call him a monster, but my mouth wasn't working right. Instead, I took a frantic look around, searching for the Nife. Sata walked out of the car, his magnetic soles clomping against the metal floor, dragging me behind him like a child's balloon on a string. I tried to grab onto something, missed a chair's arm, and was pulled out of the elevator, Nifeless. I shouldn't have ever unsheathed the damn thing.

The space station's décor liberally borrowed from science-fiction movies, with a lot of polished chrome and bright lights. Doors were circular and they opened automatically using proximity sensors. Hallways were large tubes with twenty-foot diameters, the walls rounded and smooth. A large projector flashed a WELCOME sign at us in thirty different languages. Muzak played the classic theme from *Star Wars Episode 19: Darth Jar Jar.*

"The trick is adjusting the focal length of the wormhole," Sata said as I trailed behind him. "If I zoomed out too much, I could have taken out the entire space station along with those morons. But don't get any ideas. Once I set the timer, I'm locking the focus. You won't be able to change it. Unless you can somehow make the entire space station face the opposite way, the wormhole will hit Chicago."

Sata imploded two more security guards, who were flying at us with jet packs on their backs. An alarm went off, red lights flashing. I tried to get a handhold on the ceiling, but it was smooth and I bounced off. Sata tugged me past a giant picture window, and I stared, impotent, at the enormous blue-green earth. So beautiful. So vulnerable.

Sata caught me looking.

"Don't be depressed, Talon-*kun*. There are infinite other earths, and this one is vastly overpopulated. Besides, I'm only sending them to a dinosaur planet, where they have a fighting chance. I could send them to an earth that's entirely covered in lava. Or one where it rains sulfuric acid. Or where everyone has incurable jock itch. I actually found an earth like that. As expected, the people there are grumpy, and there's an understandably high rate of suicide."

I stretched, and caught my fingers in the grating around a lighting fixture. "Are you enjoying playing God, Sata?"

"Yes. Very much so," he said, continuing to walk away. "I read the Bible in college, in a mythology class. That Old Testament God was a rascal, but He didn't have nearly the fun He could have if He'd abused his power a bit more. Ah, here we are. The air lock."

Sata came to a set of square double doors and pressed in a code on the keypad. They hissed open. I wound the jelly rope around my wrist, taking up the slack.

"Once I enter the air lock and seal the doors behind me, you won't be able to open them again until I've gone," Sata said. "So this is it, Talon. We're on the one-yard line, and I'm about to make a touchdown. If you want to stop me, this is your last chance. The clock begins . . . now."

Sata removed the TEV from his chest and flipped it around. Then he closed his eyes.

An LED—apparently for my benefit—appeared on the back of the device. It flashed 20:00, and then began to count down.

I gave the jelly rope a big tug, then released the ceiling, flinging myself at him.

FORTY-SEVEN

The look of surprise on my sensei's face told me he hadn't been expecting my attack. He barely had time to raise his sword when I was on him, wrapping my hand around his TEV strap. Then I reared back and punched him in the face.

Because of the lack of gravity, the blow didn't have my weight behind it. But I was still able to break the bastard's nose. I hit him four more times in paid succession—*pop pop pop pop*—blood exploding around his head—Sata choking on it as he gasped for air—then the *shinai* coming up and digging into my armpit.

He juiced me, a blue spark and loud *crack* accompanying the familiar jolt of pain. I released him, planting my feet on his chest, jumping away with all of my strength. I flew backward. The jelly rope stretched. Sata waved his palm in front of his face, trying to push away the floating blood. Then, just like an antique paddleball game, the rope reached its peak elasticity and I bounced right back at him.

I flew in face-first, knocking his *shinai* to the side as I latched onto his hair. Then I dropped my other arm,

locking his elbow up under my armpit so he couldn't use
the sword again. Knees digging into his sides, I released
his hair and gripped his throat, letting out a roar of anger
as I did.

I squeezed, trying to rip out his trachea. Sata made a
wonderful gagging sound, his whole body shaking, and I
concentrated on putting all of my effort into strangling the
son of a bitch.

Then I noticed the rhythmic motion to his shakes, and
how his gagging sounded, in fact, like something else.

Sata was laughing.

I brought back my hand, ready to pound his nose again.
Sata jackknifed his body and the next thing I knew I was
pinned under one of his feet, the tip of his *shinai* jammed
into my mouth and pressing against my very terrified
tongue.

"That was it?" Sata asked, still giggling. "That was all?
Such a disappointment you've been, Talon-*kun*. All your
years of training and experience, all leading up to this very
moment, and that was your best effort?" He wiped a sleeve
across his nose. "It was like being hit by a child."

"Mmmph mmnmgm," I said. That was *fuck you* with a
sword in my mouth.

I braced myself for the zap, but instead he withdrew the
shinai and punted me in the ribs. As I floated away, Sata
touched the sword tip to the jelly rope, zapping and sever-
ing it.

"Enjoy watching Chicago disappear," he said.

Then Sata walked into the air lock and closed the doors
behind him as I drifted off, unable to do anything but
watch.

I cursed myself for taking out the Nife too early. Now
was when I needed it most. Instead, it was floating around
in the lift somewhere, and the lift was fifty yards down the
hallway, which might as well have been a thousand miles

away. I flailed my arms, trying to swim through the air, with predictably pathetic results.

Momentum was taking me toward the large picture window, but too slowly. At this rate, Chicago's entire population would be eaten by dinosaurs before I even got halfway there. I looked out the reinforced glass, at the hotels and casinos tethered to the space station, their flashing neon out of place in this environment. Once Chicago disappeared, the tether would, too. Thirty thousand more people I wouldn't be able to save. If there were an award for the world's biggest loser, I wouldn't win that, either.

I'd blown it. Big-time. If I only had some antigrav shoes, or a jet pack.

A flashing billboard on the Hyatt showed an advertisement for a synthetic heroin, with ipecac nanobots in case of accidental overdose. Then it switched to an ad for FDS, now in key-lime-pie scent.

FDS. Feminine deodorant spray.

I quickly pulled the aerosol can from my shirt and gave it a shake. Still a little left. I sprayed the remaining contents behind me. There was enough accelerant left to boost my speed and change my direction. I held the button down until the can was empty, sailing through the air, toward the elevator.

Paranoia kicked in once I entered the lift car. I didn't see the Nife. If I flew into it, I could easily cut off a limb. Or worse; I could bump the Nife, and it could stick into the wall and breach the hull, which would cause the car, and possibly the space station, to lose pressure and get crushed.

I opened my eyes wide as they could stretch, looking this way and that way, trying to spot the Nife handle. Scanning the rows of seats, I noticed something floating near the floor. I kicked the ceiling, giving myself a tiny bit of push to get a closer look.

The object was the headrest Sata had knocked off. I

pushed myself off a chair, reached the rear of the car, and twisted around, wondering if I should go left or right.

Where was it? Where was the little bastard? Why did I have to pull it out? Why couldn't I have—

Then I felt it. A tiny tickling at my throat.

My whole body went rigid. Holding my breath, I glanced down my right cheek and saw the Nife handle, floating alongside my neck.

Had the blade already severed my throat? Was I already dead and didn't feel it yet?

I watched, waiting for the blood to come spurting out.

No blood came. But that was hardly reassuring. The Nife could be jammed in so deep it was plugging up the blood.

Carefully—oh, so carefully—I raised my left hand and touched the end of the handle with my thumb and index finger, careful not to nudge it any closer to my skin. I waited a moment, making sure my hand was steady, and then slowly pulled it away, like I was playing HyperJenga and the tower was ready to fall. When I got a safe distance I slapped my other hand up to my throat, expecting to feel the inside of my trachea.

I had a small scratch, nothing more.

Breathing again, I carefully sheathed the Nife, and then sighted down the hallway. Coiling my legs under me, I kicked off the wall and headed for the air lock. My trajectory was slightly off, so I made a slight correction by throwing the empty can to my left.

I was almost halfway there when more security guards showed up.

There's no feeling of vulnerability that quite compares to floating in zero-G. There's a sense of detachment when you leave solid ground, making you feel helpless. I can testify this emotion intensifies when four guys point Tasers at you. I covered my face with my forearms and they had at

me, firing round after round, Tesla lightning attacking the
entire right side of my body.

While my armor and food preservative wrap protected
me from the volts, the impact of the bullets was significant
enough to knock me off course, and I eventually butted up
against the picture window, glancing at an ad for McDon-
ald's extra-value meals, now only $79.95.

"Our Tasers have no effect!" one of the cops yelled.

No shit, Einstein.

"The man you're after is in the air lock!" I yelled above
the crackling of electricity.

Instead of answering, they fired more bullets at me. I
kept covered up, staring out of the corner of my eye at the
earth two hundred miles below me, wondering how long
Chicago had left.

I wondered if I could just wait for them to run out of
ammo. How much could they have, anyway?

The billboard changed. *Tired of faking orgasms? Get
the LLVV package now at the Chicago Sexual Center.*

"Thank you," I said to the billboard.

I began to convulse, faking being hit. They stopped firing and watched me. Eventually they turned off the power.
I remained limp, my mouth hanging open, hoping they
didn't take the opportunity to shoot me in my exposed skin.

"Is he dead?"

"I dunno. Go check."

"You go check."

"No, you."

"You assholes. I'll check."

Mr. Tough Guy walked over. When he reached to take
my pulse, I decided to give the groin shot one last try, and
lashed out with a vicious punch to his manly man bits. He
squealed, bringing up the Taser. I used him as a human
shield, putting my finger over his on the trigger, shooting
his three buddies and turning the final bullet on his leg.

I let all four do the lightning dance for a few seconds, then cut the power on his utility belt.

It took me a minute to tug off my own shoes and put on his magnetic soles. By the time I made it to the air lock, I looked through the glass in the door and saw Sata had already suited up into his skydiving outfit. The TEV had been bonded to a window overlooking the earth. The digital display read 14:45 and was ticking down the seconds.

Sata saw me standing there and walked up to the door. He hit the comm-link button.

"I thought you'd run off. You have about fourteen and a half minutes left. After I jump out of the air lock, the outside door will automatically close. I have a suit for you in the locker there. If I were you, I'd put it on and follow me. The controls are on the wristband. Or you're welcome to stay up here and watch Chicago disappear. But when the TEV goes off, the wormhole will also transport the window it's attached to, and you'll be sucked into space. And don't bother trying to remove the TEV. I mollybonded it to the reinforced glass." He smiled at me. "Good-bye, Talon. See you in Milwaukee, if you survive the jump."

He stuck his helmet onto his head, flipped down his visor, and then hit the hatch button. The outer door opened up, and Sata was shot out into open space, waving to me as he left.

Thirty seconds later the hatch closed, and I entered the same door code he'd used earlier. I raced right up to the TEV, drawing out my Nife. This was the reason I hadn't used the blade earlier—I needed it to destroy the TEV.

I slashed out.

The Nife bounced off.

I tried again, applying more pressure.

The blade wouldn't penetrate the TEV at all.

"Shit. The cover is made of nanotubes."

Naturally, the only thing a nanotube knife couldn't cut was something made out of the same material. Carbon nanotubes were created in factory labs, put together one molecule at a time. They couldn't be cut. They were made to order in whatever shape the buyer desired. I wouldn't be able to damage the TEV with anything less than a nuclear explosion.

But that didn't mean I couldn't move it.

If I cut the TEV away from the window, I could turn it toward empty space. Then Chicago wouldn't implode.

With less than thirteen minutes left, I ran to the locker and took out the space suit Sata had left for me. The material was stiff, hard to put on, and the side zipper was the thickest I'd ever seen. The boots were part of the suit, and they fit perfectly—Sata must have been anticipating this for quite some time. Once I made sure all the flaps were sealed, I popped on the helmet and fixed it to the collar.

Then I went back to the TEV, examining how it was attached. Sata had mollybonded it to the window. If I carefully sliced along the seam, I should be able to remove the TEV without breaking through the glass and sucking me out into space. It shouldn't be too hard. The glass used in space stations was reinforced, several inches thick. As long as I didn't make any colossal screwups, I should be able to get it off in time.

I placed the flat of the blade against the window, just as the air lock door opened up behind me and more cops flooded in.

They opened fire. But Sata's suit—made to withstand both the heat of reentry and a free fall through the Tesla field—weathered the barrage fine. I concentrated on making my cut slow and even, avoiding too much pressure, following the edge of the TEV.

Two inches away from finishing, some brain donor tackled me, jamming my elbow.

The Nife went right through the window, which then exploded outward, causing me, the TEV, and all the cops in the room to get pulled into the cold black void of space.

FORTY-EIGHT

When I was a kid, staring up at the sky and wishing I could be an astrominer and work on the moon, I always imagined my first spacewalk would instill me with wonder and awe. And I might have felt some wonder and awe as I hurtled away from the space station if I hadn't been screaming so loud it fogged up my visor.

I managed to get the screaming under control after only forty-seven seconds. That allowed the suit's internal rebreather to clear my visor and let me see the earth, in all of its enormous blue-green glory, as I hurtled toward it untethered through unforgiving space.

That caused another round of screaming, which I got under control much quicker than the first bout. After my visor cleared, I took some stock of my surroundings and noticed the idiot who tackled me still had his arms around my waist. I tried to pull them off, but they'd frozen solid, two blocks of flesh-colored ice. Incredibly, I'd kept hold of the Nife. I made a cut in each of his elbows—not so deep I went completely through and breached my suit—and then was able to break off his arms and send him off into the void.

I turned and watched him float away. He joined six other cops, each frozen in tragic yet semicomical positions, one guy actually holding his mouth in surprise, another in midrun like he could still get away.

The space station was a hundred yards behind me, and I continued to fly farther away from it. I swallowed, my heart in my throat. The feeling of helplessness that zero-G induced was child's play to actually being out in space, unattached to anything. It was like being dropped in the middle of the ocean with no hope of rescue.

I looked ahead, and saw the TEV only a few feet away, drifting lazily through the vacuum, its prismatic surface flashing various colors. The clock on the back read 9:42, and was still counting down. I had no idea how Sata focused the wormhole. Was it aimed at Chicago based on line of sight and trajectory, or did he program in specific coordinates? I knew only that the TEV was still pointed at the earth, and that couldn't be good. If it didn't implode Chicago, there were plenty of other habitable places it could devastate.

I had to get hold of that device.

Compartmentalizing my fear to deal with it later, I stared at the buttons on my wristband. Sata had mentioned the suit had a propulsion device. There were five buttons total, each large enough to press with my gloved finger, each with printing beneath. I switched the Nife to my bad hand and raised the wrist closer to my face so I could read. It glowed in the dark—helpful, because even with my interior helmet lamp and the light reflecting off the earth, it was dark as night out there. The five numbered words were:

1. THRUST
2. DROGUE
3. ROGALLO
4. IONIZER
5. CRUCIFORM

Of the three, the only word I understood was *thrust*. And since it was numbered "1," I decided to press it.

Immediately, I heard a hissing sound in my helmet, and my legs shot up and sent me spinning ass over head. As I twirled, I saw a white gas jetting out of the heels of my boots. I brought my knees into my chest and began to spin even faster. While the absence of gravity prevented my inner ear from jostling and causing dizziness, the effect was still very disorienting and more than a little scary. Before I hit a hundred rpm I splayed out my legs, switching from rotation to a single direction. It took a minute to figure out how to move my feet in order to fly straight. I also learned Sata had built speed controls into the soles. Lifting my toes slowed down the jets, and pointing them downward sped them up.

Once I was more or less stabilized, I had a bad moment when I realized I'd lost sight of the TEV. Fighting panic, I flew back toward the space station and the frozen copsicles, then followed their straight trajectory, forging ahead of them. I caught a glint of color, and saw the display.

7:55 . . . 7:54 . . . 7:53 . . .

Hurrying, I flexed out my toes, accelerating, rapidly catching up to the TEV. I bumped it with my bad arm, causing it to turn toward me. Not the development I'd hoped for. I reached for the TEV again, knocking it to the side and speeding past it. I kept my eyes locked on it, coming around again in an arc, and this time matched its speed before attempting a two-armed grab, the Nife still in my fist.

Once I held the device securely, I postulated which way to throw it. If I faced the lens the opposite way and sent it off into space, it couldn't transport any matter on earth. But if it had even the slightest spin when I threw it, chances were the wormhole could still hit our planet, or maybe the space station.

I slowed down, steadying my hands, ready to cast it off into the great beyond.

Luckily, I had a sudden realization and caught myself before chucking the TEV away.

The people of Boise, and the people at the elevator station, had all been sent to a dinosaur planet. But there was a good chance they were all still alive.

This TEV might be the only way to get them back to our universe. Not only could it send matter to parallel planets; its destination was already programmed in.

Of course, I had no way of understanding how it worked.

But I knew someone who did.

I tucked the TEV tightly under my arm, put one of its straps over my shoulder, and hit the gas, rocketing toward earth. Sata had a nice head start, but I wouldn't have put it past him to linger, if only to see if I could catch up. I don't know what shocked me more—his newly acquired homicidal nature, or the fact that this all seemed like a big game to him. The unrestrained glee on his face while he was imploding innocent people sickened me in a way I'd never known before.

Being a cop, I'd seen a lot of badness in the world. Since becoming a timecaster, the majority of cruelty was confined to crimes of passion, and even that trickled to nonexistence once people knew they could be held accountable at any time.

Sata was something different. Something beyond insane, temporary or permanent. As with Alter-Talon, there was something so twisted, so wrong, about his demeanor that the only word I could use to describe it was *evil*.

Had that darkness always been there? If so, how could I have missed it? If not, how could someone so good become so bad so quickly?

Then I had a thought. A revelatory thought. But I filed it away for later when I saw the exhaust plume from Sata's boot jets. As trails went, this couldn't be easier to follow; two cloudy streaks the width of my dear, departed Corvette.

I pointed my toes as far as they would go, getting an extra little burst of speed. Giving the TEV a quick glance, I saw I had a little more than five minutes before the wormhole event.

My dual goals were to find Sata and follow him to a hopefully safe landing, and to make sure when the TEV counted down to zero I had it pointed toward space.

The change was gradual, so slow I didn't notice it right away. At first, it was just a small bump against my helmet. Then my whole suit began to vibrate. Softly at first. Then in a much rougher way.

Sata's plume became larger, more dispersed. I flexed my toes to slow down, take stock of the situation.

My jets cut off, but I didn't slow down.

In fact, I sped up.

Though it was still black as ink, I realized what was happening. I was going from the thermosphere to the stratosphere, and gravity was taking over. I hit the thrust button, killing the boot jets.

My speed still increased. I was going fast. Real fast. Several hundred miles per hour fast. And the wind really began to bat me around, causing a strain on my neck and arms. I held the TEV tight to my chest, careful not to stab myself with my Nife. Ignoring the growing sense of terror building up inside of me, I managed to get the second strap onto my opposite shoulder, wearing the device as a chest plate like Sata had done. It was just in the nick of time, too. The turbulence had gotten so bad I couldn't keep my arms next to my body. I would have dropped the TEV for sure. It was all I could do to hold on to the Nife.

That was when I noticed the temperature start to rise.

At first, I'd attributed it to fear and exertion. The suit

was well insulated against freezing space, so it made sense my body heat would accumulate.

But then my cheeks began to ache, like a bad sunburn.

Atmospheric reentry.

Like all kids, I took space travel lessons in school. And like all kids, I mostly goofed off in class. So while I remembered some terms such as *drag coefficient*, *angle of attack*, and *shock wave standoff*, I couldn't remember definitions for any of them, or how they applied to my situation.

The only thing I knew for certain was that reentering earth's atmosphere caused friction, and with friction came heat, and very quickly I was going to reach a temperature of several thousand degrees Fahrenheit. Even wearing Sata's ingeniously designed space suit, I would roast alive without some sort of heat shield.

It rapidly became too hot for me to even think. My mouth went dry. My sweat evaporated, steamed up my visor, and then that baked onto the inside, leaving a thin white film.

Losing consciousness, I barely noticed something below me. A tiny red speck, in the shape of a triangle, bright red contrasting against the expansive blue-green of the earth.

Sata? Where'd he get a triangle? Why didn't I have one?

And right then, with my brain feeling like it was simmering in a Crock-Pot, I remembered what *rogallo* meant.

FORTY-NINE

In the past twenty-four hours, I'd been frightened so many times I'd lost count. But prior to these recent life-threatening events, my biggest scare had been skydiving with Vicki. While giving us a last-minute pep talk in the heliplane, our instructor had regaled us with a history of the sport, along with the many types of parachutes developed.

Rogallo, drogue, and cruciform were all chute shapes, used for different purposes. A rogallo was a fancy name for a flexible airfoil. Though made of triangular cloth, it functioned more like a wing than a parachute, and was used on hang gliders and Parasevs. Sata's triangle a few miles beneath me was a rogallo chute.

Mustering up my remaining dregs of common sense, I knew it was too soon for the rogallo, partly because it seemed like I was traveling too fast for it to work, but mostly because Sata had labeled it "3."

I hit button number "2" on my wrist instead, launching the drogue.

Drogue chutes were invented to be deployed by rapidly

moving objects, just as spacecraft, missiles, and, in this case, me.

The effect was instantaneous. Though I'd never had my limbs pulled off, I could imagine it felt similar. The drogue parachute exploded out the back of my suit and immediately reduced my speed, so fast I felt blood slosh into my hands and feet, making them swell up. The suit's infrastructure focused the brunt of the force on my shoulders and hips, which instantly ached. My vision blurred, and I swung back and forth like a pendulum, fighting not to pass out.

Eventually, thankfully, the terrible heat diminished. Inside the suit, the circulating air slowly cooled, so it no longer felt like I was breathing inside an oven. The swaying eventually evened out. I became lucid enough to pull back the TEV and check the timer.

5:23 and counting.

While the drogue had slowed me down considerably, I was still going much too fast to land. A glance upward revealed a chute that looked like a long, tapered sleeve, with a large hole in the top. If I hit the ground using only this, I'd pancake myself.

Luckily, Sata had more buttons on his clever little space suit. Keeping in sequence, I hit "3," the rogallo.

The drogue detached and a triangular wing popped out the back of my suit, immediately slowing me down even more. My angle of descent went from a straight plummet to a thirty-degree angle. But it was a smooth transition, rather than a jarring one like the drogue.

I leaned backward, cutting my angle of attack even more, reducing my speed while learning how to tilt and twist my body to go in the direction I wanted to. After a few arcs and turns, I located Sata, perhaps half a mile below me. I aimed myself toward him.

Beneath us, the earth was huge, dominating my vision. My fear of drifting solo through space was replaced by the larger fear of free-falling. Plummeting through biorecycle chutes and jumping off of fifty-story buildings was scary enough. This awesome height made me want to puke. Which, inside a helmet, wouldn't be a smart idea.

I took large, deep breaths, focusing on Sata, concentrating on getting closer. Around me, the sky was changing from black to blue. I got within a few hundred yards of Sata, and closed the distance even more. Though part of me wanted to swoop down and cut his chute to ribbons, I needed him alive if I wanted to save Chicago.

"So, Talon, I see you've managed to follow me." The speakers were in my helmet. *"What did you think of re-entry? Hot stuff, huh?"*

I wondered how to activate the microphone. Maybe it was voice-activated.

"The microphone is voice-activated," Sata said.

"I knew that," I told him.

"We'll still be in the air when Chicago transports to the parallel world. But we should be able to see it from up here."

"Guess again, asshole. I've got the TEV on me."

I patted my chest and checked the time.

2:35.

"What? You fool!"

Sata's airfoil turned a hundred eighty degrees. I altered my trajectory to get out of his flight path. He adjusted his as well, so we were both heading toward the same point. We closed the distance quickly, proof that even with the rogallos we were still falling at very high speeds.

A second before we collided, I veered right and Sata veered left, so we flew side by side.

"Give me the TEV!" he thundered, his shout making my ears hurt.

"Come get it, Grandpa."

Ducking his shoulder, Sata turned hard and slammed into

me. The impact made my teeth rattle. Both of our rogallos became entangled, and we began to plummet in a twisted, spinning mass. Sata tugged at the TEV straps across my shoulders. Without even thinking, I lashed out at his face, the Nife cutting a line across his helmet visor. He grabbed my wrist and locked his legs around my waist, squeezing my lungs to the point of bursting. I felt a sharp pain in my shoulder, and saw a metal knife blade protruding from his gloved finger. He twisted it into my flesh as I fought to push him away.

He screamed something at me, but all I could hear was the wind whistling in through the hole I'd made in his helmet. I felt his finger knife twisting inside my chest, nicking my ribs. Then he pulled out and punched the awful blade into my opposite shoulder.

I understood the point of his attack only when he withdrew the weapon. He wasn't out to harm me.

He was cutting the TEV straps.

Sata kicked away from me, dropping at a faster rate.

I don't know if he was trying to escape, or if he'd had a major wardrobe malfunction, but he left his rogallo twisted up in mine and began to free-fall again, sans chute.

He also managed to get the TEV. I watched him wave at me as he dropped into a blue-and-white storm cloud, disappearing from my sight.

I tried reaching up over my shoulder with my Nife, to cut the lines. But our two wings had tangled into a sort of propeller shape, making me spin. The wind resistance was so strong that no matter how I strained, I was unable to flip over and reach the ropes.

I tried twisting my body. Contorting my sore shoulders and pelvis. Stretching out my arms. Tucking into a ball.

Nothing worked. And the spinning became faster, and faster.

In space, spinning was confusing.

But under gravity's grasp, the fluid in my inner ears was being shaken like a snow globe, bringing disorientation, dizziness, nausea, and an overwhelming feeling of panic.

Chicago was going to implode in less than two minutes, and there was nothing I could do about it.

Then the centrifugal force became too much, and once again I began to black out.

And then I actually did black out.

Unconsciousness wasn't peaceful. Even knocked out, every synapse in my brain was firing in panic. I somehow managed to startle myself awake, and when I did I saw I'd dropped the Nife, which made me panic even more.

That meant I had only one chance left for survival.

I stared at the button on my wrist and hit "1."

Nothing happened.

I tried "2."

Nothing.

"3."

No change at all.

I stared at the last two buttons, "4" *ionizer* and "5" *cruciform*. I knew cruciform was another type of parachute, but if I hit the button now, would it get tangled up with the dual rogallo death spiral? And should I even try to hit a button out of order?

I had no idea what *ionizer* was. But at this point I had nothing else to lose.

I pressed "4."

The rogallo detached, taking its snarled twin along with it, and I once again was free-falling. All too soon I reached the storm cloud Sata had disappeared into. I was so elated to be free of the chutes that I didn't even think to question what the storm cloud was.

I found out twenty seconds later, when I drifted into it and the world became a brilliant explosion of blue.

I'd reached the Tesla field.

FIFTY

The Mastermind clutches his prize to his chest as he hits terminal velocity, falling at close to six hundred miles per hour. The slit in his visor is letting cold wind in, but he can still see if he squints, and the rebreather is still feeding him oxygen.

He smiles. The finger knife had been a last-minute addition to the suit—a precautionary measure in case the parachutes didn't detach as designed. It turned out to be a very smart move. He never would have gotten the TEV from Talon otherwise.

Who could have predicted the mouse would have a Nife? Talon had played it smart, kept it hidden until the last possible moment. But in the end, even that hadn't been enough.

Sata plummets into the Tesla field. He's already pressed the ionizer button, shielding his suit against the incredible amount of electrical energy. The whole world turns bright blue.

Bringing the TEV close to his face, Sata squints at the clock.

1:01 . . . 1:00 . . . 0:59 . . . 0:58 . . .

This next part is going to be tricky. Sata should still be able to vanquish most of Chicago, but he'll have to aim it manually. He won't be able to implode as wide of an area, but—

Sata hears a tremendous thunderclap, louder than anything he's ever experienced before, and at the same time sees a flash of superbright light.

Then he doesn't see anything at all.

Sata understands what just happened. The ionizer is supposed to form a defensive antistatic barrier around his suit. But when Talon had slashed his visor, he'd also put a hole in the ion shield. Lightning, like water, takes the path of least resistance.

The Mastermind screams.

He screams at his miscalculation.

He screams at the ruination of his calculated plan.

He screams at the mouse, who somehow managed to beat him.

But most of all, he screams in pain, because both of his eyeballs have just exploded and are leaking all over his cheeks.

FIFTY-ONE

I braced my entire body as I fell into the Tesla field. You'd think I would have gotten used to being zapped by electricity by now, having been subjected to enough volts to power a small city for a year, but the thought of the ensuing pain still made me want to curl up in a fetal position and suck my thumb.

Incredibly, the pain didn't come.

Everything became bright blue, and thousands—millions—of lightning flashes streaked sideways, diagonally, up and down, all around. Beautiful, and potentially deadly. But none of them zapped me.

I credited the ionizer button, and then tilted my body face-first, looking for Sata.

Incredibly, I found him.

Even more incredibly, he was the one curled up fetal, clutching the TEV to his chest. By dipping my shoulders I was able to increase my rate of descent. We both fell through the bottom of the Tesla field and into open sky just as I bumped into him.

The TEV went spinning off, away from us.

I stared at my mentor for a moment, saw the blood caking the inside of his visor, and wondered if he was even still alive. Then his fist shot out and he chucked me under the chin, knocking me away as he sailed off in the opposite direction.

It wasn't even a choice of what to chase. I splayed out my arms and legs to slow down, then went after the TEV.

I didn't know how much time I had left, but I figured I wouldn't have a second chance if I screwed up. The TEV was spinning like a top. Depending on how long the worm-hole stayed open, it could potentially swallow up a good portion of the earth, along with me, the moon, and any-thing else the lens passed over. I sidled up close to it and reached out a finger, giving the corner a tap. It slowed the spin enough for me to read the counter.

0:11 . . . 0:10 . . .

Rather than freak out, I brought my arms in closer to my body . . .

Increasing my speed . . .

And accidentally bumped the TEV out of reach.

0:08 . . . 0:07 . . .

The very definition of calm and cool, I once again accelerated . . .

Carefully stretched out my hand . . .

Accidentally bumping the TEV out of reach again.

I didn't get this far to lose because of panic or impa-tience. Plus, my nudges weren't a total loss. I'd managed to get it to stop spinning.

Unfortunately, the lens was now facing the earth. And, be it coincidence or some omnipotent force controlling the universe who enjoyed irony, the TEV was aiming right at Chicago.

0:05 . . . 0:04 . . .

The wind blew me off to the side. I dropped my right flank . . .

Sped up . . .

Got in close again . . .

And clasped my arms around the TEV—

—accidentally bumping it out of reach for the third time.

0:03 . . . 0:02 . . .

Fuck being careful.

I plowed into the damn thing hard, wrapped my arms around it, and aimed the lens at the giant blue expanse of Lake Michigan.

The TEV shuddered, and I heard a *whump*.

As I stared, a section in the middle of the great lake hollowed out, like a giant ice-cream scoop had been taken to it. Millions—maybe billions—of gallons of water vanished.

Then the water filled in the indentation, rushing back on all sides at once, causing the blue to turn white with an enormous splash.

Chicago was safe. Plus I still had the TEV, which could be used to bring Boise back.

I allowed myself a small grin. All in a day's work. Cue the applause.

Compared to saving eight million people at the last possible second, the remainder of the free fall should be cake. I wrapped the TEV strap around my wrist and hit button "5" for *cruciform*.

The square parachute billowed open above me—a jarring sensation but nothing I wasn't able to handle. The toggle ropes dropped down next to my hands and I grabbed them tight, braking and steering and making my way north up the coast of Lake Michigan, miles past Chicago.

Opening my chute this high above the earth's surface meant a long and turbulent descent. I spent the time alternating between adjusting my course and scanning the skies for Sata.

I didn't see him.

I postulated on his survival rate. From the blood inside his helmet, I guessed his eyes had popped in the Tesla field. He could have still released his chute and landed safely, but my fifteen-minute scan of the sky didn't reveal him.

I turned my thoughts to Vicki, Alter-Talon, Teague, Boise, and the poison coursing through my system. Hopefully I'd be able to wrap up some of these loose ends, perhaps even with the authorities on my side. Certainly there were cameras at the Arthur C. Clarke Station, which showed Sata on his rampage. It would be nice to stop running and get some actual help instead. While I couldn't figure out how the wormhole TEV worked, I had no doubt some government egghead could.

The wind got stronger, whipping me around. Though I was still a long way from safety, the adrenaline had worn off and I actually yawned. I adjusted my direction, heading toward Milwaukee and my wife.

That was when the first bolt of Tesla lightning hit me.

It was a big bolt, obviously from a Tesla Taser satellite. I should have guessed that once I fell into US airspace I was being monitored. My displacement of Lake Michigan water, instead of being viewed as a heroic act that saved a city, could have been mistaken for an attack.

Another bolt struck me, confirming my hypothesis. Luckily, Sata's hypersuit deflected the charge. But I knew TTS would only be the first strike. Next would probably be—

—missiles. Two of them. Ground to air, coming up fast. I stared down between my legs and watched them rocket up at me, trailing long plumes of gray smoke.

FIFTY-TWO

Some days a guy just can't catch a break.

If the TTS had locked onto me, the missiles had locked on as well. I guessed them to be airburst, which meant they wouldn't even need to hit me to kill me. They would explode within a few hundred feet, the shock wave and shrapnel ripping me to shreds.

I tried to recall if anything in my peace officer training dealt with dodging missiles while parachuting at fifty thousand feet, and came up empty. But I hadn't gone this far to get shot out of the sky like a fat, lazy duck.

Pulling up the TEV to chest level, I fumbled with the counter, trying to find a button or knob to reset the countdown. Sata wouldn't make it obvious. But there had to be some way to program it, some way to reset the wormhole.

I glanced beneath me. The missiles had gotten much bigger, and I could hear the roar of their engines. I didn't have much time left.

The normal TEVs—the ones that didn't transport matter to dinosaur planets—worked by tuning in to the fabric of spacetime. When I pet the bunny and found the octeract point, I did it through concentration and slight adjustments of the control knob.

This TEV didn't have a control knob. Or did it?

What if the knob wasn't physical?

I remembered when Sata set the device. He'd done so without touching anything. He'd closed his eyes, and the LED had begun its countdown.

I closed my eyes as well, letting my brain stretch out into infinity, trying to block out the missiles, the environment, and all physical sensation. Not the easiest thing to do while parachuting, exhausted, and terrified, but I didn't have time to fail. Instead of manipulating a knob, I imagined it, fine-tuning until my mind was flooded with light and the bunny appeared.

I pictured the bunny with a timer on its head that displayed 0:03.

When I opened my eyes, the TEV displayed three seconds, and was counting down.

The missiles were within airburst range. I pointed the lens and held my breath.

The counter reached 0:00.

The TEV shuddered.

The missiles disappeared. So did another chunk of Lake Michigan. I hoped I hadn't hit any boaters.

"Can anyone hear me?" I asked. I had no idea what radio frequency the helmet microphone was tuned to, or how far its range was, but it was worth a shot. "This is Talon Avalon. I'm carrying a device that can destroy the entire city."

"This is the Chicago Coast Guard," came the response. *"What are your demands?"*

Demands? "Uh, it would be nice if you stopped firing missiles at me."

"Why are you shooting your device at Lake Michigan?"

"It's not my device. It belongs to Michio Sata. He programmed it to destroy Chicago, and I jumped out of a space station to stop him."

No answer.

"Hello?"

I wondered if I'd gone out of range. I checked around for more missiles, but didn't see any. Maybe they actually listened.

Leaving the TEV to hang from my wrist once again, I altered my course, continuing on to Milwaukee.

"Avalon, this is Mayor George W. Dailey. You really think you can force your demands on the great city of Chicago and get away with it?"

"My only demand is for you to stop shooting missiles at me."

"We don't negotiate with terrorists, Avalon. And we won't bend in the face of extortion."

"What am I extorting?"

"You're scum, Avalon. There isn't a place on earth you'll be able to hide. We'll hunt you down like the rat you are."

So much for getting the authorities on my side.

"Listen up, Mayor Dipshit, because I'm only going to say this once. Leave. Me. Alone. Any further attempt to talk to me, shoot at me, or otherwise engage me in any way will be viewed as an attack and will be dealt with harshly."

More silence.

"Hello? Mayor Asshole? You there?"

"Look, Mr. Avalon, my legal advisors have informed me that I may have come off a bit, um, harsh, and they'd like me to once again ask what your demands are. Under no circumstances do we want to provoke you any in way."

I didn't trust politicos, especially Chicago politicos. But if they thought I was a real threat, maybe they'd give me some breathing room.

"Here's what I want, Dailey. I want you guys to check out the video from the space elevator station earlier today. I also want you to locate Neil Winston and interrogate him. He's in Zelda Peterson's apartment at thirteen twenty-two Wacker."

"What do you want us to ask him?"

"Ask him what he knows."

"Anything else?"

I thought it over. "Yeah. I want my neighbor, Norm Chomsky, to go on the six o'clock news tonight, and apologize to me for being a dick."

"Which channel?"

"All of them. And better make it national news."

"Is that all?"

"That's all. Now, stay out of my way, and don't try to contact me again. My device is wired to my heartbeat. Any attempt to attack me will destroy fifty square miles."

"You have my word I'll do everything in my power to see your demands are met."

Satisfied I'd be left alone, I drifted toward Milwaukee to save Vicki and face my doppelganger.

FIFTY-THREE

I was sure my every move was being watched when I landed without incident on a rocky beach several miles south of Milwaukee. I disconnected the chute, watching it blow into the water, and then retied the TEV to my chest.

The authorities apparently believed the "wired to my heartbeat" bullshit and gave me a wide berth. I kept my space suit on just in case someone got cute with the Tesla satellites, but had to remove my helmet to call Vicki. It was nice to breathe fresh air again, and listening to the waves lap against the shore was tranquil, almost peaceful.

"Hello?"

Hearing my wife's voice brought tears to my eyes.

"Vicki? Are you okay?"

"Talon? Why are you calling me from the bathroom?"

My whole body tensed up. "Vicki, listen to me carefully. That's not me in the bathroom. You have to get out of there."

"What are you talking about?"

"Run away. Right now."

"You're not making sense. I'm with you right now."

"The man you're with looks like me, but he isn't me. He's the killer the cops are after. Tell me where you are right now."

"*I'm at—*"

"*Who are you talking to?*"

I froze. I would recognize that voice anywhere.

It was mine.

"*No one,*" Vicki said.

"*Is that him on the headphone?*" Alter-Talon asked.

"*Who?*"

I heard a slap. My heart shrunk.

"*Stop being coy, bitch. Is that you, Talon?*"

I closed my eyes, picturing him with his ear pressed to Vicki's.

"It's me," I said.

"*I haven't heard anything about Chicago disappearing. Sata underestimated you. Is he dead?*"

Talking to myself ranked as one of the strangest experiences of my life.

"I don't know."

"*Doesn't matter. He served his purpose.*"

"Which was?"

"*To bring you to me. I've got your wife, and the antidote. How far are you from Milwaukee?*"

"An hour. Maybe less."

"*Meet us at the abandoned brewery on the outskirts of dissytown. You have forty-five minutes. Come alone, no weapons. Any funny stuff—*"

I heard another slap, and Vicki cried out.

"*You understand?*"

I did my best to keep my voice steady. "Why are you doing this?"

"*You'll find out soon enough.*"

"*Talon, I love—*"

Vicki's words were cut off. I imagined the bastard pinching her ear to hang up.

I stood there for a moment, impotent, wondering how this was all going to end. Sata seemed to be motivated by nothing other than insanity, and I'd assumed Alter-Talon was similarly bent. But he didn't sound like he was having fun. He seemed controlled. Calculated.

This guy wanted something from me. And I wasn't sure I wanted to know what it was.

A squadron of heliplanes passed overhead, in a classic military wedge formation. I had no doubt they had something to do with me, and could only hope Mayor Dailey could convince the cops in Wisconsin to leave me alone.

Zipping open a side flap on my suit, I tugged the DT from my utility belt and found my current location. Eleven point four miles to the brewery. I also did a quick GPS search for me and Vicki, coming up empty. Alter-Talon must have worn an obfuscation disk over his chip, just like I did, and he had probably put one on my wife as well.

I broke into a jog, running up the beach, climbing some concrete steps to street level, then borrowing a bio-fuel scooter from a very rude woman who knew so many dirty synonyms for *rectum* she would have made Harry McGlade blush.

It took half an hour of maddening stop-and-go traffic before I made it to Milwaukee's dissytown. During the trip my imagination conjured horrible scenarios of Alter-Talon hurting Vicki. I'd dealt with a lot of abuse over the last twenty-four hours, but there was nothing that could be done to me worse than hurting my wife.

By the time I motored into the ranks of the disenfranchised, I was ready to strangle anyone who looked at me cross-eyed. Like Rockford's dissytown, this one was filled with a lot of dirty folks looking confused, shell-shocked, and deviant. More crumbling buildings. More crushed dreams. And no BHVs to speak of, at least not any as attractive as Yummi and her cohorts.

I kept one eye on my DT, steering around piles of garbage

and making my way to the brewery. I stopped in front of an alley, trying to determine my best route, when a gang approached.

Six of them, dressed like a homeless hyperhockey team, complete with filthy pads and sticks stained with dried blood.

"Nice bike," their leader said. "Why don't you give it to me, then get the fuck out of our neighborhood."

I checked my DT. Four minutes to get to the brewery. I didn't have time to uncork a bottle of smack-down on these punks, much as they probably deserved it.

"Where's the brewery?" I asked.

"You say something, butthead?"

They couldn't hear me with the helmet on. I yanked it off.

All six stepped back, and the leader raised his hands in supplication.

"Talon! Shit, I'm sorry, man. I didn't know it was you."

"The brewery," I repeated.

"You know it's right down the street here."

"Where?"

He pointed. "End of the block. On the left. Look, you're not pissed or nothing, are you? How can we make it up to you, buddy?"

I considered sending him and his droogs to the dinosaur planet, but I had a feeling I wasn't the Talon they were afraid of. Alter-Talon had been here, and apparently left a serious impression.

"Beat each other up," I ordered.

By the time I put my helmet back on, they were kicking the shit out of one another. I motored past. With one minute remaining I ditched the bike and walked through the front door of the Milwaukee Brewing Company.

The interior was quiet, dark, warehouse-sized. I flipped open my visor and tapped my eyelid, bringing on infrared. Nothing stood out. I switched to night vision, creeping silently past rusty old lauter tuns that stretched to the ceiling, the foul smell of mildew assaulting my nostrils.

My headphone rang, and I answered.

"Keep going, straight ahead. At the end of the walkway, there's a door."

"Where's Vicki?"

I heard a slap, and my wife whimpered. I was going to rip out this guy's spine and stab him through the heart with it.

He hung up. I moved a bit quicker, but stayed cautious. When I got to the aforementioned door, I tapped my AVCL back to infrared, and spotted the heat signatures of three people behind the door, all standing in the center of the room.

Flipping down my helmet visor, I turned the knob and entered.

Unlike the dank, decay, and filth I'd just walked through, this room was brightly lit and clean. It resembled the infirmary at Yummi's parking farm, down to the two metal patient tables. There was also a tray topped with wicked-looking knives, clamps, and tools. Several expensive-looking pieces of medical equipment stood between the tables, beeping and making machine sounds.

Alter-Talon wore what he had in the timecast transmissions: black jumpsuit, black gloves. To his left was a tall, thin man in a white lab coat. He was bald, and had thick glasses that magnified his blue eyes to three times their normal size. To Alter-Talon's right . . .

"Vicki."

"Talon."

She was handcuffed to a metal pipe. I hurried to her, yanking off my helmet and letting it fall, hugging her tight, never wanting to let go. We both said, "I love you," and, "I'm sorry," several times. When I pulled back to kiss her, I noticed her black eye.

I turned on Alter-Talon, feeling myself grow very cold.

"Well, hello there, handsome," Alter-Talon said.

When I took a step toward him he held up a small black device.

"Hold it! Any closer and Vicki's dead."

I halted, fighting the urge to rip his face off. "What have you done?"

"My associate, Dr. Coursey, has implanted a small bomb in Vicki's molar. I press this button, it blows her head off."

"You're bluffing." I turned to my wife. "Vicki?"

She nodded slowly. "He attached something to my tooth."

"It won't actually blow her head off," Dr. Coursey said. He had a German accent. "Just blow a big hole in her neck, tearing through the carotid artery. I've done trial runs on several dissys. Death occurs within twenty seconds."

My desire to tear both of them limb from limb wrestled with the need to control my rage. Through clenched teeth I managed to say, "What do you want?"

Alter-Talon smiled, and it was an ugly thing to behold. He tossed the black detonator to Dr. Coursey, then raised one of his gloved hands. Using the other, he peeled the glove off.

The odor hit me before he even finished. Rotting meat, even worse than I'd smelled in the biorecycle chute. When he tossed the glove away, I saw his fingers and couldn't help but flinch at the sight. The flesh was infected, sloughing off in strips. In the case of his thumb, the bone protruded from his skin.

"To start with," Alter-Talon said, "I want your hands."

FIFTY-FOUR

I stared, trying to make sense of what he'd just said.

"My hands?"

Talon wiggled his ruined fingers, one of the nails falling off. "My other hand is even worse. This is my sixth set of transplants. It always ends in the same way. My body rejects the cadaver donors, and they begin to rot while still attached. Can you guess where I lost them?"

I thought back, years ago, to the bomb I defused under the snack table at the retirement home. I nodded.

"You pulled the red wire," Alter-Talon said. "I pulled the blue. Shredded my hands all the way up to my elbows."

I followed his line of thinking. "And the donors don't work, so you looked for a perfect genetic match."

"I searched the multiverse for one, and found you."

This went beyond my mentor just being crazy from steroid abuse. "Sata didn't find you randomly," I stated.

"No. I found him. I killed Aunt Zelda for him, and destroyed Boise because he asked me to."

"Boise wasn't destroyed. It was sucked into a wormhole and sent to a planet filled with dinosaurs."

"On your earth, it was. In my parallel universe, I sent it to an earth without any atmosphere. They're all dead."

"You lousy SMF," I said, clenching my fists.

"So the people of our Boise are still alive?" Vicki asked.

Alter-Talon shrugged. "I guess. Those who haven't been eaten yet."

I shook my head, amazed. "And you did all of this, just for my hands?"

"It's actually more than that. After all these years of taking higher and higher doses of experimental immuno-suppressant drugs, my body has begun to reject more than just the transplants. Both of my feet are now rotting. And so is a part very near and dear to me."

He patted his groin.

"So you want my hands, my feet . . . and my junk?"

Dr. Coursey patted the metal table. "We'll make you as comfortable as possible during the procedure. If you co-operate, we're even willing to let you live. Both you, and your wife."

"Maybe you'll have better luck with cadaver parts than I've had," Alter-Talon said.

I stared at Vicki. She seemed scared, and sad, but also determined.

"Don't do it," she said. "He's a lunatic who killed half a million people."

"I can't let you die, Vicki."

"A half million, Talon. I'm not worth it. Neither of us are."

"You're worth more to me than everyone else on the planet put together, Vicki."

"We're both going to die anyway, Talon. I couldn't bear knowing this psycho was running around free, committing genocide."

"I promise, no more genocide," Alter-Talon said. "Cross my heart." He dragged a bloody fingertip over his chest. "Besides, you really don't have a choice. The nanopoison in your system will kill you unless I give you the antidote. I'm going to get your parts, alive or dead. I hold all the cards here."

This was going to end badly, no matter how it ended. But if there was even the slightest chance I could save Vicki's life, I'd do it. Even if it meant living without hands, feet, and Talon Jr.

"I love you," I said to her.

"How much?"

"More than anything else."

"Promise me something, then," she implored.

"Anything."

"Promise me if, given the choice, you'd save Boise over me."

"Vicki . . ."

"Half a million are already dead. Don't let it be a million. Please. Not because of me."

Her eyes got teary. Mine probably did, too.

"I promise," I said.

Vicki lifted up her chin, tilting her head to the right. Her gaze was rock-steady. I understood what she wanted. Though it made me sick, I gave her a nod.

"You know what you have to do," my wife said. "Make it count."

Without dwelling on it, I threw a haymaker, cracking her in the jaw with everything I had. Then I spun around and kicked Alter-Talon in the face, knocking him backward.

He staggered, then caught his footing.

"Kill the bitch!" he screamed.

I turned. Dr. Coursey lifted up the detonator, his thumb pressing the button just as a small white projectile—trailing a thin line of blood—hit him in the face.

The bomb Vicki spit at him exploded with the sound of a firecracker, but packed considerably more power. Dr. Coursey fell, but both hands weren't enough to stop the geyser erupting from the hole in his neck.

I faced Alter-Talon again, but he was already running toward Vicki, the TEV off his chest and clenched in his hand.

"This isn't over," he said. He held the device at arm's length, pointing it toward himself and my wife.

Vicki and I locked eyes.

Just as I cried out, "No!" he and Vicki imploded, vanishing into a wormhole.

Alter-Talon's TEV dropped to the floor.

I stared at the space where they'd disappeared, wondering what to do next. My knuckles still hurt from punching the woman I loved. Dr. Coursey coughed, gagged, and bled out on the floor of the brewery.

I picked up Alter-Talon's TEV. Like Sata's, it reflected light in a prism, and lacked dials and controls. But I'd learned how to use it while free-falling. I could follow Vicki and Alter-Talon into his world, and get her back.

Just as I was getting ready to mentally tune in to the octeract point, I caught myself and touched the TEV on my chest. This one was programmed to transport matter to the dinosaur planet. I'd promised Vicki, only a few seconds ago, that, if given the chance, I'd save Boise over her.

I wasn't one to break my promises. And if I went after her, without trying to return Boise to this universe, she'd never forgive me.

WTF was I supposed to do? Save the woman I loved, or sacrifice her life, and mine (since the poison was slowly killing me), in order to save five hundred thousand innocent people?

What would you do?

I made my decision. Then I closed my eyes, pet the bunny, and stepped through the wormhole into a parallel universe.

GLOSSARY

In the future, tech and acronyms rule the day . . .

AFAIK—As far as I know/knew.

AVCL—All-vision contact lens. Allows user to see in a variety of conditions.

BHV—Bleeding heart volunteer.

Biofuel—Fuel made from animal and plant lipids and starches, along with the methane released when composting.

Bōgu—Kendo armor, consisting of a *dô* (chest plate), *kote* (belt), *tare* (gloves), and *men* (helmet).

BRB—Be right back.

Carbon nanotube—The strongest substance known to man, created in molecular strings by factory labs.

Chip—A microchip implanted in the wrists of all people at birth, it serves as identification, a universal key, and a debit card.

CPD—Chicago Peace Department, aka the cops.

Credits—In a cashless society, a credit is the digital representation of a US dollar, existing solely as data.

CWII—The second US Civil War of 2034.

Dissy—One of the disenfranchised. Someone who rejects the modern way of living and exists off the grid without paying taxes.

DT—Digital tablet, a pocket computer.

Duckets—Paper money.

EPF—Electronic perimeter fence, used to keep suspects in a designated area.

Frog legs—Artificial, flexible spring stilts, used as leg extenders in powerbocking to run faster and jump higher.

Fuct—Screwed.

Genipet—A genetically altered pet.

GPS—Global positioning satellite.

Hang up—A vocal command to disconnect a headphone call, also synonymous with *good-bye*.

Headphone—An ear/brain implant allowing phone calls without phones.

Hobo—The act and equipment used to jump onto a moving train.

Intranet—Three hundred petabytes of stored information—every bit of knowledge and media from the history of mankind—that exists preinstalled on every DT.

IRL—In real life.

IRT—In real time.

Kermit—A pedestrian who powerbocks, using frog leg extensions on their feet.

LEO—Low-earth orbit.

Nife—A carbon nanotube knife, only a few nanometers thick.

P&P bars—Clubs that sell pot and pills.

Pet the bunny—Slang for tuning in to the fabric of space-time using a TEV.

PrOn—Pornography.

Roids—Steroids. Those who use roids are known as *roiders*.

Shinai—A sword used in the Japanese martial art kendo.

SLP—State-licensed prostitute, aka *social workers*.

SMF—Sick motherfucker.

Space elevator—A woven rope of carbon nanotubes, tethered to the earth on one end and a low-earth orbit satellite on the other, which allows for inexpensive travel into space.

Tachyon—A subatomic particle that can travel faster than the speed of light.

Tesla field—A generated electromagnetic field surrounding the earth that supplies cordless electric power.

TEV—Tachyon emission visualizer. A timecaster's viewfinder into the past.

TG—Transgender.

Timecaster—A peace officer who uses TEVs to record past events and solve crimes.

TTS—Tesla Taser satellite.

UFSE—The universal search application for the intranet, aka *uffsee* and Use the Fucking Search Engine.

Utopeon—A taxpaying citizen.

Van Damme—Slang term for a timecaster.

WTF—What the fuck.

WYSIWYW—What you see is what you want.

New from Hugo and Nebula award-winning author

ROBERT J. SAWYER

The final book in the WWW trilogy

000111001010101000000001011111101010000000101000101010000001011101010010101010

WWW:WONDER

000111001010101000000001011111101010000000101000101010000001011101010010101010

The advent of Webmind—a vast consciousness that spontaneously emerged from the infrastructure of the World Wide Web—is changing *everything*. From curing cancer to easing international tensions, Webmind seems a boon to humanity.

But Colonel Peyton Hume, the Pentagon's top expert on artificial intelligence, is convinced Webmind is a threat. He turns to the hacker underground to help him bring Webmind down. But soon hackers start mysteriously vanishing. Is Webmind killing them before they can mount an attack?

Caitlin Decter—the once-blind sixteen-year-old math genius who discovered Webmind—desperately tries to protect her friend. Can this new world of wonder survive—or will everything, Webmind included, come crashing down?

M795T1110

Now available from
CHARLES STROSS

"Stross gives his readers a British superspy
with a long-term girlfriend, no fashion sense,
and an aversion to martinis."
—*San Francisco Chronicle*

THE FULLER MEMORANDUM
A Laundry Files Novel

When a top secret dossier known as the Fuller Memorandum vanishes—along with his boss—Bob Howard is determined to discover exactly what the memorandum contained (and perhaps clear his boss's name). But Bob runs afoul of Russian agents, ancient demons, and the apostles of a hideous faith who have plans to raise a very unpleasant undead entity known as the Eater of Souls.

Now Bob must use all of his skills to learn the secret of the Fuller Memorandum in order to save the world—and avoid becoming an item on the Eater of Souls's dinner menu . . .

M652T0311

ALASTAIR REYNOLDS

TERMINAL WORLD

In a far-distant future, an enforcement agent named
Quillon has been living incognito in the last human
city of Spearpoint, working as a pathologist in the
district morgue. But when a near-dead angel drops
onto his dissection table, his world is wrenched
apart.

For the angel is a winged post-human from
Spearpoint's Celestial Levels, and with the dying body comes bad news: Quillon must leave his
home and travel into the cold and hostile lands beyond the city.

penguin.com